THE CASTLE OF OTRANTO

HORACE WALPOLE, fourth earl of Orford, was the son of Robert Walpole, twice Prime Minister of Britain. Born in 1717, he was educated at Eton and King's College, Cambridge. In 1739 he set off on his Grand Tour with the poet Thomas Gray, travelling throughout France and Italy. On his return to England in 1741 he became MP for Callington in Cornwall, and later for Castle Rising and King's Lynn, remaining in Parliament until 1768. His father died in 1745 and in 1747 he moved to Twickenham, where he bought the house he named Strawberry Hill. Here, in his 'little Gothic castle', he lived at the centre of a literary and political society.

Walpole established a private printing press at Strawberry Hill in 1757, and published Gray's Pindaric Odes, *The Progress of Poesy* and *The Bard*. He also published some of his own works, including *A Catalogue of the Royal and Noble Authors of England* (1758), *Fugitive Pieces* (1758) and *Anecdotes of Painting in England* (1762). *The Castle of Otranto* was published under a pseudonym in 1764 and launched the fashion for the Gothic romance in England. *Historic Doubts on the Life and Reign of King Richard the Third*, a defence of Richard, and *The Mysterious Mother*, a tragic drama, appeared in 1768. Walpole is also remembered for the vast collection of his letters to a wide circle of correspondents, dealing with politics, art, literature and social gossip, as well as firsthand accounts of the Jacobite rebellion and other subjects of great historical significance.

Horace Walpole died in 1797, having succeeded his nephew as Earl of Orford in 1791. His memoirs were kept in a sealed chest until 1818, and were later published as *Memoirs of the Last Ten Years of the Reign of George the Second* (1822) and *Memoirs of the Reign of King George III* (1845).

MICHAEL GAMER is Associate Professor of English at the University of Pennsylvania and author of *Romanticism and the Gothic: Genre, Reception and Canon Formation* (Cambridge University Press, 2000). With Jeffrey Cox, he is editor of *Romantic Period Drama: An Anthology* (Broadview Press, forthcoming 2002).

HORACE WALPOLE

The Castle of Otranto

Edited with an Introduction and Notes by
MICHAEL GAMER

PENGUIN BOOKS

PENGUIN BOOKS

Published by the Penguin Group
Penguin Books Ltd, 80 Strand, London WC2R 0RL, England
Penguin Putnam Inc., 375 Hudson Street, New York, New York 10014, USA
Penguin Books Australia Ltd, 250 Camberwell Road, Camberwell, Victoria 3124, Australia
Penguin Books Canada Ltd, 10 Alcorn Avenue, Toronto, Ontario, Canada M4V 3B2
Penguin Books India (P) Ltd, 11 Community Centre, Panchsheel Park, New Delhi – 110 017, India
Penguin Books (NZ) Ltd, Cnr Rosedale and Airborne Roads, Albany, Auckland, New Zealand
Penguin Books (South Africa) (Pty) Ltd, 24 Sturdee Avenue, Rosebank 2196, South Africa

Penguin Books Ltd, Registered Offices: 80 Strand, London WC2R 0RL, England

www.penguin.com

This edition first published 2001
4

Editorial matter copyright © Michael Gamer, 2001
All rights reserved

The moral right of the editor has been asserted

Set in 10/12.5 pt Monotype Ehrhardt
Typeset by Rowland Phototypesetting Ltd,
Bury St Edmunds, Suffolk
Printed in Great Britain by Clays Ltd, St Ives plc

CONTENTS

CHRONOLOGY

1717   *24 September*: Born at Arlington Street, London, third son of Robert Walpole and Catherine Shorter Walpole. The Walpole family's acquisition of their estate at Houghton dates from the thirteenth century.

1721   Robert Walpole becomes 'Prime Minister' to George I in the aftermath of the South Sea Bubble. His own profits from these transactions are colossal.

1727–34   *26 April 1727*: Attends Eton, where he meets Thomas Ashton, Thomas Gray and Richard West. The four call themselves the 'Quadruple Alliance'. *1 June 1727*: Meets George I, who departs for Hanover two days later and dies within a fortnight.

1735–9   Attends King's College, Cambridge. *Summer 1737*: Death of Lady Walpole. After six months Robert Walpole marries his mistress, Maria Skerrett, who dies in 1738.

1739–41   *29 March 1739*: Walpole and Gray embark on a Grand Tour, during which Walpole begins writing the letters on which much of his fame rests. While abroad, Walpole is elected to Parliament for the borough of Callington in Cornwall. He will remain MP for Callington until 1754, after which he continues in Parliament as MP to Castle Rising until 1757 and King's Lynn until 1768. *May 1741*: Walpole and Gray quarrel in Italy and return separately.

1741–2   *14 September 1741*: Arrives in London to find Robert Walpole's majority in Parliament seriously reduced. *11 February 1742*: Robert Walpole resigns the office of Prime Minister

vii

and is made Earl of Orford; he also secures for Horace Walpole places at the Exchequer worth £2,000 per year, making him independent for life. *23 March*: First speech in the House of Commons, in defence of his father.

1743   Begins *Aedes Walpolianae*, a catalogue of paintings owned by his father, finishing the first draft on 24 August.

1745   *18 March*: Death of Robert Walpole, who leaves to Horace Walpole the lease of the London house on Arlington Street, £5,000, and the office of Collector of the Customs, worth £1,000 per year. *November*: Walpole reconciled with Gray.

1746   Begins writing for the *Museum*. *April*: The Jacobite rebellion, begun in the autumn of 1745, ends with the defeat of Charles Edward Stuart by William, Duke of Cumberland, at the Battle of Culloden.

1747   Begins writing a series of anonymous political essays for *Old England or the Broadbottom Journal* and, in the following year, for the *Remembrancer*. *Aedes Walpolianae* printed privately. *May*: Leases 'Chopp'd-Straw Hall', in Twickenham, which he purchases in the following year and renames 'Strawberry Hill'.

1748   Walpole's 'Epistle to Thomas Ashton from Florence', 'The Beauties' and his Epilogue to *Tamerlane* published in the first volumes of James Dodsley's *Collection of Poems*. *18 September*: Writes to Horace Mann requesting return of his letters to use as raw material for a history of his own times; these requests become a regular feature of his correspondences.

1749   *28 September*: In a letter to George Montagu, Walpole for the first time indicates his intention to transform Strawberry Hill into a Gothic castle.

1750   Thomas Gray sends the completed *Elegy Written in a Country Churchyard* to Walpole, who circulates the poem in manuscript among friends. When Gray receives word that an unauthorized version will be published in the *Magazine of Magazines*, he asks Walpole to make amends by seeing the poem through the press. It is published in 1751 and is a smash hit.

1751   First stage of building at Strawberry Hill, completed 1753. Walpole convinces Gray to publish a small edition of poetry. In this year Walpole also begins writing his *Memoirs*.

1752   Second edition of *Aedes Walpolianae* published.

1753   *February*: Writes the first of nine essays for the *World*, a periodical published by Robert Dodsley. *March*: Dodsley publishes *Designs by Mr. R. Bentley, for Six Poems by Mr. T. Gray*.

1755   First attack of gout. The second occurred in 1760, and thereafter was chronic.

1757   *25 June*: Erects a printing press at Strawberry Hill, the first private printing press in England. *3 August*: The press's first publication is *Odes by Mr. Gray*. In an attempt to save Admiral Byng from execution, Walpole publishes anonymously his successful political pamphlet *A Letter from Xo Ho, a Chinese Philosopher at London, to His Friend Lien Chi at Peking* through London publisher N. Middleton, thus establishing his practice of never using the Strawberry Hill Press to publish political works.

1758   *15 April*: *Catalogue of Royal and Noble Authors*, 2 vols., printed at Strawberry Hill (300 copies). *13 July*: *Fugitive Pieces* printed at Strawberry Hill (200 copies). *September*: Begins second stage of building at Strawberry Hill, completed 1763.

1760   *26 October*: Death of George II.

1762   Begins publishing his *Anecdotes of Painting* and *A Catalogue of Engravers*, 5 vols. (1762–71), at Strawberry Hill.

1764   *11 April*: Because of his opposition to the general warrant arrest of John Wilkes, Walpole's cousin Henry Seymour Conway is dismissed from command of his regiment and from his place as Groom of the Bedchamber. *June*: Begins work on *The Castle of Otranto*. *6 August*: Completes *The Castle of Otranto*. *24 December*: *The Castle of Otranto* published by T. Lownds (500 copies).

1765   An abridgment of *The Castle of Otranto* appears in the *Universal Magazine*. *11 April*: Second edition of *The Castle of Otranto* published in London by William Bathoe and T. Lownds (500 copies). Pirated versions of both the first and second editions appear in Dublin. *August*: Departs for Paris, where he befriends Madame du Deffand and is fêted by Parisian literary society. He will visit Paris again in 1767, 1769, 1771 and 1775.

1766   Third edition of *The Castle of Otranto* published in London by W. Bathoe.

1767   A French translation of *The Castle of Otranto* is published in Amsterdam and Paris.

1768   *1 February*: *Historic Doubts on the Life of King Richard the Third* published in London by Dodsley. *6 August*: *The Mysterious Mother* printed at Strawberry Hill and privately distributed (fifty copies). Walpole retires from Parliament at the end of the year.

1771   Begins third stage of building at Strawberry Hill; most of it is completed in 1774, with the Beauclerc Tower finished in 1776.

1773   Walpole anonymously sends the manuscript for his comic afterpiece, *Nature Will Prevail*, to George Colman at the Haymarket Theatre. Colman shelves the play through lack of interest.

1774   *A Description of the Villa of Horace Walpole* printed at Strawberry Hill (100 copies).

1777   Unjustly blamed in the *Monthly Review* for the death of Thomas Chatterton.

1778   George Colman discovers that Walpole is the author of *Nature Will Prevail* and expresses interest in performing it at the Haymarket Theatre. Walpole declines. The play débuts finally in a performance commanded by the king and queen, and is acted seven times in 1778. It is performed thereafter in 1779 and 1781–6, for a total of twenty-eight performances.

1779   *January*: Defends his conduct towards Chatterton in *A Letter to the Editor of the Miscellanies of Thomas Chatterton*, printed at Strawberry Hill (200 copies).

1781   *May*: Facing the threat of a pirated publication of *The*

Mysterious Mother, Walpole allows Dodsley to print the play for publication. When no piracy appears, Walpole suppresses its publication. *17 November*: Robert Jephson's dramatic adaptation of *The Castle of Otranto*, *The Count of Narbonne*, produced successfully (twenty-one nights) at the Theatre Royal, Covent Garden. The text of the play will be printed five times in the decade, and will appear in nearly every standard collection of British drama published in the nineteenth century.

1782   Fourth edition of *The Castle of Otranto* published in London by James Dodsley. *A Letter to the Editor of the Miscellanies of Chatterton* printed in four instalments in the *Gentleman's Magazine*.

1784   Publishes a second, expanded edition of *A Description of the Villa of Horace Walpole* at Strawberry Hill Press (200 copies).

1786   Fifth edition of *The Castle of Otranto* published by James Dodsley.

1788   Mary and Agnes Berry move with their father to Twickenham and befriend Walpole, with Mary Berry eventually serving as his literary executor. Writes *Reminiscences, written in 1788, for the amusement of Miss Mary and Miss Agnes Berry*.

1791   *February*: Another pirated edition of *The Mysterious Mother* is threatened from a Dublin bookseller. After some grumbling Walpole allows it to be published. A London reprint of the edition soon follows. During the year, two editions of *The Castle of Otranto* appear, one printed by Dodsley and the other beautifully printed and illustrated in Parma by Bodoni. *5 December*: Becomes the fourth Earl of Orford.

1792   Finishes writing his *Memoirs*.

1793   Two new editions of *The Castle of Otranto* published, one by Wenman & Hodgson in London and one by Himbourg in Berlin.

1794   *The Castle of Otranto* reprinted, with large omissions, in the *New Wonderful Magazine, and Marvellous Chronicle* 4 (1794), pp. 117–40.

1795   An Italian translation of *The Castle of Otranto* printed in London by George Sivrac.

1796   Jeffery's Edition of *The Castle of Otranto* published. Its illustrations carry headings in Italian, and stress the book's elegance and ethereal quality.

1797   French translation of *The Castle of Otranto*, entitled *Isabelle et Theodore*, published in Paris by Lepetit. *2 March*: Dies in London, aged eighty. Buried at Houghton. Walpole leaves his *Memoirs* ready for publication in a sealed chest, which his will decrees cannot be opened until 1818. They are eventually published as *Memoirs of the Last Ten Years of the Reign of George the Second* (Vols. VII–VIII of *The Works of Horatio Walpole* (London, 1822)) and *Memoirs of the Reign of George III* (London, 1845).

1798   Publication of *Works of Horatio Walpole, Earl of Orford*, ed. Mary Berry, 9 vols., by John Murray. Vols. I–V appear in 1798; Vol. VI in 1818; Vols. VII–VIII in 1822; and Vol. IX in 1825.

INTRODUCTION

1. Reception

Since its first publication in 1764, *The Castle of Otranto* has rarely, if ever, been out of print, and over 130 editions precede this one.[1] Few books of fiction have surpassed its sustained popularity in the history of literary publishing; even fewer can claim so central an influence on the history of the novel or on late eighteenth-century prose romance. Appearing a quarter of a century before Gothic fiction became a popular literary form, Walpole's story is startling for the way in which it assembles, almost prophetically, an array of generic devices recognizable to any reader familiar with *Frankenstein* (1818), *Northanger Abbey* (1818), *Wuthering Heights* (1847) or *Dracula* (1897). The fatal prophecy against Manfred's house, the supernatural visitations attending it, and the Draconian attempts of Manfred to combat both found their way into countless late eighteenth- and early nineteenth-century fictions, including those of Anna Letitia Barbauld, Clara Reeve, Ann Radcliffe, Matthew Lewis, W. H. Ireland, Charlotte Dacre and Charles Robert Maturin. In addition, the book's breathless pace and mysterious opening, packed with unexplainable happenings and sinister portents, anticipate later detective and sensation fiction. Most influential and evocative of all, of course, has been the icon of the castle, transformed in Walpole's handling from a locus of safety into a place of sexual transgression and supernatural visitation, of secret passageways and political intrigue. With its adjacent monastery, it is a place that harbours guilty secrets and unlawful desires, a fortress not for keeping people out but for keeping them in. Modern readers, therefore, will find in

Walpole's Gothic structures the prototypes not only for other Gothic fictions like *The Mysteries of Udolpho* (1794) and *Melmoth the Wanderer* (1820), but also for twentieth-century films as popular and disparate as *Nosferatu* (1922), *Rebecca* (1940), *Alien* (1979) and *The Name of the Rose* (1986).

Yet in its immediate reception and in the many appraisals that have followed, critical responses to *The Castle of Otranto* and to its author have been consistently mixed, characterized by a recognizable blend of pleasure and bewilderment, admiration and discomfort. Early nineteenth-century anthologies of the British novel, for example, included Walpole's romance almost without exception; yet when Anna Letitia Barbauld chose in 1810 to include it in her monumental series *The British Novelists*, she began by pointing uneasily to its popularity with younger readers and by expressing reservations about its cultural value. Walpole's 'slight performance', as she called it, may have been 'one of the first of the modern productions founded on appearances of terror' and may have shown 'a livelier play of fancy' than most of its successors, but these virtues did not entirely excuse the supernatural fiction that it apparently had inspired: 'it is calculated to make a great impression on those who relish the fictions of the *Arabian Tales*, and similar performances . . . Since this author's time, from the perusal of Mrs Radcliffe's productions and some of the German tales, we may be said to have "supped full with horrors".'[2]

A year later, another essay on Walpole and *The Castle of Otranto* appeared, this time published in an Edinburgh edition of the novel edited by Walter Scott.[3] Like Barbauld, Scott expressed reservations about the source of *Otranto*'s popularity and its frequent recourse to the supernatural before moving on to more enthusiastic praise; but there the similarities between the two essays ended. No longer (as in Barbauld's description) a slight, spirited work written by a dilettante in eight days, *The Castle of Otranto* in Scott's treatment constituted a daring synthesis of historical realism and unfettered imaginative liberty. Scott, therefore, presents Walpole as at once an eccentric dreamer, an insightful antiquarian, and a gifted and imaginative historian. Tapping 'that secret and reserved feeling of love for the marvelous and supernatural, which occupies a hidden corner in almost every one's bosom',[4]

Walpole's antiquarian knowledge, Scott argued, had allowed him the coup of introducing apparitions seamlessly into a carefully historicized setting:

The association of which we have spoken [that of overcoming rational disbelief in the supernatural] is of a nature peculiarly delicate, and subject to be broken and disarranged. It is, for instance, almost impossible to build such a modern Gothic structure as shall impress us with the feelings we have endeavoured to describe. It may be grand, or it may be gloomy; it may excite magnificent or melancholy ideas; but it must fail in bringing forth the sensation of supernatural awe, connected with halls that have echoed to the sounds of remote generations, and have been pressed by the footsteps of those who have long since passed away. Yet Horace Walpole has attained in composition, what, as an architect, he must have felt beyond the power of his art. The remote and superstitious period in which his scene is laid, the art with which he has furnished forth its Gothic decorations, the sustained, and, in general, dignified tone of feudal manners, prepare us gradually for the favourable reception of prodigies, which, though they could not really have happened at any period, were consistent with the belief of all mankind at that time in which the action is placed.[5]

Coming from a writer traditionally credited with inventing the historical novel – whose estate Abbotsford was modelled, in many ways, on Walpole's own Strawberry Hill – Scott's tribute probably should not surprise us. That Scott should agree with Barbauld (herself an early theorist and practitioner of supernatural fiction[6]) in so many particulars while differing so markedly on *Otranto*'s cultural significance, however, is at once unexpected and yet typical of the book's varied critical reception. It remains one of the few works of fiction to draw strong praise and censure from so many authors of note, boasting famous dismissals by William Hazlitt and Thomas Babington Macaulay and encomiums from writers as different from one another as Lord Byron and Ann Yearsley.[7] Scott's celebration may be the one more often quoted in scholarly essays and editions, but twenty-first-century readers will find themselves surprised by the justness of Barbauld's observations, particularly her fascination with the volume's slightness and theatricality and her representation of it as 'the sportive effusion of a man of genius, who throws the reins loose upon the neck of his imagination'.[8] If readers have found difficulty finding stable footing when reading Walpole's romance, their uneasiness has stemmed at least in part from its unsettling combination of careful historicism and imaginative outrageousness, of solemnity and burlesque.

In addition to these difficulties of irony and tone, *The Castle of Otranto*'s first reviewers were forced to cope with the ruse of its initial publication. Anxious over the book's reception, Walpole had disguised its first edition by publishing it under the pseudonym of 'William Marshall, Gent.' and by having Thomas Lownds print and sell the work rather than doing so at his own press at Strawberry Hill. Walpole then added a bogus Preface that still reads as one of the work's triumphs, burlesquing scholarly tone and gleefully attending to minute details of the forgery. Writing in the persona of Marshall, Walpole declares *Otranto* to be an English translation of a sixteenth-century text printed in Naples in 1529 and written by one 'ONUPHRIO MURALTO, Canon of the Church of St. NICHOLAS at OTRANTO' (see p. 1). He then proceeds to give this genealogy an extra twist, surmising Onuphrio Muralto to have taken as the source of his narrative a tale originally written during the Crusades. Walpole's Preface even provides an account of the work's probable religious and political origins, speculating it to be a document of the Italian Counter-Reformation: 'It is not unlikely that an artful priest ... might avail himself of his abilities as an author to confirm the populace in their ancient errors and superstitions' (see p. 5). The sum is a fabrication whose complex historicism is typical of Walpole's sense of humour, since to pull off the forgery in convincing fashion he must impersonate an eighteenth-century Catholic English country gentleman translating a militant sixteenth-century Neapolitan priest appropriating (for religious and political ends) a thirteenth-century local history. With this elaborate frame and a few additional observations on its dramatic excellence and the difficulties of translating Italian into English, *The Castle of Otranto* appeared in masquerade on Christmas Eve of 1764.

The immediate response was not auspicious. Perhaps suspicious of the book's holiday publication date, the *Critical Review* reacted defensively. It flatly condemned the book's subject matter and, after displaying its own command of antiquarian knowledge, cavalierly refused to judge its authenticity: 'whether he speaks seriously or ironically, we neither know nor care. The publication of any work, at this time, in England composed of such rotten materials, is a phœnomenon we cannot account for'.[9] The *Monthly Review* chose a more charitable course, recommending the book as a historical curiosity and as 'a work of genius, evincing great dramatic powers, and exhibiting fine views of nature'.[10] When Walpole's second edition showed the work to be a modern production with pretensions to literary innovation, however, the *Monthly* was forced to recant its judgement:

While we considered it as [a translation from an ancient writer], we could readily excuse its preposterous phœnomena, and consider them as sacrifices to a gross and unenlightened age. – But when, as in this edition, the Castle of Otranto is declared to be a modern performance, that indulgence we afforded to the foibles of a supposed antiquity, we can by no means extend to the singularity of a false taste in a cultivated period of learning. It is, indeed, more than strange, that an Author, of a refined and polished genius, should be an advocate for re-establishing the barbarous superstitions of Gothic devilism![11]

No doubt the *Monthly*'s irritation stemmed from a dislike of being made to look foolish. Still, its response is worth examining for what it yields about the literary culture into which Walpole published his romance. Strikingly, none of the immediate responses to *The Castle of Otranto* allowed for the possibility that a cultivated mind could enjoy reading, let alone be capable of writing, such a book. In the above quotation, the *Monthly Review*'s objections arise out of assumptions about its role as a respectable and enlightened literary journal. The reviewer, John Langhorne, appears especially keen to separate his own 'period of cultivated learning' from past ages, and especially from *Otranto*'s culture of chivalry and its 'barbarous superstitions of Gothic devilism'. What is interesting here is the way in which imagining this kind of gulf between superstitious past and enlightened present brings with it other assumptions about readerly pleasure. From the *Monthly*'s relative position of enlightenment, it is unwilling on some fundamental level to believe that rational readers or writers can take pleasure in supernatural representations. Its first review, therefore, had instead presented *The Castle of Otranto* as a historical curiosity, and within this framework had invited readers to discern a recognizable human nature transcending history and overcoming the most egregious superstition. Put another way, the *Monthly Review*'s stance of finding pleasure in *Otranto*'s 'fine views of nature' while being repulsed by its barbarism allowed for the accompanying belief that noble, laudable aspects of human nature could transcend the centuries while other, less desirable aspects could not.

The *Monthly*'s applause in its first review had arisen, then, from the narrative of historical progress it had been able to impose on Walpole's book. In doing so, it wielded a story that recurs in critical writing frequently during the second half of the eighteenth century, shaping debates about the function of the supernatural not only in fiction but also on the stage.[12] We find it operating even in the responses of Walpole's own circle of friends – as with George 'Gilly' Williams, who felt *Otranto*'s archaic setting and subject matter to be so patently absurd and innately uninteresting that 'no boarding-school Miss of thirteen could get half through without yawning'.[13] We see it also in the accounts of more flexible and sympathetic readers like William Mason, who could not fathom the idea that the book was a modern production. Writing to Walpole immediately after the publication of the book's second edition, Mason confessed that, 'When a friend of mine to whom I had recommended *The Castle of Otranto* returned it me with some doubts of its originality, I laughed him to scorn, and wondered he could be so absurd as to think that anybody nowadays had imagination enough to invent such a story.'[14] In the face of such statements, we can begin to grasp how completely the assumptions of readers like Mason could be challenged by the revelation that *The Castle of Otranto* was not an ancient text but a 'Gothic story' (the subtitle Walpole affixed to *Otranto*'s second edition) by a modern author. To understand the particular nerves that Walpole's book struck we need to consider the social position of its inventor and his relation to this historically specific question of 'imagination', since Walpole brought both to bear on his attempts to transform how his contemporaries read prose fiction and understood its function.

2. The 'Master of Otranto'

With the appearance of its second edition, *The Castle of Otranto* ceased
to be written by a zealous priest from bygone times. Its author became
instead a living, mature man of forty-seven years of age, a Member of
Parliament of nearly twenty-five years' standing, and the son of a
celebrated Prime Minister. Part of *The Castle of Otranto*'s contemporary
reception, then, has always been tied to Walpole's notoriety as a public
figure, since readers and reviewers alike were forced to ask what it
meant for a man of such eminence to write such a book. Educated at
Eton and Cambridge, Horace Walpole had grown up during the height
of Robert Walpole's power. As Walpole's biographers have suggested,
his social position no doubt helped to render his time at Eton free of
the usual bullying and brutality associated with the school in the
eighteenth century, and made his Grand Tour a heady, exuberant and
formative experience.[15] While travelling in Italy in 1740 with his
childhood friend Thomas Gray, Walpole mixed with its best society,
befriending diplomats like Horace Mann and taking great pleasure in
purchasing works of art for his father's extensive collection at his
country estate Houghton in Norwich. Elected to Parliament while
abroad, Walpole arrived back in England in September of 1741
expecting to take his seat in the House of Commons and his place
among London's élite. His first speech six months after his arrival,
however, could hardly have accorded less with his expectations. In that
time, Robert Walpole's government had fallen after over two decades
in power. Consequently, Walpole's first address was in defence of his
father who, in the wake of his resignation, faced multiple allegations of
corruption. With this reversal of fortune, Horace Walpole's involvement in parliamentary matters over the next decades was intermittent
and behind the scenes. Rather than acting as a direct participant in
affairs of state, he moved between the role of periodic strategist and
pamphleteer and that of perpetual observer and chronicler. Steadfastly
loyal to his father's memory, his first book was a catalogue of the
paintings Robert Walpole had collected and housed at Houghton,
entitled *Aedes Walpolianae*, written in 1743 and printed privately in

1747. Walpole's later *Memoirs*, begun in 1751 and forty-one years in the writing, constitutes a textual version of this lifelong work of defending the family's political legacy.[16]

Over the next years Walpole wrote primarily as a gentleman author and elegant essayist, publishing when it suited him and taking pleasure in helping to publish the works of his friends. Three of his early poems – 'Epistle to Thomas Ashton from Florence', 'The Beauties' and an Epilogue to *Tamerlane* – appeared in 1748 in the first volumes of James Dodsley's *Collection of Poems*, which also featured Gray's first published work. After this joint appearance, Walpole spent considerable energy over the next decade persuading Gray to publish more poetry and over-seeing its production and reception. The *Elegy Written in a Country Churchyard* appeared in 1751 to great applause; *Designs by Mr. R. Bentley, for Six Poems by Mr. T. Gray* (featuring elaborate rococo illustrations by Walpole's friend Richard Bentley) appeared two years later. It is no accident that when Walpole opened the Strawberry Hill Press in 1757, he chose *Odes by Mr. Gray* (1757) as its first published work.

In spite of this sustained interest in writing and publishing poetry, however, Walpole emerged in the 1740s and 1750s primarily as a prose writer – one capable of moving between savage parody, graceful elegance and pointed observation. His first essays, written for magazines such as the *Museum* and the *World*, were determinedly frivolous and deliberately at odds with the moral essays of Samuel Johnson and with the serious tone of periodicals like the *Gentleman's Magazine*. The 'Advertisement to the History of Good Breeding' and 'On the Relative Simplicity of Gothic Manners to Our Own', for example, indulged in parody and burlesque. Others, like the 'Scheme for Raising a large Sum of Money by Message Cards and Notes', were at once more outrageous and more intellectual, and showed Walpole developing ideas that would prove central to the literary and aesthetic projects that culminated in *The Castle of Otranto*:

The notion I have of a *Museum* is an Hospital for every Thing that is *singular*; whether the Thing have acquired Singularity, from having escaped the Rage of Time; from any natural Oddness in itself; or from being so insignificant that nobody ever thought it worth their while to produce any more of the same

Sort. Intrinsic Value has little or no Property in the merit of *curiosities* . . . If the Learned World could be so happy as to discover a *Roman*'s old Shoe (provided the Literati were agreed it were a Shoe, and not a leathern Casque, a drinking Vessel, a balloting Box, or an empress's Head Attire), such Shoe would immediately have the Entrée into any collection in *Europe*.[17]

This notion of singularity and uniqueness informs most of Walpole's writing and publishing in these years. The Strawberry Hill Press, moreover, provided him with a means of bypassing the usual channels of book printing and bookselling when he chose to do so. Abjuring both profit and politics when choosing manuscripts for publication, the press quickly acquired a reputation for publishing books fundamentally different from those available elsewhere.

In his own compositions Walpole appears often to have been driven by a similar desire for innovation even when writing anonymous partisan tracts for other presses. His successful political satire, *A Letter from Xo Ho, a Chinese Philosopher at London, to His Friend Lien Chi at Peking* (N. Middleton, 1757), anticipated later works like Robert Southey's *Letters from England by Don Manuel Alvarez Espriella* (1807), while his *Catalogue of Royal and Noble Authors* (Strawberry Hill Press, 1758) was one of the first books of its kind. It was for his groundbreaking *Anecdotes of Painting* (Strawberry Hill, 1762), however, that Walpole became best known before the success of *The Castle of Otranto*. At once a treasure-trove of information and a sustained assessment of English painting, the book shows Walpole moving at ease between the minutiae of historical research and engaging, arresting writing. W. S. Lewis puts the matter succinctly: 'It was an instant success. Gibbon spoke of his "minute curiosity and acuteness." Strangers wrote to him with gratitude and volunteered additions and corrections for the next edition. It was no wonder that this work was so popular: it was new, informative, and entertaining . . . [and] laid the foundations for an historical study of the Fine Arts in England.'[18]

One of the difficulties readers have faced when attempting to come to grips with Walpole's writings and reputation has stemmed from his diversity of interests and this fondness of 'Singularity'. For nineteenth-century historian and essayist Thomas Babington Macaulay, Walpole's eccentricity and determination to be considered a gentleman author who wrote with ease on many subjects smacked of affectation and effeminacy. '[None] but an unhealthy and disorganized mind,' he argued, 'could have produced such literary luxuries.'[19] Likely the most influential assessment of Walpole ever written, Macaulay's account derives its persuasiveness from its ability to present Walpole's work and life as projections of a single set of affectations that, while assembled and put on like masks, nevertheless comprise Walpole's character.[20] Whether by reading Walpole's correspondence, wandering through Strawberry Hill, or perusing the volumes published by its press, one nevertheless imbibes the same aesthetic experience:

The motto which he prefixed to this *Catalogue of Royal and Noble Authors*, might have been inscribed with perfect propriety over the door of every room in his house, and on the titlepage of every one of his books. 'Dove diavolo, Messer Ludovico, avete pigliate tante coglionere?' ['Where the devil, Sir Ludovico, did you collect so many imbecilities?'] In his villa, every compartment is a museum; every piece of furniture is a curiosity; there is something strange in the form of a shovel; there is a long story belonging to the bell-rope. We wander among a profusion of rarities, of trifling intrinsic value, but so quaint in fashion, or connected with such remarkable names and events that they may well detain our attention for a moment. A moment is enough.[21]

Deriving much of its rancour from his own sense of professionalism, Macaulay's distaste arises out of a belief not just that Walpole's interests are 'unhealthy', but that they also constitute an affront to artistic seriousness and therefore a denigration of appropriate authorship. Yet what Macaulay dismissed pejoratively as a 'profusion of rarities' in Walpole's life and works has been reappraised by twentieth-century literary historians as a body of innovative writing of unparalleled range, one typical of the generation of Samuel Johnson and Hester Thrale Piozzi and surpassing even that of Oliver Goldsmith. Between 1747 and his death in 1797, Walpole wrote and published several poems, a historical romance, a tragedy, a comic afterpiece, a book of art history, a bibliographic study, a memoir, a diary, a description of his own house, several catalogues of paintings, political pamphlets, fables and fairy tales. After his death his executors published what remains an authoritative political history of late eighteenth-century Britain and perhaps the most famous body of correspondence ever written.[22]

Even in the face of this voluminous output, it is fair to say that Walpole was equally famous in his lifetime for his achievements as a collector and architect. At the time of his death his collection of miniature and print portraits was arguably the best ever assembled in Britain. His villa Strawberry Hill, moreover, was without question the most famous house of its kind. Like *The Castle of Otranto*, which, though often called the first Gothic novel, was in many ways anticipated by the poetry of William Collins and novels like Tobias Smollett's *Ferdinand Count Fathom* (1753) and Thomas Leland's *Longsword* (1762), Strawberry Hill was more influential than entirely original. While not the first attempt to appropriate Gothic architecture into a domestic setting, it effectively revived Gothic as a popular architectural style.[23] In 1748 Walpole had purchased the original Chopp'd-Straw Hall and its five acres in Twickenham because of its nearness to London and its attractive location on the banks of the Thames. He did not start remodelling until 1751, and for that purpose commandeered the help of friends John Chute (who transformed much of the exterior) and Richard Bentley (who brought to Walpole's interiors the same extravagant flair with which he had illustrated Gray's poems). Calling themselves 'The Committee', the three transformed the house, quadrupling its original size in a little over a decade and adding battlements, turrets, cloisters, stained glass, fireplaces and other fixtures to give it the effect of a medieval castle. Their work, moreover, was decidedly unlike Robert Walpole's Palladian estate at Houghton, largely because Strawberry Hill's small size and irregular design dictated different choices of architectural style and materials. Where Houghton achieved its effects through stone, grand rooms and columns, Strawberry Hill used theatrical devices like *trompe-l'oeil* painting and materials like plaster and papier mâché. Writing to Horace Mann in 1750, Walpole explained that '[t]he Grecian is only proper for magnificent and public buildings. Columns and all their beautiful ornaments look ridiculous when crowded into a closet or a cheesecake house. The variety is little, and admits no charming irregularities.'[24]

By the end of its second stage of building in 1763, Strawberry

Hill had already become a celebrated attraction, further gaining in reputation as the century closed. A telling measure of its popularity occurs in *The Ambulator: or, A Pocket Companion in a Tour Round London* (1800), which devotes five pages to Strawberry Hill while allocating only two to the British Museum.[25] While the steadily increasing stream of visitors to his villa forced Walpole later in his life to print rules for admission, he also openly encouraged the attention that the house conferred on him by twice printing a description of it and its contents.[26] This transformation of house into textual form was hardly accidental. As early as 1765 Walpole began to encourage friends and readers to associate Strawberry Hill with the setting of *The Castle of Otranto* by playfully referring to the villa as 'Otranto' and himself as 'The Master of Otranto'.[27] More importantly, he repeatedly associated the house with *Otranto*'s composition:

Your partiality to me and Strawberry have I hope inclined you to excuse the wildness of the story. You will even have found some traits to put you in mind of this place. When you read of the picture quitting its panel, did not you recollect the portrait of Lord Falkland all in white in my gallery? Shall I even confess to you what was the origin of my romance? I waked one morning in the beginning of last June from a dream, of which all I could recover was, that I had thought myself in an ancient castle (a very natural dream for a head filled like mine with Gothic story) and that on the uppermost bannister of a great staircase I saw a gigantic hand in armour. In the evening I sat down and began to write, without knowing in the least what I intended to say or relate. The work grew on my hands, and I grew fond of it – add that I was very glad to think of anything rather than politics – In short I was so engrossed with my tale, which I completed in less than two months, that one evening I wrote from the time I had drunk my tea, about six o'clock, till half an hour after one in the morning, when my hand and fingers were so weary, that I could not hold the pen to finish the sentence, but left Matilda and Isabella talking, in the middle of a paragraph.[28]

The dream, pointedly, is 'a very natural dream' within the surroundings of Strawberry Hill, one that opposes Gothic story, Gothic villa and Gothic dream to their 'modern' and 'rational' counterparts. In this sense, Walpole's account of his romance's origin constructs a fairly elaborate analogy, one in which the same differences that distinguish

Strawberry Hill from other eighteenth-century houses also distinguish *The Castle of Otranto* from other contemporary fiction. House and text stand, here and elsewhere, as analogous expressions of the same singular urge, serving as both excuse for, and vindication of, one another. It is within the surroundings of Strawberry Hill and this notion of complementarity that we should understand *The Castle of Otranto*'s choice of aesthetics and its narrative strategies, particularly its fondness for dreamlike setting and theatrical effect.

3. 'Two Kinds of Romance'

However much it might have begun as a random exercise in composition, *The Castle of Otranto* exhibits in its opening pages the purposiveness of a manifesto. Walpole's narrative of the book originating in a dream, suggestive as it has been to explorations of consciousness in Gothic fiction,[29] is more than counterbalanced by the critical accounts he provided in the book's second Preface and in his own correspondence. The story's opening lines, furthermore, with their strong allegiance to fairy tales, signal a departure from established forms of eighteenth-century fiction, while the miraculous events frequently invoke and subvert literary conventions in ways that smack of anti-romances like Charlotte Lennox's *The Female Quixote* (1752). Here, however, the conventions that are being subverted are not those of romance (as with Lennox) but those of formal realism. Walpole may open, for example, with an unwilling bride left at the altar, but he does not devote his ensuing pages (as one might expect in a novel) to providing that bride's 'history' or to describing the chain of individual motivations and contingent events that brought about the occurrence. Instead, he provides a supernatural spectacle – the groom Conrad 'dashed to pieces, and almost buried under an enormous helmet, an hundred times more large than any casque ever made for human being' (p. 18) – that obliterates the possibility of rational explanation and raises more questions than it answers. We see similar strategies at work as well in the book's almost allegorical handling of character. Even in the case of his most fully developed character, Manfred, Walpole spends considerably more time describing Manfred's strategic decisions than the internal processes that produce them. *The Castle of Otranto*'s supernatural agents, moreover, contribute to this strategy, actively thwarting the very kinds of characterization that form a staple of the fiction of Defoe and Richardson and even of the social satires of Henry Fielding, Charlotte Lennox and Tobias Smollett. All of Manfred's plotting and re-plotting, his gifts for calculating probabilities and responding to contingencies, fail because he is presented with a fixed narrative and fate that no amount of character, no attention to detail, and no amount of strategizing can avert.

If the ruse of Walpole's first Preface governed how *The Castle of Otranto*'s first edition was received, the critical discourse with which he opens the Preface to the second edition has proven equally influential with modern readers. Part of its persuasiveness is more than understandable; Walpole's description of the book, as 'an attempt to blend the two kinds of romance, the ancient and the modern' (see p. 9), does capture its innovative combination of supernaturalism and psychological realism, of chivalric romance and modern novel. His Epigraph, moreover, tellingly revises Horace's *Ars Poetica* to express *Otranto*'s aesthetic ends. While the original Horace translates roughly into 'Idle fancies shall be shaped like a sick man's dream so that neither foot nor head can be assigned to a single shape,' Walpole's rewriting of the Latin changes the meaning of the final words to 'nevertheless head and foot are assigned to a single shape'.[30]

What Walpole's critical statements do *not* adequately capture are the ways his text consistently transgresses the conventions of both fictional traditions rather than compromising between them – an assertion suggested elsewhere by Walpole in a letter to Madame du Deffand:

Let the critics have their say: I shall not be vexed: it was not written for this age, which wants nothing but cold reason. I own to you, and you will think me madder than ever, that of all my works it is the only one in which I pleased myself: I let my imagination run: my visions and my passions kindled me. I wrote it in defiance of rules, critics, and philosophies: and it seems to me all the better for that.[31]

Stated in the terms of his second preface, Walpole's 'defiance' arises from his belief that the critical 'rules' separating ancient and modern romance are more artificial than any fiction that could result from their indiscriminate mixing. In the place of such strictures he offers the counter-argument that his generic mixture of the supernatural and the mundane, of broad comedy and classical tragedy, is both appropriate and natural because it functions as a formal expression of medieval consciousness and culture. A modern critic, E. J. Clery, describes the various historicisms at work here nicely: 'Rationally speaking, ghosts and goblins are not *true*, but when they appear in the literary artifacts of past ages, they are *true to history*, accurate representations of an obsolete system of belief: a stance we might call *exemplary* historicism.'[32] Walpole puts this matter of the nature of history more ironically, provocatively insisting within *The Castle of Otranto*'s historicized setting, 'My rule was nature' (p. 10).

Writing within the literary culture of the 1760s, Walpole's confident celebration of *The Castle of Otranto*'s 'nature' owes a considerable debt to Richard Hurd's *Letters on Chivalry and Romance* (1762), a text that helped to revive the status of medieval 'Gothic' literature and architecture in the second half of the eighteenth century. Published only two years before Walpole's romance, Hurd's study had argued for the fundamental similarity of Homeric epic and 'Gothic' metrical romance. From this 'remarkable correspondency', Hurd had proceeded to make a striking defence of the formal logic of the Gothic:

When an architect examines a Gothic structure by Grecian rules, he finds nothing but deformity. But the Gothic architecture has its own rules, by which when it comes to be examined, it is seen to have its merit, as well as the Grecian ... The same observation holds of the two sorts of poetry. Judge of the *Faery Queen* by the classic models, and you are shocked by its disorder: consider it with an eye to its Gothic original, and you find it regular. The unity and simplicity of the former are more complete: but the latter has that sort of unity and simplicity, which results from its nature. The *Faery Queen*, then, as a Gothic poem, derives its METHOD, as well as the other characters of its composition, from the established modes and ideas of chivalry.[33]

Walpole's appropriation of key ideas in Hurd's *Letters* has understandably been important to modern assessments[34] of *The Castle of Otranto*, providing a sense of its intellectual underpinnings and anticipated readership. As the attacks on Voltaire in its second Preface suggest, Walpole was more than willing to repackage Hurd's arguments in the language of anti-French sentiment and in the logic of cultural nationalism. Given Macaulay's later condemnation of Walpole as 'the most Frenchified English writer of the eighteenth century',[35] his recourse to national chauvinism here strongly suggests a desire to mitigate reader and reviewer censure that might have otherwise resulted from the initial ruse of its first edition. The criticisms of Voltaire, after all, could just as easily have been directed against his own countrymen David Garrick and Nahum Tate, whose popular stage versions of Shakespeare had frequently purged scenes perceived to be at odds with the overall tone of the play in question.

Apart from this decision to represent his romance as homage to the natural genius of the national Bard, other political currents run through *The Castle of Otranto* as well. Walpole's account of the book's composition as a kind of therapy against a particularly bad year in Parliament has been well documented,[36] as have been the correspondences between Manfred's tyranny and aspects of Walpole's own life, particularly George III's treatment of Walpole's cousin Henry Seymour Conway. Other commentators have called attention to the almost Oedipal family violence that pervades the text, finding in Manfred's political downfall a kind of political exorcism by Walpole of his father.[37] It is when we remind ourselves of Walpole's fondness for masquerade and ventriloquism, however, that we begin to sense the extent of Walpole's deep play in *The Castle of Otranto* with issues of defiance and transgression, whether literary or political. For if the character of Manfred raises questions concerning the nature of Walpole's identification with the psychology of power, then Walpole's impersonation of the translator 'William Marshall, Gent.' presents us with an equally striking piece of political theatre. Walpole's politics throughout his life were resolutely Whig, in part out of loyalty to his father and in part because of his innate suspicion of power and those who held it. Yet within the fiction of *The Castle of Otranto*'s first edition, Marshall is unquestionably Tory and likely an old Jacobite supporter of the Stuart monarchy. Standing at the head of 'an ancient catholic family in the north of England' (p. 5),

Marshall discovers, translates and publishes a tract of the Italian Counter-Reformation. The story, furthermore, dramatizes the restoration of a wrongfully ousted ruler and the downfall of a usurping house after three generations in power, one in which Manfred's position as the grandson of the usurper Ricardo corresponds nicely to George III's position as the grandson of the first Hanoverian king of Great Britain. Given the horror Walpole expressed in his correspondence during the 1745 Jacobite rebellion, his reasons for choosing a figure like Marshall are difficult to ascertain. Unlike the 'artful priest' he supposedly translates, Marshall functions in Walpole's representation as neither a figure of allegory nor an object of ridicule, and falls equally far from embodying Jacobite parody or from functioning as a fictional means of acting out fantasies of political defiance. He does, however, form part of Walpole's sense of aesthetic subversion and knowing impropriety – what Macaulay criticized as perversion and what recent commentators have characterized as an obsession with surface, performance and counterfeiting.[38]

For Susan Sontag, Strawberry Hill (and Gothic fiction more generally) embodies the essence of 'camp' because each displays a nostalgic affection for its source materials and a self-conscious 'love of the exaggerated, the "off"'.[39] Such 'off' moments in *The Castle of Otranto* have been noted by even its earliest readers. They occur in the book's superfluous details (as when Bianca notes that no one has slept in the chamber below them 'since the great astrologer that was your brother's tutor drowned himself' (p. 38)), in its habit of setting conventions against one another (as when the chivalry-mad Theodore unchivalrously pledges himself both to Matilda and to Isabella because he cannot tell the two heroines apart), and in its crucial scenes (as when the statue of Alphonso the Good ludicrously bleeds from its nose). Such occasions most often show Walpole gesturing to literary conventions yet refusing to wield (or oppose) them with propriety. Responding to these unstable moments in the text, readers as far-ranging as Clara Reeve, Walter Scott and William Hazlitt all noted that Walpole's ghosts often undermined the very effects they were supposed to produce. They appeared too often, or else were too large, too substantial, too *corporeal*. Hazlitt's distaste is especially telling. Calling Walpole's supernatural 'the pasteboard machinery of a pantomime', he characterizes it as too obtrusive and too artificial to produce authentic terror in its reader. Lacking appropriate sublimity and seriousness, Walpole's ghosts 'are a matter-of-fact impossibility; a fixture, and no longer a phantom'.[40] Such formulations nicely anticipate the critical assessments of Robert Miles and Jerrold Hogle, who, while differing from one another in the questions they ask of Walpole's texts, none the less isolate Walpole's self-consciousness about questions of authenticity as emblematic of Gothic writing more generally.[41] For Miles, Walpole's romance is not only about uncovering correct genealogies; it also thematizes such questions of lineage by putting forward a false account of its own origins and then insisting on its veracity. Hogle finds a similar practice of counterfeiting – and a similar nostalgia about literary and class origins – in Walpole's ghosts, which parade as medieval Italian spirits while gesturing with every action to Shakespeare. Hogle's term, 'the Ghost of the Counterfeit', recalls not only Macaulay's disgust for Walpole's 'masks within masks' but also Sontag's notion that *The Castle of Otranto* presents us not with ghosts but rather with 'ghosts' – what Hazlitt calls 'chimeras . . . begot upon shadows and dim likenesses'.[42]

It is this sense of inherent irony and self-conscious artifice – that one is somehow not meeting with characters and things but rather with performances of characters and representations of things – that has so often produced the revulsion of critics like Macaulay and the excitement of writers like Sontag. Addressing Walpole's habit of infusing his text with allusions to Shakespeare and other works, Robert Mack finally attaches the word 'parody' to Walpole's text – but not 'parody' in its usual sense:

Otranto is parody not in the sense that it seeks to deride or to mock the characteristics and language of Shakespearean drama, but parody rather in the more etymologically precise sense of the word. It is a literal *para-odos*, a complementary 'song' to be heard not in place of, but alongside the original. It asks its readers to carry their knowledge of the entire corpus of Shakespeare's drama to the work so that those very readers can themselves fill in the narrative gaps in the volume with the resonance of a shared theatrical tradition.[43]

The same can be said for the position of theatre and performance in *The Castle of Otranto* as well. While Walpole's first reviewers sensed that they were reading an eighteenth-century forgery and not a medieval romance, because of small historical errors in the text, twenty-first-century readers will discover *Otranto*'s eighteenth-century origins in the sentimental and overblown acting styles of its character-performers. The blushes, sighs and fainting spells of Walpole's heroines, and the dark brow and moody stalking of Manfred, are as much a part of the theatre of Garrick as is the spectacle in which Manfred's servant reports the death of Conrad:

The servant, who had not staid long enough to have crossed the court to Conrad's apartment, came running back breathless, in a frantic manner, his eyes staring, and foaming at the mouth. He said nothing, but pointed to the court. The company were struck with terror and amazement. The princess Hippolita, without knowing what was the matter, but anxious for her son, swooned away. (p. 18)

This focus on sentiment and emotional gesture – on representing the *expression* of emotional conflict rather than on describing its internal processes – provides us with another way of understanding the self-consciousness of Walpole's narrative style and characterization. That an inveterate theatre-goer and author of an acclaimed tragedy (*The Mysterious Mother*) and a successful comic afterpiece (*Nature Will Prevail*) should construct character theatrically rather than novelistically should not surprise us. Similar observations can be made about *Otranto*'s narrative structure. Its five chapters and general fidelity to the classical unities of the drama make it resemble a five-act tragedy far more than an eighteenth-century romance. Certainly Walpole cultivated the association; in his first Preface to *Otranto* he noted playfully: 'It is a pity that he did not apply his talents to what they were evidently proper for, the theatre' (p. 7).

Responding to Walpole's cue, we may wish to attend to the seemingly endless ghosts, counterfeits and masks in *The Castle of Otranto* by investigating the degree to which they are informed by a logic of performance and by the cultural history of Georgian theatre and opera. For Charles Beecher Hogan and Anne Williams, such a suggestion opens up a number of fruitful possibilities for understanding how and why Walpole's book has troubled its readers for so long. Locating the aesthetics of *The Castle of Otranto* in *opera seria*, Williams reimagines Strawberry Hill and the romance it inspired as essentially theatrical: 'For Walpole, Gothic is always just that, performances, its structures always full of imitation, disguise, and *travesti*.'[44] Looking to late eighteenth-century dramas of spectacle and the invention of melodrama in the early nineteenth century, Hogan's assessment is equally sweeping and suggestive. 'The grandfather of the Gothic novel,' he concludes, 'was also the grandfather of the Gothic play.'[45]

We might wish to reverse this pronouncement, however, when we consider *The Castle of Otranto*'s sustained popularity and influence. Commentators on Walpole and the Gothic have often been puzzled by the seemingly inexplicable gap between the publication of *Otranto* (1764) and the later popularity of Gothic fiction and drama in the 1780s and 1790s, wondering why such an explosively popular genre should have taken nearly twenty years to gain its hold on British imaginations. Examining its publication history a final time, we see only one significant span of years (1767–81) in which no printing of *The Castle of Otranto* occurred – perhaps the only time the book might ever have been out of print. This single dry spell was ended by the stage success of Robert Jephson's *The Count of Narbonne* (1781), an adaptation of *The Castle of Otranto* to which Walpole contributed many hours of his time hoping for its success. He was not disappointed. Performed twenty-one times during its initial run, *The Count of Narbonne* was the hit of the 1781–2 theatrical season and held the stage for the next two decades. With Jephson's success, a fresh edition of *The Castle of Otranto* was called for in 1782, and thereafter the book experienced a similar, sustained popularity: it received fourteen printings in English between 1782 and 1800; spawned numerous imitations; and acquired its status as a foundational work of Gothic fiction. Certainly the Gothic novel gave rise to the Gothic play, but the suggestion here is that Jephson's adaptation invited readers to do more than merely take up Walpole's romance again and read it alongside its theatrical representation. The sustained popularity of both points to a symbiosis between Gothic text and Gothic drama – one that anticipates the Gothic's later returns in film and digital media, and that is present since the first Gothic 'revival' of the genre Jephson and Walpole helped to construct.

Notes

1. See A. T. Hazen, *A Bibliography of Horace Walpole* (New Haven: Yale University Press, 1947), pp. 52–67; and W. S. Lewis, Introduction to Walpole, *The Castle of Otranto*, ed. W. S. Lewis (London and New York: Oxford University Press, 1964), pp. vii–viii.

2. See Appendix, no. 11, p. ii. By 'German tales' Barbauld refers not only to German works popular in Britain in the 1790s, like K. F. Kahlert's *The Necromancer, or a Tale of the Black Forest* (1794) and Gottfried August Bürger's oft-translated poem *Lenore* (1774), but also to English celebrations of German supernaturalism like Matthew Lewis's *The Monk* (1796) and Charlotte Dacre's *Zofloya* (1805).

3. See Appendix, no. 12. Scott later reprinted the essay for *Ballantyne's Novelist's Library*, ed. and intro. Walter Scott, 10 vols. (London: Hurst, Robinson & Co., 1821–4).

4. See Appendix, no. 12, p. xvii.

5. Ibid., pp. xx–xxi.

6. Barbauld's *Miscellaneous Pieces in Prose* (London: J. Johnson, 1773), written with her brother John Aiken, contains a theoretical essay on suspense ('On the Pleasure Derived from Objects of Terror') and a supernatural short story ('Sir Bertrand, a Fragment').

7. See Appendix: Early Responses to *The Castle of Otranto*.

8. See Appendix, no. 11, p. i.

9. See Appendix, no. 1, p. 51.

10. See Appendix, no. 2, p. 99.

11. See Appendix, no. 4, p. 394.

12. See especially Robert P. Reno, 'James Boaden's *Fontainville Forest* and Matthew Lewis's *The Castle Spectre*: Challenges of the Supernatural Ghost on the Late Eighteenth-Century Stage', *Eighteenth-Century Life* 9 (1984), pp. 95–106; and Further Reading, Clery.

13. See Further Reading, Lewis, *The Yale Edition of Horace Walpole's Correspondence* (hereinafter referred to as *Correspondence*), Vol. 30, p. 177.

14. Ibid., Vol. 28, p. 5.

15. See Further Reading, Kallich, Ketton-Cremer, and Mowl.

16. By Walpole's injunction, the manuscripts of the *Memoirs* were not published until nearly three decades after his death.

17. *Museum* 2 (1746), pp. 46–7.

18. See Further Reading, Lewis, *Horace Walpole: The A. W. Mellon Lectures in the Fine Arts 1960*, p. 155.

19. See Appendix, no. 17, p. 227.

20. Ibid., esp. p. 227: 'His features were covered by mask within mask. When the outer disguise of obvious affectation was removed, you were still as far as ever from seeing the real man.'

21. Ibid., p. 239.

22. See Further Reading, Ketton-Cremer and Lewis (*Correspondence*).

23. As a revived architectural style, Gothic was first popularized by the engravings that appeared in Thomas and Batty Langley's *Gothic Architecture, Improved*, which was first published in 1741 under the title of *Ancient Architecture*. Walpole criticized the Langleys' attempts to graft Gothic decorations on to classical forms. Other early attempts, like those of Lord Brooke at Warwick Castle, failed in Walpole's mind for similar reasons, while Saunderson Miller's work at Wroxton simply collapsed.

24. Walpole to Horace Mann, 25 February 1750 (*Correspondence*, Vol. 20, p. 127).

25. See *The Ambulator: or, A Pocket Companion in a Tour Round London* (London: J. Scatcherd, 1800), pp. 14–15, 198–202.

26. See Walpole, *Journal of the Printing-Office at Strawberry Hill*, ed. Paget Toynbee (London: Constable & Houghton Mifflin, 1923). Under 1784 the entry reads 'printed a page of rules for admission to see my House', but does not indicate how many copies were printed. See also Walpole, *A Description of the Villa of Mr. Horace Walpole* (Twickenham: Strawberry Hill, 1774; 2nd edition, 1784).

27. See Walpole to William Cole, 9 March 1765 (*Correspondence*, Vol. 1, p. 88); Walpole to Horace Mann, 18 November 1771 (ibid., Vol. 23, pp. 349–51); and Walpole to Mme du Deffand, 27 January 1775 (ibid., Vol. 6, p. 145). Angry over Walpole's refusal to believe his forgeries genuine, Thomas Chatterton later wrote a long diatribe against the 'Baron of Otranto', which formed the basis of the later controversy over Walpole's role in Chatterton's death (ibid., Vol. 15, pp. xvi–xvii).

28. Walpole to William Cole, 9 March 1765 (*Correspondence*, Vol. 1, p. 88). See also Walpole, *A Description of the Villa of Mr. Horace Walpole*, p. iv.

29. See Further Reading, Guest, Harfst, Kiely and Punter.

30. This was first noted in W. S. Lewis, Introduction to *The Castle of Otranto*, pp. 12–13.

31. Walpole to Mme du Deffand, 13 March 1767. This translation quoted from Stephen Gwynn, *The Life of Horace Walpole* (London: Thorton Butterworth, 1932), p. 191.

32. See Further Reading, Clery, p. 54.

33. Richard Hurd, *Letters on Chivalry and Romance*, ed. Edith J. Morley (London: Henry Frowde, 1911), pp. 94, 118–19.

34. See Further Reading, Clery, Guest and Kiely.

35. See Appendix, no. 17, p. 233.

36. See Further Reading, Fothergill, Ketton-Cremer and Samson.

37. See Further Reading, Harfst and Haggerty.

38. See Further Reading, Hogan, Hogle, Sedgwick and Williams.

39. See Further Reading, Sontag, p. 108.

40. See Appendix, no. 15.

41. See Further Reading, Miles and Hogle.

42. See Appendix, no. 15.

43. Robert Mack, Introduction to Walpole, *The Castle of Otranto and Hieroglyphic Tales* (London: J. M. Dent, 1993), p. xx.

44. See Further Reading, Williams, p. 115.

45. See Further Reading, Hogan, p. 237.

FURTHER READING

Books and Articles:

Baldick, Chris, ed., *The Oxford Book of Gothic Tales* (Oxford and New York: Oxford University Press, 1992). Aims to provide a survey of Gothic short fiction from the late eighteenth century to the present day.

Bedford, Kristina, ' "This Castle Hath a Pleasant Seat": Shakespearean Allusion in *The Castle of Otranto*', *English Studies in Canada* XIV (1988), pp. 415–33. An exhaustive exploration of Walpole's writings about, and borrowings from, Shakespeare.

Brown, Marshall, 'A Philosophical View of the Gothic Novel', *Studies in Romanticism* 26 (1987), pp. 275–301. Considers Gothic fiction by Walpole and others in relation to eighteenth-century philosophical discourses.

Chalcraft, Anna, *A Paper House: Horace Walpole at Strawberry Hill* (Beverley: Highgate, 1998). A selection of Walpole's letters interspersed with commentary on the construction and cultural significance of Strawberry Hill.

Clery, E. J., *The Rise of Supernatural Fiction 1762–1800* (Cambridge: Cambridge University Press, 1995). This material history of Gothic and supernatural fiction devotes two chapters to Walpole and *Otranto*: Ch. 3, 'The Advantages of History', places Walpole's hoax with the first edition in the context of popular antiquarianism in the 1760s and the various historicisms it practised; Ch. 4, 'Back to the Future', reads *Otranto* within contemporary re-imaginings (Richard Hurd, James Stuart and Adam Smith) of chivalry and feudalism as 'a distinctive stage in historical evolution with a prevailing mode of subsistence giving rise to characteristic social, intellectual and political structures' (p. 68).

Cox, Jeffrey, ed., *Seven Gothic Dramas, 1789–1825* (Athens, OH: Ohio University Press, 1992). An anthology of Gothic drama with a substantial and cogent Introduction that addresses Walpole as an important precursor to this kind of spectacular drama.

Fothergill, Brian, *The Strawberry Hill Set: Horace Walpole and His Circle* (London: Faber & Faber, 1983). A biographical account of Walpole, focusing on his many friendships.

Frank, Frederick S., *Guide to the Gothic II: An Annotated Bibliography of Criticism, 1983–1993* (Lanham, MD, and London: The Scarecrow Press, Inc., 1995). An exhaustive bibliography of recent critical writing on the Gothic.

Guest, Harriet, 'The Wanton Muse: Politics and Gender in Gothic Theory after 1760', *Beyond Romanticism: New Approaches to Texts and Contexts, 1780–1832*, ed. Stephen Copley and John Whale (London and New York: Routledge, 1992), pp. 118–39. This article focuses on early theories of Gothic; on their ambivalent gendering and how they define a 'territory of . . . pleasure in terms that do not readily yield their political affiliation' (p. 119). These early theories provided a marked contrast to those affiliated with Gothic texts in the 1790s.

Haggerty, George E., 'Literature and Homosexuality in the Late Eighteenth Century: Walpole, Beckford and Lewis', *Studies in the Novel* 18 (1986), pp. 341–52. Explores the relation between Gothic fiction and the homosexuality of three of its primary eighteenth-century male practitioners.

Harfst, Betsy Perteit, *Horace Walpole and the Unconscious: An Experiment in Freudian Analysis* (New York: Arno, 1980). This published dissertation 'attempts to expose the unconscious repressions which could have been responsible for the erratic behavior of Horace Walpole . . . and to determine the relationship between these repressions and his romantic works' (p. i).

Hogan, Charles Beecher, 'The "Theatre of Geo. 3" ', *Horace Walpole: Writer, Politician, and Connoisseur*, ed. Warren Hunting Smith (New

Haven and London: Yale University Press, 1967), pp. 227–40. This article establishes Walpole's interest in both reading plays and attending the theatre as a foundation for reading *The Castle of Otranto*, ultimately arguing that '[t]he grandfather of the Gothic novel was also the grandfather of the Gothic play . . . Far more than *The Mysterious Mother* or *Nature Will Prevail* its form is dramatic; so is its theme; so are its characters' (p. 237).

Hogle, Jerrold, 'The Ghost of the Counterfeit and the Genesis of the Gothic', *Gothick Origins and Innovations*, ed. Allan Lloyd Smith and Victor Sage (Amsterdam and Atlanta: Rodopi, 1994), pp. 23–33. This playful essay interprets Walpole's (and Gothic fiction's) obsession with forgeries and counterfeited signs through the work of Jean Baudrillard, Gilles Deleuze and Félix Guattari, focusing particularly on their contention that with the advent of mercantile and capitalist culture one sees a widening gulf between sign and signifier.

Kallich, Martin, *Horace Walpole* (New York: Twayne, 1971). This study of Walpole's literary historical importance gives primacy to his published writings rather than to his letters.

Ketton-Cremer, R. W., *Horace Walpole: A Biography*, 3rd edition (London: Methuen, 1964). First published in 1940, this remains the most recent standard biography of Walpole.

Kiely, Robert, *The Romantic Novel in England* (Cambridge, MA: Harvard University Press, 1972). This book devotes its opening chapter to *The Castle of Otranto*, stressing the book's relation to epic and eighteenth-century politics, and its interest in Catholicism and the irrational.

Kliger, Samuel, *The Goths in England: A Study in Seventeenth- and Eighteenth-Century Thought* (Cambridge, MA: Harvard University Press, 1952). This foundational study connects Gothic Revival aesthetics of the eighteenth century to seventeenth-century political debates about the nature of parliamentary prerogative, arguing that 'the history of the "Gothic" begins not in the eighteenth but in the seventeenth century, not in aesthetic but in political discussion'.

Lewis, W. S., *Horace Walpole: The A. W. Mellon Lectures in the Fine Arts 1960* (London: Rupert Hart-Davis, 1961). Five readable and cogent introductory lectures on Walpole's 'Family', 'Friends', 'Politics', 'Strawberry Hill' and 'Works'.

Lewis, W. S., ed., *The Yale Edition of Horace Walpole's Correspondence*, 48 vols. (New Haven: Yale University Press; London: Oxford University Press, 1937–83). The monumental edition of Horace Walpole's correspondence.

McKinney, David, 'The Castle of My Ancestors: Horace Walpole and Strawberry Hill', *British Journal for Eighteenth-Century Studies* 13 (1990), pp. 199–214. This article focuses upon Walpole's construction of Strawberry Hill as a genealogical monument that evoked an idealized past whose glory is transferred to Walpole and his family.

Miles, Robert, *Gothic Writing, 1750–1820: A Genealogy* (London and New York: Routledge, 1993). Defining Gothic as a heterogeneous aesthetic crossing the genres, this book devotes a chapter to Walpole's (and the Gothic's) self-reflexive fixation upon questions of lineage and descent.

Mowl, Timothy, *Horace Walpole: The Great Outsider* (London: John Murray, 1996). This most recent biography of Walpole takes issue with earlier treatments of Walpole's homosexuality by W. S. Lewis, R. W. Ketton-Cremer and others; it is most persuasive in its treatment of Walpole's Grand Tour and his relationship with Lord Lincoln.

Napier, Elizabeth, *The Failure of Gothic: Problems of Disjunction in an Eighteenth-Century Literary Form* (Oxford: Clarendon Press, 1987). Napier's book argues that modern critical readings of Gothic fiction have been characterized by 'imprecision and extremes' (p. 4), and attributes this phenomenon to the instability (what she calls the 'failure') of the genre itself.

Punter, David, *The Literature of Terror: A History of Gothic Fictions from 1765 to the Present Day: Volume 1: The Gothic Tradition* (London and New York: Longman, 1980; 2nd edition, 1996). A foundational study of the Gothic from both Freudian and Marxist approaches, treating its persistent themes, its relation to other contemporary aesthetic movements, and its various transformations and their contexts.

Sabor, Peter, ed., *Horace Walpole: The Critical Heritage* (London and New York: Routledge & Kegan Paul, 1987). An anthology of Walpole's contemporary, nineteenth- and twentieth-century critical reception.

Samson, John, 'Politics Gothicized: The Conway Incident and *The Castle of Otranto*', *Eighteenth-Century Life* 10 (1986), pp. 145–58. Countering the widespread assumption that Walpole wrote *The Castle of Otranto* as an escape from politics, this essay argues that 'the book evinces a startling infusion of the characters, events, and ideas in Walpole's political life in 1764' (p. 145).

Sedgwick, Eve Kosofsky, *The Coherence of Gothic Conventions*, 2nd edition (New York: Methuen, 1986). This book provides an account of the relation between Gothic conventions and the ways in which its practitioners wield language and structure narrative.

Sontag, Susan, 'Notes on Camp', *Against Interpretation* (New York: Farrar, Strauss & Giroux, 1966). Also printed in *A Susan Sontag Reader*, intro. Elizabeth Hardwick (Harmondsworth: Penguin Books, 1983), pp. 105–19.

Watt, Ian P., 'Time and the Family in the Gothic Novel: *The Castle of Otranto*', *Eighteenth-Century Life* 10 (1986), pp. 159–71. Watt reads *Otranto*'s concern with genealogies and retribution not only to suggest that '[t]he very word "Gothic" suggests that the genre has got something to do with time' (p. 159), but also to argue that 'the essence of *The Castle of Otranto*' is its dramatization of the supernatural ability of a family's various pasts to impose themselves upon the present (p. 161).

Williams, Anne, 'Monstrous Pleasures: Horace Walpole, Opera, and the Conception of Gothic', *Gothic Studies* 2 (April 2000), pp. 104–18. This article explores Walpole's fondness for opera and grounds *The Castle of Otranto* and the Gothic in operatic travesty, theatricality and subject matter.

On-Line Resources:

Gothic Literature: What the Romantics Read, ed. Douglass Thomson (URL: http://www2.gasou.edu/facstaff/dougt/gothic.htm). Explores William Blake's, Lord Byron's, Samuel Coleridge's, John Keats's, Percy Bysshe Shelley's and William Wordsworth's acquaintance with Gothic writing, and provides a bibliography on the subject.

The Lewis Walpole Library. Curator of site: Anthony Melillo <anthony.melillo@yale.edu> (URL: http://www.library.yale. edu/Walpole). A small site providing information for visiting the Lewis Walpole Library in Farmington, Connecticut, as well as for conducting research there.

The Literary Gothic, ed. Jack G. Voller (URL: http://www.litgothic. com). A general guide to the Gothic on the world-wide web, featuring an excellent bibliography of electronic texts and general resources.

The Sickly Taper, ed. Frederick Frank (URL: http://www.toolcity. net/~ffrank). A site dedicated to Gothic bibliography that extends Frank's *Guide to the Gothic*.

Sublime Anxiety: The Gothic Family and the Outsider, (URL: http:// www.lib.virginia.edu/exhibits/gothic). An exhibition at the University of Virginia library curated by Natalie Regensburg exploring the literary, economic and social history of Gothic writing, with sections on 'Women and the Gothic', 'Imperialism', 'Mystery and the Detective' and other subjects.

Women Romantic-Era Writers, ed. Adriana Craciun (URL: http:// www.nottingham.ac.uk/~aezacweb/wrew.htm). A wide-ranging site providing substantial resources for people interested in Gothic women writers and their female contemporaries.

A NOTE ON THE TEXT

The Castle of Otranto was printed frequently during Horace Walpole's lifetime. Its first edition of 500 copies appeared 24 December 1764; the second, also of 500 copies, appeared 11 April 1765. Subsequent editions or reprintings followed in 1766 (third edition), 1782 (fourth edition), 1786 (fifth edition), 1791 (a reprint of the fifth edition and a sixth edition published in Parma, Italy, by Bodoni), 1793 (two printings), 1794, 1796 and 1797. French translations appeared in 1767 and 1797, Italian in 1794 and 1795. A. T. Hazen provides an exhaustive listing of all editions of Walpole's works in *A Bibliography of Horace Walpole* (New Haven: Yale University Press, 1947).

The basis for this edition's text of *The Castle of Otranto* is the version printed in *The Works of Horatio Walpole, Earl of Orford*, 5 vols. (London: G. G. & J. Robinson, and J. Edwards, 1798), Vol. 2, pp. 1–90. Walpole had begun printing his collected works as early as 1768 or 1770 (see *Correspondence*, Vol. 42, pp. 371–3), and the text of *The Castle of Otranto* appearing in his collected *Works* was the last that he prepared for publication. While strongly resembling the second edition of 1765, it corrects earlier typographical errors and makes many small alterations, particularly of punctuation. Except in the case of obvious errors I have preserved Walpole's spelling and punctuation.

THE

Castle of Otranto,

A

STORY

Translated by

WILLIAM MARSHALL,[1] Gent.

From the Original ITALIAN of

ONUPHRIO MURALTO,[2]

Canon of the Church of St. NICHOLAS[3]
at OTRANTO

LONDON:
Printed for THO. Lownds in Fleet-Street.
MDCCLXIV

[*Title-page of the first edition*]

THE

Castle of Otranto,

A

GOTHIC STORY.

————*Vanæ*

Fingentur species, tamen ut Pes, & Caput uni Reddantur formæ.[1] ————

HOR.

THE SECOND EDITION

LONDON:

Printed for WILLIAM BATHOE in the *Strand,*
and THOMAS LOWNDS in *Fleet-Street.*

M.DCC.LXV.

[*Title-page of the second edition*]

PREFACE TO THE FIRST EDITION

The following work was found in the library of an ancient catholic family in the north of England.[1] It was printed at Naples,[2] in the black letter,[3] in the year 1529.[4] How much sooner it was written does not appear. The principal incidents are such as were believed in the darkest ages of christianity; but the language and conduct have nothing that savours of barbarism. The style is the purest Italian.[5] If the story was written near the time when it is supposed to have happened, it must have been between 1095, the æra of the first crusade, and 1243,[6] the date of the last, or not long afterwards. There is no other circumstance in the work that can lead us to guess at the period in which the scene is laid: the names of the actors are evidently fictitious,[7] and probably disguised on purpose: yet the Spanish names of the domestics seem to indicate that this work was not composed until the establishment of the Arragonian kings in Naples[8] had made Spanish appellations familiar in that country. The beauty of the diction, and the zeal of the author, [moderated however by singular judgment] concur to make me think that the date of the composition was little antecedent to that of the impression. Letters were then in their most flourishing state in Italy, and contributed to dispel the empire of superstition, at that time so forcibly attacked by the reformers. It is not unlikely that an artful priest might endeavour to turn their own arms on the innovators; and might avail himself of his abilities as an author to confirm the populace in their ancient errors and superstitions. If this was his view, he has certainly acted with signal address. Such a work as the following would enslave a hundred vulgar minds beyond half the books of controversy that have been written from the days of Luther[9] to the present hour.

This solution of the author's motives is however offered as a mere conjecture. Whatever his views were, or whatever effects the execution of them might have, his work can only be laid before the public at present as a matter of entertainment. Even as such, some apology for it is necessary. Miracles, visions, necromancy, dreams, and other preternatural events, are exploded now even from romances. That was not the case when our author wrote; much less when the story itself is supposed to have happened. Belief in every kind of prodigy was so established in those dark ages, that an author would not be faithful to the *manners* of the times who should omit all mention of them. He is not bound to believe them himself, but he must represent his actors as believing them.

If this *air* of the *miraculous* is excused, the reader will find nothing else unworthy of his perusal. Allow the possibility of the facts, and all the actors comport themselves as persons would do in their situation. There is no bombast, no similes, flowers,[10] digressions, or unnecessary descriptions. Every thing tends directly to the catastrophe. Never is the reader's attention relaxed. The rules of the drama[11] are almost observed throughout the conduct of the piece. The characters are well drawn, and still better maintained. Terror, the author's principal engine, prevents the story from ever languishing; and it is so often contrasted by pity, that the mind is kept up in a constant vicissitude of interesting passions.[12]

Some persons may perhaps think the characters of the domestics too little serious for the general cast of the story; but besides their opposition to the principal personages, the art of the author is very observable in his conduct of the subalterns. They discover many passages essential to the story, which could not be well brought to light but by their *naïveté* and simplicity: in particular, the womanish terror and foibles of Bianca, in the last chapter, conduce essentially towards advancing the catastrophe.

It is natural for a translator to be prejudiced in favour of his adopted work. More impartial readers may not be so much struck with the beauties of this piece as I was. Yet I am not blind to my author's defects. I could wish he had grounded his plan on a more useful moral than this; that *the sins of fathers are visited on their children to the third and fourth generation.*[13] I doubt whether in his time, any more than at present, ambition curbed its appetite of dominion from the dread of so remote a punishment. And yet this moral is weakened by that less direct insinuation, that even such anathema may be diverted by devotion to saint Nicholas. Here the interest of the monk plainly gets the better of the judgment of the author. However, with all its faults, I have no doubt but the English reader will be pleased with a sight of this performance. The piety that reigns throughout, the lessons of virtue that are inculcated, and the rigid purity of the sentiments, exempt this work from the censure to which romances are but too liable.[14] Should it meet with the success I hope for, I may be encouraged to re-print the original Italian, though it will tend to depreciate my own labour. Our language falls far short of the charms of the Italian, both for variety and harmony. The latter is peculiarly excellent for simple narrative. It is difficult in English *to relate* without falling too low or rising too high; a fault obviously occasioned by the little care taken to speak pure language in common conversation. Every Italian or Frenchman of any rank piques himself on speaking his own tongue correctly and with choice. I cannot flatter myself with having done justice to my author in this respect: his style is as elegant as his conduct of the passions is masterly. It is pity that he did not apply his talents to what they were evidently proper for, the theatre.

I will detain the reader no longer but to make one short remark. Though the machinery is invention, and the names of the actors imaginary, I cannot but believe that the ground-work of the story is founded on truth. The scene is undoubtedly laid in some real castle.[15] The author seems frequently, without design, to describe particular parts. *The chamber,* says he, *on the right-hand; the door on the left-hand; the distance from the chapel to Conrad's apartment:* these and other passages are strong presumptions that the author had some certain building in his eye. Curious persons, who have leisure to employ in such researches, may possibly discover in the Italian writers the foundation on which our author has built. If a catastrophe, at all resembling that which he describes, is believed to have given rise to this work, it will contribute to interest the reader, and will make The Castle of Otranto a still more moving story.

PREFACE TO THE SECOND EDITION

The favourable manner in which this little piece has been received by the public,[1] calls upon the author to explain the grounds on which he composed it. But before he opens those motives, it is fit that he should ask pardon of his readers for having offered his work to them under the borrowed personage of a translator. As diffidence of his own abilities, and the novelty of the attempt, were his sole inducements to assume that disguise, he flatters himself he shall appear excusable. He resigned his performance to the impartial judgment of the public; determined to let it perish in obscurity, if disapproved; nor meaning to avow such a trifle, unless better judges should pronounce that he might own it without a blush.

It was an attempt to blend the two kinds of romance, the ancient and the modern. In the former all was imagination and improbability: in the latter, nature is always intended to be, and sometimes has been, copied with success. Invention has not been wanting; but the great resources of fancy have been dammed up, by a strict adherence to common life. But if in the latter species Nature has cramped imagination, she did but take her revenge, having been totally excluded from old romances. The actions, sentiments, conversations, of the heroes and heroines of ancient days were as unnatural as the machines employed to put them in motion.

The author of the following pages thought it possible to reconcile the two kinds. Desirous of leaving the powers of fancy at liberty to expatiate through the boundless realms of invention, and thence of creating more interesting situations, he wished to conduct the mortal agents of his drama according to the rules of probability;[2] in short, to make them think, speak and act, as it might be supposed mere men and women would do in extraordinary positions. He had observed, that in all inspired writings, the personages under the dispensation of miracles, and witnesses to the most stupendous phenomena, never lose sight of their human character: whereas in the productions of romantic story, an improbable event never fails to be attended by an absurd dialogue. The actors seem to lose their senses the moment the laws of nature have lost their tone. As the public have applauded the attempt, the author must not say he was entirely unequal to the task he had undertaken: yet if the new route he has struck out shall have paved a road for men of brighter talents, he shall own with pleasure and modesty, that he was sensible the plan was capable of receiving greater embellishments than his imagination or conduct of the passions could bestow on it.

With regard to the deportment of the domestics, on which I have touched in the former preface, I will beg leave to add a few words. The simplicity of their behaviour, almost tending to excite smiles, which at first seem not consonant to the serious cast of the work, appeared to me not only not improper, but was marked designedly in that manner. My rule was nature.[3] However grave, important, or even melancholy, the sensations of princes and heroes may be, they do not stamp the same affections[4] on their domestics: at least the latter do not, or should not be made to express their passions in the same dignified tone. In my humble opinion, the contrast between the sublime[5] of the one, and the *naïveté* of the other, sets the pathetic of the former in a stronger light. The very impatience which a reader feels, while delayed by the coarse pleasantries of vulgar actors from arriving at the knowledge of the important catastrophe he expects, perhaps heightens, certainly proves that he has been artfully interested in, the depending event. But I had higher authority than my own opinion for this conduct. The great master of nature, Shakespeare, was the model I copied. Let me ask if his tragedies of Hamlet and Julius Caesar would not lose a considerable share of the spirit and wonderful beauties, if the humour of the grave-diggers, the fooleries of Polonius, and the clumsy jests of the Roman citizens were omitted, or vested in heroics?[6] Is not the eloquence of Antony, the nobler and affectedly-unaffected oration of Brutus, artificially exalted by the rude bursts of nature from the mouths of their auditors? These touches remind one of the Grecian sculptor, who, to convey the idea of a Colossus within the dimensions of a seal, inserted a little boy measuring his thumb.

No, says Voltaire[7] in his edition of Corneille,[8] this mixture of buffoonery and solemnity is intolerable. — Voltaire is a genius[9] – but not of Shakespeare's magnitude. Without recurring to disputable authority, I appeal Voltaire to himself. I shall not avail myself of his former encomiums on our mighty poet; though the French critic has twice translated the same speech in Hamlet,[10] some years ago in admiration, latterly in derision; and I am sorry to find that his judgment grows weaker, when it ought to be farther matured. But I shall make use of his own words, delivered on the general topic of the theatre, when he was neither thinking to recommend or decry Shakespeare's practice; consequently at a moment when Voltaire was impartial. In the preface to his Enfant prodigue, that exquisite piece of which I declare my admiration, and which, should I live twenty years longer, I trust I should never attempt to ridicule, he has these words, speaking of comedy, [but equally applicable to tragedy, if tragedy is, as surely it ought to be, a picture of human life; nor can I conceive why occasional pleasantry ought more to be banished from the tragic scene, than pathetic seriousness from the comic] *On y voit un melange de serieux et de plaisanterie, de comique et de touchant;* souvent même une seule avanture *produit tous ces contrastes. Rien n'est si commun qu'une maison dans laquelle* un pere gronde, un fille occupée de sa passion pleure; *le fils se moque des deux, et quelques parens prennent part differemment à la scene, &c. Nous n'inferons pas de là que toute comedie doive avoir des scenes de bouffonnerie et des scenes attendrissantes: il y a beaucoup de tres bonnes pieces où il ne regne que de la gayeté; d'autres toutes serieuses; d'autres melangées: d'autres où l'attendrissement va jusques aux larmes:* il ne faut donner l'exclusion à aucun genre: *et si l'on me demandoit, quel genre est le meilleur, je repondrois, celui qui est le mieux traité.*[11] Surely if a comedy may be *toute serieuse*, tragedy may now and then, soberly, be indulged in a smile. Who shall proscribe it? Shall the critic, who in self-defence declares that *no kind* ought to be excluded from comedy, give laws to Shakespeare?

I am aware that the preface from whence I have quoted these passages does not stand in monsieur de Voltaire's name, but in that of his editor; yet who doubts that the editor and author were the same person?[12] Or where is the editor, who has so happily possessed himself of his author's style and brilliant ease of argument? These passages were indubitably the genuine sentiments of that great writer. In his epistle to Maffei, prefixed to his Merope,[13] he delivers almost the same opinion, though I doubt with a little irony. I will repeat his words, and then give my reason for quoting them. After translating a passage in Maffei's Merope, monsieur de Voltaire adds, *Tous ces traits sont naïfs: tout y est convenable à ceux que vous introduisez sur la scene*, et aux moeurs que vous leur donnez. *Ces familiarités naturelles eussent été, à ce que je crois, bien reçues dans Athenes; mais Paris et notre parterre veulent une autre espece de simplicité*.[14] I doubt, I say, whether there is not a grain of sneer in this and other passages of that epistle; yet the force of truth is not damaged by being tinged with ridicule. Maffei was to represent a Grecian story: surely the Athenians were as competent judges of Grecian manners, and of the propriety of introducing them, as the parterre[15] of Paris. On the contrary, says Voltaire [and I cannot but admire his reasoning] there were but ten thousand citizens at Athens, and Paris has near eight hundred thousand inhabitants, among whom one may reckon thirty thousand judges of dramatic works. — Indeed! — But allowing so numerous a tribunal, I believe this is the only instance in which it was ever pretended that thirty thousand persons, living near two thousand years after the era in question, were, upon the mere face of the poll, declared better judges than the Grecians themselves of what ought to be the manners of a tragedy written on a Grecian story.

I will not enter into a discussion of the *espece de simplicité*, which the *parterre* of Paris demands, nor of the shackles with which *the thirty thousand judges* have cramped their poetry, the chief merit of which, as I gather from the repeated passages in The New Commentary on Corneille, consists in vaulting in spite of those fetters; a merit which, if true, would reduce poetry from the lofty effort of imagination, to a puerile and most contemptible labour – *difficiles nugæ*[16] with a witness! I cannot help however mentioning a couplet, which to my English ears always sounded as the flattest and most trifling instance of circumstantial propriety; but which Voltaire, who has dealt so severely with nine parts in ten of Corneille's works, has singled out to defend in Racine;[17]

> *De son appartement cette porte est prochaine,*
> *Et cette autre conduit dans celui de la reine.*[18]

In English,

> To Caesar's closet through this door you come,
> And t'other leads to the queen's drawing-room.

Unhappy Shakespeare! hadst thou made Rosencrans inform his compeer Guildenstern of the ichnography[19] of that palace of Copenhagen, instead of presenting us with a moral dialogue between the prince of Denmark and the grave-digger, the illuminated pit of Paris would have been instructed *a second time* to adore thy talents.

The result of all I have said, is to shelter my own daring under the cannon of the brightest genius this country, at least, has produced. I might have pleaded, that having created a new species of romance, I was at liberty to lay down what rules I thought fit for the conduct of it: but I should be more proud of having imitated, however faintly, weakly, and at a distance, so masterly a pattern, than to enjoy the entire merit of invention, unless I could have marked my work with genius as well as with originality. Such as it is, the public have honoured it sufficiently, whatever rank their suffrages allot to it.

SONNET

To the Right Honourable Lady Mary Coke.[1]

The gentle maid, whose hapless tale
These melancholy pages speak;
Say, gracious lady, shall she fail
To draw the tear adown thy cheek?

No; never was thy pitying breast
Insensible to human woes;
Tender, though firm, it melts distrest
For weaknesses it never knows.

Oh! guard the marvels I relate
Of fell ambition scourg'd by fate,
   From reason's peevish blame:
Blest with thy smile, my dauntless sail
I dare expand to fancy's gale,
   For sure thy smiles are fame.
                    H. W.

CHAPTER I

Manfred, prince of Otranto, had one son and one daughter: the latter, a most beautiful virgin, aged eighteen, was called Matilda. Conrad, the son, was three years younger, a homely youth, sickly, and of no promising disposition; yet he was the darling of his father, who never showed any symptoms of affection to Matilda. Manfred had contracted a marriage for his son with the marquis of Vicenza's daughter, Isabella; and she had already been delivered by her guardians into the hands of Manfred, that he might celebrate the wedding as soon as Conrad's infirm state of health would permit. Manfred's impatience for this ceremonial was remarked by his family and neighbours. The former, indeed, apprehending the severity of their prince's disposition, did not dare to utter their surmises on this precipitation. Hippolita, his wife, an amiable lady, did sometimes venture to represent the danger of marrying their only son so early, considering his great youth, and greater infirmities; but she never received any other answer than reflections on her own sterility, who had given him but one heir. His tenants and subjects were less cautious in their discourses: they attributed this hasty wedding to the prince's dread of seeing accomplished an ancient prophecy, which was said to have pronounced, *That the castle and lordship of Otranto should pass from the present family, whenever the real owner should be grown too large to inhabit it.* It was difficult to make any sense of this prophecy; and still less easy to conceive what it had to do with the marriage in question. Yet these mysteries, or contradictions, did not make the populace adhere the less to their opinion.

Young Conrad's birth-day was fixed for his espousals. The company was assembled in the chapel of the castle, and every thing ready for beginning the divine office, when Conrad himself was missing. Manfred, impatient of the least delay, and who had not observed his son retire, dispatched one of his attendants to summon the young prince. The servant, who had not staid long enough to have crossed the court to Conrad's apartment, came running back breathless, in a frantic manner, his eyes staring, and foaming at the mouth. He said nothing, but pointed to the court. The company were struck with terror and amazement. The princess Hippolita, without knowing what was the matter, but anxious for her son, swooned away. Manfred, less apprehensive than enraged at the procrastination of the nuptials, and at the folly of his domestic, asked imperiously, what was the matter? The fellow made no answer, but continued pointing towards the court-yard; and at last, after repeated questions put to him, cried out, Oh, the helmet! the helmet! In the mean time some of the company had run into the court, from whence was heard a confused noise of shrieks, horror, and surprise. Manfred, who began to be alarmed at not seeing his son, went himself to get information of what occasioned this strange confusion. Matilda remained endeavouring to assist her mother, and Isabella staid for the same purpose, and to avoid showing any impatience for the bridegroom, for whom, in truth, she had conceived little affection.

The first thing that struck Manfred's eyes was a group of his servants endeavouring to raise something that appeared to him a mountain of sable plumes. He gazed without believing his sight. What are ye doing? cried Manfred, wrathfully: Where is my son? A volley of voices replied, Oh, my lord! the prince! the prince, the helmet! the helmet! Shocked with these lamentable sounds, and dreading he knew not what, he advanced hastily — But what a sight for a father's eyes! – He beheld his child dashed to pieces, and almost buried under an enormous helmet, an hundred times more large than any casque ever made for human being, and shaded with a proportionable quantity of black feathers.

The horror of the spectacle, the ignorance of all around how this misfortune had happened, and above all, the tremendous phœnomenon before him, took away the prince's speech. Yet his silence lasted longer than even grief could occasion. He fixed his eyes on what he wished in vain to believe a vision; and seemed less attentive to his loss, than buried in meditation on the stupendous object that had occasioned it. He touched, he examined the fatal casque; nor could even the bleeding mangled remains of the young prince divert the eyes of Manfred from the portent before him. All who had known his partial fondness for young Conrad, were as much surprised at their prince's insensibility, as thunderstruck themselves at the miracle of the helmet. They conveyed the disfigured corpse into the hall, without receiving the least direction from Manfred. As little was he attentive to the ladies who remained in the chapel: on the contrary, without mentioning the unhappy princesses his wife and daughter, the first sounds that dropped from Manfred's lips were, Take care of the lady Isabella.

The domestics, without observing the singularity of this direction, were guided by their affection to their mistress to consider it as peculiarly addressed to her situation, and flew to her assistance. They conveyed her to her chamber more dead than alive, and indifferent to all the strange circumstances she heard, except the death of her son. Matilda, who doated on her mother, smothered her own grief and amazement, and thought of nothing but assisting and comforting her afflicted parent. Isabella, who had been treated by Hippolita like a daughter, and who returned that tenderness with equal duty and affection, was scarce less assiduous about the princess; at the same time endeavouring to partake and lessen the weight of sorrow which she saw Matilda strove to suppress, for whom she had conceived the warmest sympathy of friendship. Yet her own situation could not help finding its place in her thoughts. She felt no concern for the death of young Conrad, except commiseration; and she was not sorry to be delivered from a marriage which had promised her little felicity, either from her destined bridegroom, or from the severe temper of Manfred, who, though he had distinguished her by great indulgence, had imprinted her mind with terror, from his causeless rigour to such amiable princesses as Hippolita and Matilda.

While the ladies were conveying the wretched mother to her bed, Manfred remained in the court, gazing on the ominous casque, and regardless of the crowd which the strangeness of the event had now assembled around him. The few words he articulated tended solely to enquiries, whether any man knew from whence it could have come? Nobody could give him the least information. However, as it seemed to be the sole object of his curiosity, it soon became so to the rest of the spectators, whose conjectures were as absurd and improbable as the catastrophe itself was unprecedented. In the midst of their senseless guesses a young peasant, whom rumour had drawn thither from a neighbouring village, observed that the miraculous helmet was exactly like that on the figure in black marble of Alfonso the Good,[1] one of their former princes, in the church of St. Nicholas. Villain! What sayest thou! cried Manfred, starting from his trance in a tempest of rage, and seizing the young man by the collar: How darest thou utter such treason? Thy life shall pay for it. The spectators, who as little comprehended the cause of the prince's fury as all the rest they had seen, were at a loss to unravel this new circumstance. The young peasant himself was still more astonished, not conceiving how he had offended the prince: yet recollecting himself, with a mixture of grace and humility, he disengaged himself from Manfred's gripe,[2] and then, with an obeisance[3] which discovered more jealousy of innocence, than dismay, he asked with respect, of what he was guilty! Manfred, more enraged at the vigour, however decently exerted, with which the young man had shaken off his hold, than appeased by his submission, ordered his attendants to seize him, and, if he had not been withheld by his friends whom he had invited to the nuptials, would have poignarded[4] the peasant in their arms.

During this altercation some of the vulgar spectators had run to the great church which stood near the castle, and came back open-mouthed, declaring the helmet was missing from Alfonso's statue. Manfred, at this news, grew perfectly frantic; and, as if he sought a subject on which to vent the tempest within him, he rushed again on the young peasant, crying, Villain! monster! sorcerer! 'tis thou hast slain my son! The mob, who wanted some object within the scope of their capacities on whom they might discharge their bewildered reasonings, caught the words from the mouth of their lord, and re-echoed, Ay, ay; 'tis he, 'tis he: he has stolen the helmet from good Alfonso's tomb, and dashed out the brains of our young prince with it: – never reflecting how enormous the disproportion was between the marble helmet that had been in the church, and that of steel before their eyes; nor how impossible it was for a youth, seemingly not twenty, to wield a piece of armour of so prodigious a weight.

The folly of these ejaculations brought Manfred to himself: yet whether provoked at the peasant having observed the resemblance between the two helmets, and thereby led to the farther discovery of the absence of that in the church; or wishing to bury any fresh rumour under so impertinent a supposition; he gravely pronounced that the young man was certainly a necromancer, and that till the church could take cognizance of the affair, he would have the magician, whom they had thus detected, kept prisoner under the helmet itself, which he ordered his attendants to raise, and place the young man under it; declaring he should be kept there without food, with which his own infernal art might furnish him.

It was in vain for the youth to represent against this preposterous sentence: in vain did Manfred's friends endeavour to divert him from this savage and ill-grounded resolution. The generality were charmed with their lord's decision, which to their apprehensions carried great appearance of justice, as the magician was to be punished by the very instrument with which he had offended: nor were they struck with the least compunction at the probability of the youth being starved, for they firmly believed that by his diabolical skill he could easily supply himself with nutriment.

Manfred thus saw his commands even cheerfully obeyed; and appointing a guard with strict orders to prevent any food being conveyed to the prisoner, he dismissed his friends and attendants, and retired to his own chamber, after locking the gates of the castle, in which he suffered none but his domestics to remain.

In the mean time, the care and zeal of the young ladies had brought the princess Hippolita to herself, who amidst the transports of her own sorrow frequently demanded news of her lord, would have dismissed her attendants to watch over him, and at last enjoined Matilda to leave her, and visit and comfort her father. Matilda, who wanted no affectionate duty to Manfred, though she trembled at his austerity, obeyed the orders of Hippolita, whom she tenderly recommended to

Isabella; and enquiring of the domestics for her father, was informed that he was retired to his chamber, and had commanded that nobody should have admittance to him. Concluding that he was immersed in sorrow for the death of her brother, and fearing to renew his tears by the sight of his sole remaining child, she hesitated whether she should break in upon his affliction; yet solicitude for him, backed by the commands of her mother, encouraged her to venture disobeying the orders he had given; a fault she had never been guilty of before. The gentle timidity of her nature made her pause for some minutes at his door. She heard him traverse his chamber backwards and forwards with disordered steps; a mood which increased her apprehensions. She was however just going to beg admittance, when Manfred suddenly opened his door; and as it was now twilight, concurring with the disorder of his mind, he did not distinguish the person, but asked angrily who it was? Matilda replied trembling, My dearest father, it is I, your daughter. Manfred, stepping back hastily, cried, Begone, I do not want a daughter; and, flinging back abruptly, clapped the door against the terrified Matilda.

She was too well acquainted with her father's impetuosity to venture a second intrusion. When she had a little recovered the shock of so bitter a reception, she wiped away her tears, to prevent the additional stab that the knowledge of it would give to Hippolita, who questioned her in the most anxious terms on the health of Manfred, and how he bore his loss. Matilda assured her he was well, and supported his misfortune with manly fortitude. But will he not let me see him? said Hippolita mournfully: Will he not permit me to blend my tears with his, and shed a mother's sorrows in the bosom of her lord? Or do you deceive me, Matilda? I know how Manfred doated on his son: Is not the stroke too heavy for him? Has he not sunk under it? – You do not answer me – Alas! I dread the worst! – Raise me, my maidens: I will, I will see my lord. Bear me to him instantly; he is dearer to me even than my children. Matilda made signs to Isabella to prevent Hippolita's rising; and both these lovely young women were using their gentle violence to stop and calm the princess, when a servant on the part of Manfred arrived, and told Isabella that his lord demanded to speak with her.

With me! cried Isabella. Go, said Hippolita, relieved by a message from her lord: Manfred cannot support the sight of his own family. He thinks you less disordered than we are, and dreads the shock of my grief. Console him, dear Isabella, and tell him I will smother my own anguish rather than add to his.

It was now evening; the servant who conducted Isabella bore a torch before her. When they came to Manfred, who was walking impatiently about the gallery, he started and said hastily, Take away that light, and begone. Then shutting the door impetuously, he flung himself upon a bench against the wall, and bade Isabella sit by him. She obeyed trembling. I sent for you, lady, said he, – and then stopped under great appearance of confusion. My lord! – Yes, I sent for you on a matter of great moment, resumed he: – Dry your tears, young lady – you have lost your bridegroom: – yes, cruel fate, and I have lost the hopes of my race! – But Conrad was not worthy of your beauty. – How! my lord, said Isabella; sure you do not suspect me of not feeling the concern I ought? My duty and affection would have always – Think no more of him, interrupted Manfred; he was a sickly puny child, and heaven has perhaps taken him away that I might not trust the honours of my house on so frail a foundation. The line of Manfred calls for numerous supports. My foolish fondness for that boy blinded the eyes of my prudence – but it is better as it is. I hope in a few years to have reason to rejoice at the death of Conrad.

Words cannot paint the astonishment of Isabella. At first she apprehended that grief had disordered Manfred's understanding. Her next thought suggested that this strange discourse was designed to ensnare her: she feared that Manfred had perceived her indifference for his son: and in consequence of that idea she replied, Good my lord, do not doubt my tenderness; my heart would have accompanied my hand. Conrad would have engrossed all my care; and wherever fate shall dispose of me, I shall always cherish his memory, and regard your highness and the virtuous Hippolita as my parents. Curse on Hippolita! cried Manfred: forget her from this moment, as I do. In short, lady, you have missed a husband undeserving of your charms: they shall now be better disposed of. Instead of a sickly boy, you shall have a husband in the prime of his age, who will know how to value your beauties, and who may expect a numerous offspring. Alas, my lord, said Isabella, my mind is too sadly engrossed by the recent catastrophe in your family to think of another marriage. If ever my father returns, and it shall be his pleasure, I shall obey, as I did when I consented to give my hand to your son: but until his return permit me to remain under your hospitable roof, and employ the melancholy hours in assuaging yours, Hippolita's, and the fair Matilda's affliction.

I desired you once before, said Manfred angrily, not to name that woman; from this hour she must be a stranger to you, as she must be to me: – in short, Isabella, since I cannot give you my son, I offer you myself. – Heavens! cried Isabella, waking from her delusion, what do I hear! You, my lord! You! My father in law! the father of Conrad! the husband of the virtuous and tender Hippolita! – I tell you, said Manfred imperiously, Hippolita is no longer my wife; I divorce her from this hour. Too long has she cursed me by her unfruitfulness: my fate depends on having sons, – and this night I trust will give a new date to my hopes. At those words he seized the cold hand of Isabella, who was half-dead with fright and horror. She shrieked, and started from him. Manfred rose to pursue her; when the moon, which was now up, and gleamed in at the opposite casement, presented to his sight the plumes of the fatal helmet, which rose to the height of the windows, waving backwards and forwards in a tempestuous manner, and accompanied with a hollow and rustling sound. Isabella, who gathered courage from her situation, and who dreaded nothing so much as Manfred's pursuit of his declaration, cried, Look, my lord! see heaven itself declares against your impious intentions! – Heaven nor hell shall impede my designs, said Manfred, advancing again to seize the princess. At that instant the portrait of his grandfather, which hung over the bench where they had been sitting, uttered a deep sigh and heaved its breast.[5] Isabella, whose back was turned to the picture, saw not the motion, nor knew whence the sound came, but started and said, Hark, my lord! what sound was that? and at the same time made towards the door. Manfred, distracted between the flight of Isabella, who had now reached the stairs, and his inability to keep his eyes from the picture, which began to move, had however advanced some steps after her, still looking backwards on the portrait, when he saw it quit its pannel, and descend

on the floor with a grave and melancholy air. Do I dream? cried
Manfred returning, or are the devils themselves in league against me?
Speak, infernal spectre! Or, if thou art my grandsire, why dost thou
too conspire against thy wretched descendent, who too dearly pays for
– Ere he could finish the sentence the vision sighed again, and made a
sign to Manfred to follow him. Lead on! cried Manfred; I will follow
thee to the gulph of perdition.[6] The spectre marched sedately, but
dejected, to the end of the gallery, and turned into a chamber on the
right hand. Manfred accompanied him at a little distance, full of anxiety
and horror, but resolved. As he would have entered the chamber, the
door was clapped-to with violence by an invisible hand. The prince,
collecting courage from this delay, would have forcibly burst open the
door with his foot, but found that it resisted his utmost efforts. Since
hell will not satisfy my curiosity, said Manfred, I will use the human
means in my power for preserving my race; Isabella shall not escape
me.

That lady, whose resolution had given way to terror the moment
she had quitted Manfred, continued her flight to the bottom of the
principal staircase. There she stopped, not knowing whither to direct
her steps, nor how to escape from the impetuosity of the prince. The
gates of the castle she knew were locked, and guards placed in the
court. Should she, as her heart prompted her, go and prepare Hippolita
for the cruel destiny that awaited her, she did not doubt but Manfred
would seek her there, and that his violence would incite him to double
the injury he meditated, without leaving room for them to avoid the
impetuosity of his passions. Delay might give him time to reflect on
the horrid measures he had conceived, or produce some circumstance
in her favour, if she could for that night at least avoid his odious
purpose. — Yet where conceal herself! How avoid the pursuit he
would infallibly make throughout the castle! As these thoughts passed
rapidly through her mind, she recollected a subterraneous passage
which led from the vaults of the castle to the church of saint Nicholas.
Could she reach the altar before she was overtaken, she knew even
Manfred's violence would not dare to profane the sacredness of the
place; and she determined, if no other means of deliverance offered, to
shut herself up for ever among the holy virgins, whose convent was

contiguous to the cathedral. In this resolution, she seized a lamp that burned at the foot of the staircase, and hurried towards the secret passage.

The lower part of the castle was hollowed into several intricate cloisters; and it was not easy for one under so much anxiety to find the door that opened into the cavern. An awful silence reigned throughout those subterraneous regions, except now and then some blasts of wind that shook the doors she had passed, and which grating on the rusty hinges were re-echoed through that long labyrinth of darkness. Every murmur struck her with new terror; – yet more she dreaded to hear the wrathful voice of Manfred urging his domestics to pursue her. She trod as softly as impatience would give her leave, – yet frequently stopped and listened to hear if she was followed. In one of those moments she thought she heard a sigh. She shuddered, and recoiled a few paces. In a moment she thought she heard the step of some person. Her blood curdled; she concluded it was Manfred. Every suggestion that horror could inspire rushed into her mind. She condemned her rash flight, which had thus exposed her to his rage in a place where her cries were not likely to draw any body to her assistance. – Yet the sound seemed not to come from behind; – if Manfred knew where she was, he must have followed her: she was still in one of the cloisters, and the steps she had heard were too distinct to proceed from the way she had come. Cheered with this reflection, and hoping to find a friend in whoever was not the prince; she was going to advance, when a door that stood a-jar, at some distance to the left, was opened gently; but ere her lamp, which she held up, could discover who opened it, the person retreated precipitately on seeing the light.

Isabella, whom every incident was sufficient to dismay, hesitated whether she should proceed. Her dread of Manfred soon outweighed every other terror. The very circumstance of the person avoiding her, gave her a sort of courage. It could only be, she thought, some domestic belonging to the castle. Her gentleness had never raised her an enemy, and conscious innocence bade her hope that, unless sent by the prince's order to seek her, his servants would rather assist than prevent her flight. Fortifying herself with these reflections, and believing, by what she could observe, that she was near the mouth of the subterraneous cavern, she approached the door that had been opened; but a sudden gust of wind that met her at the door extinguished her lamp, and left her in total darkness.

Words cannot paint the horror of the princess's situation. Alone in so dismal a place, her mind imprinted with all the terrible events of the day, hopeless of escaping, expecting every moment the arrival of Manfred, and far from tranquil on knowing she was within reach of somebody, she knew not whom, who for some cause seemed concealed thereabouts, all these thoughts crowded on her distracted mind, and she was ready to sink under her apprehensions. She addressed herself to every saint in heaven, and inwardly implored their assistance. For a considerable time she remained in an agony of despair. At last, as softly as was possible, she felt for the door, and, having found it, entered trembling into the vault from whence she had heard the sigh and steps. It gave her a kind of momentary joy to perceive an imperfect ray of clouded moonshine gleam from the roof of the vault, which seemed to be fallen in, and from whence hung a fragment of earth or building, she could not distinguish which, that appeared to have been crushed inwards. She advanced eagerly towards this chasm, when she discerned a human form standing close against the wall.

She shrieked, believing it the ghost of her betrothed Conrad. The figure advancing, said in a submissive voice, Be not alarmed, lady; I will not injure you. Isabella, a little encouraged by the words and tone of voice of the stranger, and recollecting that this must be the person who had opened the door, recovered her spirits enough to reply, Sir, whoever you are, take pity on a wretched princess standing on the brink of destruction: assist me to escape from this fatal castle, or in few moments I may be made miserable for ever. Alas! said the stranger, what can I do to assist you? I will die in your defence; but I am unacquainted with the castle, and want — Oh! said Isabella, hastily interrupting him, help me but to find a trap-door that must be hereabout, and it is the greatest service you can do me; for I have not a minute to lose. Saying these words she felt about on the pavement, and directed the stranger to search likewise for a smooth piece of brass inclosed in one of the stones. That, said she, is the lock, which opens with a spring, of which I know the secret. If I can find that, I may escape – if not, alas, courteous stranger, I fear I shall have involved you in my misfortunes: Manfred will suspect you for the accomplice of my flight, and you will fall a victim to his resentment. I value not my life, said the stranger; and it will be some comfort to lose it in trying to deliver you from his tyranny. Generous youth, said Isabella, how shall I ever requite — As she uttered those words, a ray of moonshine streaming through a cranny of the ruin above shone directly on the lock they sought – Oh, transport! said Isabella, here is the trap-door! and taking out a key, she touched the spring, which starting aside discovered an iron ring. Lift up the door, said the princess. The stranger obeyed; and beneath appeared some stone steps descending into a vault totally dark. We must go down here, said Isabella: follow me; dark and dismal as it is, we cannot miss our way; it leads directly to the church of saint Nicholas – But perhaps, added the princess modestly, you have no reason to leave the castle, nor have I farther occasion for your service; in few minutes I shall be safe from Manfred's rage – only let me know to whom I am so much obliged. I will never quit you, said the stranger eagerly, till I have placed you in safety – nor think me, princess, more generous than I am: though you are my principal care — The stranger was interrupted by a sudden noise of voices that seemed approaching, and they soon distinguished these words: Talk not to me of necromancers; I tell you she must be in the castle; I will find her in spite of enchantment. – Oh, heavens! cried Isabella, it is the voice of Manfred! Make haste, or we are ruined! and shut the trap-door after you. Saying this, she descended the steps precipitately; and as the stranger hastened to follow her, he let the door slip out of his hands: it fell, and the spring closed over it. He tried in vain to open it, not having observed Isabella's method of touching the spring, nor had he many moments to make an essay.[7] The noise of the falling door had been heard by Manfred, who, directed by the sound, hastened thither, attended by his servants with torches. It must be Isabella, cried Manfred before he entered the vault; she is escaping by the subterraneous passage, but she cannot have got far. – What was the astonishment of the prince, when, instead of Isabella, the light of the torches discovered to him the young peasant, whom he thought confined under the fatal helmet! Traitor! said Manfred, how camest thou here? I thought thee in durance above in the court. I am no traitor, replied the young man boldly, nor am I answerable for your thoughts. Presumptuous villain! cried Manfred, dost thou provoke my wrath? Tell me; how hast thou escaped from above? Thou hast corrupted thy guards, and their lives shall answer it. My poverty, said the peasant calmly, will disculpate[8] them: though the ministers of a tyrant's wrath, to thee they are faithful, and but too willing to execute the orders which you unjustly imposed upon them. Art thou so hardy as to dare my vengeance? said the prince – but tortures shall force the truth from thee. Tell me, I will know thy accomplices. There was my accomplice! said the youth smiling, and pointing to the roof. Manfred ordered the torches to be held up, and perceived that one of the cheeks of the enchanted casque had forced its way through the pavement of the court, as his servants had let it fall over the peasant, and had broken through into the vault, leaving a gap through which the peasant had pressed himself some minutes before he was found by Isabella. Was that the way by which thou didst descend? said Manfred. It was, said the youth. But what noise was that, said Manfred, which I heard as I entered the cloister? A door clapped, said the peasant: I heard it as well as you. What door? said Manfred hastily. I am not acquainted with your castle, said the peasant; this is the first time I ever entered it; and this vault the only part of it within which I ever was. But I tell thee, said Manfred [wishing to find out if the youth had discovered the trap-door] it was this way I heard the noise: my servants heard it too. – My lord, interrupted one of them officiously, to be sure it was the trap-door, and he was going to make his escape. Peace! blockhead, said the prince angrily; if he was going to escape, how should he come on this side? I will know from his own mouth what noise it was I heard. Tell me truly; thy life depends on thy veracity. My veracity is dearer to me than my life, said the peasant; nor would I purchase the one by forfeiting the other. Indeed! young philosopher! said Manfred contemptuously: tell me then, what was the noise I heard? Ask me what I can answer, said he, and put me to death instantly if I tell you a lie. Manfred, growing impatient at the steady valour and indifference of the youth, cried, Well then, thou man of truth! answer; was it the fall of the trap-door that I heard? It was, said the youth. It was! said the prince; and how didst thou come to know there was a trap-door here? I saw the plate of brass by a gleam of moonshine, replied he. But what told thee it was a lock? said Manfred: How didst thou discover the secret of opening it? Providence,[9] that delivered me from the helmet, was able to direct me to the spring of a lock, said he. Providence should have gone a little farther, and have placed thee out of the reach of my resentment, said Manfred: when Providence had taught thee to open the lock, it abandoned thee for a fool, who did not know how to make use of its favours. Why didst thou not pursue the path pointed out for thy escape? Why didst thou shut the trap-door before thou hadst descended the steps? I might ask you, my lord, said the peasant, how I, totally unacquainted with your castle, was to know that those steps led to any outlet? but I scorn to evade your questions. Wherever those steps lead to, perhaps I should have explored the way – I could not be in a worse situation than I was. But the truth is, I let the trap-door fall: your immediate arrival followed. I had given the alarm – what imported it to me whether I was seized a minute sooner or a minute later? Thou art a resolute villain for thy years, said Manfred – yet on reflection I suspect thou dost but trifle with me: thou hast not yet told me how thou didst open the lock. That I will show you, my lord, said the peasant; and taking up a fragment of stone that had fallen from above, he laid himself on the trap-door, and began to beat on the piece of brass that covered it; meaning to gain time for the escape of the princess. This presence of mind, joined to the frankness of the youth, staggered Manfred. He even felt a disposition towards pardoning one who had been guilty of no crime. Manfred was not one of those savage tyrants who wanton in cruelty unprovoked. The circumstances of his fortune had given an asperity to his temper, which was naturally humane; and his virtues were always ready to operate, when his passion did not obscure his reason.

While the prince was in this suspense, a confused noise of voices echoed through the distant vaults. As the sound approached, he distinguished the clamour of some of his domestics, whom he had dispersed through the castle in search of Isabella, calling out, Where is my lord? Where is the prince? Here I am, said Manfred, as they came nearer; have you found the princess? The first that arrived replied, Oh, my

lord! I am glad we have found you. – Found me! said Manfred: have
you found the princess? We thought we had, my lord, said the fellow
looking terrified – but – But what? cried the prince: has she escaped?
– Jaquez and I, my lord – Yes, I and Diego, interrupted the second,
who came up in still greater consternation – Speak one of you at a time,
said Manfred; I ask you, where is the princess? We do not know, said
they both together: but we are frightened out of our wits. – So I think,
blockheads, said Manfred: what is it has scared you thus? – Oh, my
lord! said Jaquez, Diego has seen such a sight! your highness would
not believe our eyes. – What new absurdity is this? cried Manfred –
Give me a direct answer, or by heaven – Why, my lord, if it please
your highness to hear me, said the poor fellow; Diego and I – Yes, I
and Jaquez, cried his comrade – Did not I forbid you to speak both at
a time? said the prince: You, Jaquez, answer; for the other fool seems
more distracted than thou art; what is the matter? My gracious lord,
said Jaquez, if it please your highness to hear me; Diego and I, according
to your highness's orders, went to search for the young lady; but being
comprehensive[10] that we might meet the ghost of my young lord, your
highness's son, God rest his soul, as he has not received christian burial
– Sot![11] cried Manfred in a rage, is it only a ghost then that thou hast
seen? Oh, worse! worse! my lord! cried Diego: I had rather have seen
ten whole ghosts. – Grant me patience! said Manfred; these blockheads
distract me – Out of my sight, Diego! And thou, Jaquez, tell me in one
word, art thou sober? art thou raving? Thou wast wont[12] to have some
sense: has the other sot frightened himself and thee too? Speak; what
is it he fancies he has seen? Why, my lord, replied Jaquez trembling, I
was going to tell your highness, that since the calamitous misfortune
of my young lord, God rest his soul! not one of us your highness's
faithful servants, indeed we are, my lord, though poor men; I say, not
one of us has dared to set a foot about the castle, but two together: so
Diego and I, thinking that my young lady might be in the great gallery,
went up there to look for her, and tell her your highness wanted
something to impart to her. – O blundering fools! cried Manfred: and
in the mean time she has made her escape, because you were afraid of
goblins! Why, thou knave! she left me in the gallery; I came from
thence myself. – For all that, she may be there still for aught[13] I know,

said Jaquez; but the devil shall have me before I seek her there again!
– Poor Diego! I do not believe he will ever recover it! Recover what?
said Manfred; am I never to learn what it is has terrified these rascals?
But I lose my time; follow me, slave! I will see if she is in the gallery.
– For heaven's sake, my dear good lord, cried Jaquez, do not go to the
gallery! Satan himself I believe is in the great chamber next to the
gallery. – Manfred, who hitherto had treated the terror of his servants
as an idle panic, was struck at this new circumstance. He recollected
the apparition of the portrait, and the sudden closing of the door at the
end of the gallery – his voice faltered, and he asked with disorder, what
is in the great chamber? My lord, said Jaquez, when Diego and I came
into the gallery, he went first, for he said he had more courage than I.
So when we came into the gallery, we found nobody. We looked under
every bench and stool; and still we found nobody. – Were all the
pictures in their places? said Manfred. Yes, my lord, answered Jaquez;
but we did not think of looking behind them. – Well, well! said
Manfred; proceed. When we came to the door of the great chamber,
continued Jaquez, we found it shut. – And could not you open it? said
Manfred. Oh! yes, my lord, would to heaven we had not! replied he –
Nay, it was not I neither, it was Diego: he was grown fool-hardy, and
would go on, though I advised him not – If ever I open a door that is
shut again – Trifle not, said Manfred shuddering, but tell me what you
saw in the great chamber on opening the door. – I! my lord! said Jaquez,
I saw nothing; I was behind Diego; – but I heard the noise. – Jaquez,
said Manfred in a solemn tone of voice, tell me, I adjure thee by the
souls of my ancestors, what it was thou sawest; what it was thou
heardst? It was Diego saw it, my lord, it was not I, replied Jaquez; I
only heard the noise. Diego had no sooner opened the door, than he
cried out and ran back – I ran back too, and said, Is it the ghost? The
ghost! No, no, said Diego, and his hair stood on end – it is a giant, I
believe; he is all clad in armour, for I saw his foot and part of his leg,[14]
and they are as large as the helmet below in the court. As he said these
words, my lord, we heard a violent motion and the rattling of armour,
as if the giant was rising; for Diego has told me since, that he believes
the giant was lying down, for the foot and leg were stretched at length
on the floor. Before we could get to the end of the gallery, we heard

the door of the great chamber clap behind us, but we did not dare turn back to see if the giant was following us – Yet now I think on it, we must have heard him if he had pursued us – But for heaven's sake, good my lord, send for the chaplain and have the castle exorcised, for, for certain, it is enchanted. Ay, pray do, my lord, cried all the servants at once, or we must leave your highness's service. – Peace, dotards! said Manfred, and follow me; I will know what all this means. We! my lord! cried they with one voice; we would not go up to the gallery for your highness's revenue.[15] The young peasant, who had stood silent, now spoke. Will your highness, said he, permit me to try this adventure? My life is of consequence to nobody: I fear no bad angel, and have offended no good one. Your behaviour is above your seeming, said Manfred; viewing him with surprise and admiration – hereafter I will reward your bravery – but now, continued he with a sigh, I am so circumstanced, that I dare trust no eyes but my own – However, I give you leave to accompany me.

Manfred, when he first followed Isabella from the gallery, had gone directly to the apartment of his wife, concluding the princess had retired thither. Hippolita, who knew his step, rose with anxious fondness to meet her lord, whom she had not seen since the death of their son. She would have flown in a transport mixed of joy and grief to his bosom; but he pushed her rudely off, and said, Where is Isabella? Isabella! my lord! said the astonished Hippolita. Yes, Isabella; cried Manfred imperiously; I want Isabella. My lord, replied Matilda, who perceived how much his behaviour had shocked her mother, she has not been with us since your highness summoned her to your apartment. Tell me where she is, said the prince; I do not want to know where she has been. My good lord, said Hippolita, your daughter tells you the truth: Isabella left us by your command, and has not returned since: – but, my good lord, compose yourself: retire to your rest: this dismal day has disordered you. Isabella shall wait your orders in the morning. What, then you know where she is? cried Manfred: tell me directly, for I will not lose an instant – And you, woman, speaking to his wife, order your chaplain to attend me forthwith. Isabella, said Hippolita calmly, is retired I suppose to her chamber: she is not accustomed to watch at this late hour. Gracious my lord, continued she, let me know what has disturbed you: has Isabella offended you? Trouble me not with questions, said Manfred, but tell me where she is. Matilda shall call her, said the princess – sit down, my lord, and resume your wonted fortitude. – What, art thou jealous of Isabella, replied he, that you wish to be present at our interview? Good heavens! my lord, said Hippolita, what is it your highness means? Thou wilt know ere many minutes are passed, said the cruel prince. Send your chaplain to me, and wait my pleasure here. At these words he flung out of the room in search of Isabella; leaving the amazed ladies thunder-struck with his words and frantic deportment, and lost in vain conjectures on what he was meditating.

Manfred was now returning from the vault, attended by the peasant and a few of his servants whom he had obliged to accompany him. He ascended the stair-case without stopping till he arrived at the gallery, at the door of which he met Hippolita and her chaplain. When Diego had been dismissed by Manfred, he had gone directly to the princess's apartment with the alarm of what he had seen. That excellent lady, who no more than Manfred doubted of the reality of the vision, yet affected to treat it as a delirium of the servant. Willing, however, to save her lord from any additional shock, and prepared by a series of griefs not to tremble at any accession to it; she determined to make herself the first sacrifice, if fate had marked the present hour for their destruction. Dismissing the reluctant Matilda to her rest, who in vain sued for leave to accompany her mother, and attended only by her chaplain, Hippolita had visited the gallery and great chamber: and now, with more serenity of soul than she had felt for many hours, she met her lord, and assured him that the vision of the gigantic leg and foot was all a fable; and no doubt an impression made by fear, and the dark and dismal hour of the night, on the minds of his servants: She and the chaplain had examined the chamber, and found every thing in the usual order.

Manfred, though persuaded, like his wife, that the vision had been no work of fancy, recovered a little from the tempest of mind into which so many strange events had thrown him. Ashamed too of his inhuman treatment of a princess, who returned every injury with new marks of tenderness and duty, he felt returning love forcing itself into his eyes – but not less ashamed of feeling remorse towards one, against whom he was inwardly meditating a yet more bitter outrage, he curbed the yearnings of his heart, and did not dare to lean even towards pity. The next transition of his soul was to exquisite villainy. Presuming on the unshaken submission of Hippolita, he flattered himself that she would not only acquiesce with patience to a divorce, but would obey, if it was his pleasure, in endeavouring to persuade Isabella to give him her hand – But ere he could indulge this horrid hope, he reflected that Isabella was not to be found. Coming to himself, he gave orders that every avenue to the castle should be strictly guarded, and charged his domestics on pain of their lives to suffer nobody to pass out. The young peasant, to whom he spoke favourably, he ordered to remain in a small chamber on the stairs, in which there was a pallet-bed,[16] and the key of which he took away himself, telling the youth he would talk with him in the morning. Then dismissing his attendants, and bestowing a sullen kind of half-nod on Hippolita, he retired to his own chamber.

CHAPTER 2

Matilda, who by Hippolita's order had retired to her apartment, was ill-disposed to take any rest. The shocking fate of her brother had deeply affected her. She was surprised at not seeing Isabella: but the strange words which had fallen from her father, and his obscure menace to the princess his wife, accompanied by the most furious behaviour, had filled her gentle mind with terror and alarm. She waited anxiously for the return of Bianca, a young damsel that attended her, whom she had sent to learn what was become of Isabella. Bianca soon appeared, and informed her mistress of what she had gathered from the servants, that Isabella was no where to be found. She related the adventure of the young peasant, who had been discovered in the vault, though with many simple additions from the incoherent accounts of the domestics; and she dwelled principally on the gigantic leg and foot which had been seen in the gallery-chamber. This last circumstance had terrified Bianca so much, that she was rejoiced when Matilda told her that she would not go to rest, but would watch till the princess should rise.

The young princess wearied herself in conjectures on the flight of Isabella, and on the threats of Manfred to her mother. But what business could he have so urgent with the chaplain? said Matilda. Does he intend to have my brother's body interred privately in the chapel? Oh! madam, said Bianca, now I guess. As you are become his heiress, he is impatient to have you married: he has always been raving for more sons; I warrant he is now impatient for grandsons. As sure as I live, madam, I shall see you a bride at last. Good madam, you won't cast off your faithful Bianca: you won't put Donna Rosara over me, now you are a great princess? My poor Bianca, said Matilda, how fast your thoughts amble! I a great princess! What hast thou seen in Manfred's behaviour since my brother's death that bespeaks any increase of tenderness to me? No, Bianca, his heart was ever a stranger to me – but he is my father, and I must not complain. Nay, if heaven shuts my father's heart against me, it overpays my little merit in the tenderness of my mother – O that dear mother! Yes, Bianca, 'tis there I feel the rugged temper of Manfred. I can support his harshness to me with patience; but it wounds my soul when I am witness to his causeless severity towards her. Oh, madam, said Bianca, all men use their wives so, when they are weary of them. – And yet you congratulated me but now, said Matilda, when you fancied my father intended to dispose of me. I would have you a great lady, replied Bianca, come what will. I do not wish to see you moped[1] in a convent, as you would be if you had your will, and if my lady your mother, who knows that a bad husband is better than no husband at all, did not hinder you. – Bless me! what noise is that? Saint Nicholas forgive me! I was but in jest. It is the wind, said Matilda, whistling through the battlements in the tower above: you have heard it a thousand times. Nay, said Bianca, there was no harm neither in what I said: it is no sin to talk of matrimony – And so, madam, as I was saying; if my lord Manfred should offer you a handsome young prince for a bridegroom, you would drop him a curtsy, and tell him you would rather take the veil. Thank heaven! I am in no such danger, said Matilda: you know how many proposals for me he has rejected. – And you thank him, like a dutiful daughter, do you, madam? – But come, madam; suppose, to-morrow morning he was to send for you to the great council-chamber, and there you should find at his elbow a lovely young prince, with large black eyes, a smooth white forehead, and manly curling locks like jet; in short, madam, a young hero resembling the picture of the good Alfonso in the gallery, which you sit and gaze at for hours together. – Do not speak lightly of that picture, interrupted Matilda sighing: I know the adoration with which I look at that picture is uncommon – but I am not in love with a coloured pannel. The character of that virtuous prince, the veneration with which my mother has inspired me for his memory, the orisons[2] which I know not why she has enjoined me to pour forth at his tomb, all have concurred to persuade me that some how or other my destiny is linked with something relating to him. – Lord! madam, how should that be? said Bianca: I have always heard that your family was no way related to his: and I am sure I cannot conceive why my lady, the princess, sends you in a cold morning, or a damp evening, to pray at his tomb: he is no saint by the almanack.[3] If you must pray, why does not she bid you address yourself to our great saint Nicholas? I am sure he is the saint I pray to for a husband. Perhaps my mind would be less affected, said Matilda, if my mother would explain her reasons to me: but it is the mystery she observes, that inspires me with this – I know not what to call it. As she never acts from caprice, I am sure there is some fatal secret at bottom – nay, I know there is: in her agony of grief for my brother's death she dropped some words that intimated as much. – Oh, dear madam, cried Bianca, what were they? No, said Matilda: if a parent lets fall a word, and wishes it recalled, it is not for a child to utter it. What! was she sorry for what she had said? asked Bianca. – I am sure, madam, you may trust me. – With my own little secrets, when I have any, I may, said Matilda; but never with my mother's: a child ought to have no ears or eyes but as a parent directs. Well! to be sure, madam, you was born to be a saint, said Bianca, and there's no resisting one's vocation: you will end in a convent at last. But there is my lady Isabella would not be so reserved to me: she will let me talk to her of young men; and when a handsome cavalier has come to the castle, she has owned to me that she wished your brother Conrad resembled him. Bianca, said the princess, I do not allow you to mention my friend disrespectfully. Isabella is of a cheerful disposition, but her soul is pure as virtue itself. She knows your idle babbling humour, and perhaps has now and then encouraged it, to divert melancholy, and to enliven the solitude in which my father keeps us. – Blessed Mary! said Bianca starting, there it is again! – Dear madam, do you hear nothing? – This castle is certainly haunted! – Peace! said Matilda, and listen! I did think I heard a voice – but it must be fancy; your terrors I suppose have infected me. Indeed! indeed! madam, said Bianca, half-weeping with agony, I am sure I heard a voice. Does any body lie in the chamber beneath? said the princess. Nobody has dared to lie there, answered Bianca, since the great astrologer that was your brother's tutor drowned himself. For certain, madam, his ghost and the young prince's are now met in the chamber below – for heaven's sake let us fly to your mother's apartment! I charge you not to stir, said Matilda. If they are spirits in pain, we may ease their sufferings by questioning them.[4] They can mean no hurt to us, for we have not injured them – and if they should, shall we be more safe in one chamber than in another? Reach me my beads; we will say a prayer, and then speak to them. Oh, dear lady, I would not speak to a ghost for the world, cried Bianca. – As she said those words, they heard the casement of the little chamber below Matilda's open. They listened attentively, and in few minutes thought they heard a person sing, but could not distinguish the words. This can be no evil spirit, said the princess in a low voice: it is undoubtedly one of the family – open the window, and we shall know the voice. I dare not indeed, madam, said Bianca. Thou art a very fool, said Matilda, opening the window gently herself. The noise the princess made was however heard by the person beneath, who stopped, and, they concluded, had heard the casement open. Is any body below? said the princess: if there is, speak. Yes, said an unknown voice. Who is it? said Matilda. A stranger, replied the voice. What stranger? said she; and how didst thou come there at this unusual hour, when all the gates of the castle are locked? I am not here willingly, answered the voice – but pardon me, lady, if I have disturbed your rest: I knew not that I was overheard. Sleep had forsaken me: I left a restless couch, and came to waste the irksome hours with gazing on the fair approach of morning, impatient to be dismissed from this castle. Thy words and accents, said Matilda, are of a melancholy cast: if thou art unhappy, I pity thee. If poverty afflicts thee, let me know it; I will mention thee to the princess, whose beneficent soul ever melts for the distressed; and she will relieve thee. I am indeed unhappy, said the stranger; and I know not what wealth is: but I do not complain of the lot which heaven has cast for me: I am young and healthy, and am not ashamed of owing my support to myself – yet think me not proud, or that I disdain your generous offers. I will remember you in my orisons, and will pray for blessings on your gracious self and your noble mistress – If I sigh, lady, it is for others, not for myself. Now I have it, madam, said Bianca whispering to the princess. This is certainly the young peasant; and by my conscience he

39

is in love! — Well, this is a charming adventure! – Do, madam, let us sift him.[5] He does not know you, but takes you for one of my lady Hippolita's women. Art thou not ashamed, Bianca? said the princess: what right have we to pry into the secrets of this young man's heart? He seems virtuous and frank, and tells us he is unhappy: are those circumstances that authorize us to make a property of[6] him? How are we entitled to his confidence? Lord! madam, how little you know of love! replied Bianca: why, lovers have no pleasure equal to talking of their mistress. And would you have *me* become a peasant's confidante? said the princess. Well then, let me talk to him, said Bianca: though I have the honour of being your highness's maid of honour, I was not always so great: besides, if love levels ranks, it raises them too: I have a respect for any young man in love. – Peace, simpleton! said the princess. Though he said he was unhappy, it does not follow that he must be in love. Think of all that has happened to-day, and tell me if there are no misfortunes but what love causes. Stranger, resumed the princess, if thy misfortunes have not been occasioned by thy own fault, and are within the compass of the princess Hippolita's power to redress, I will take upon me to answer that she will be thy protectress. When thou art dismissed from this castle, repair to holy father Jerome at the convent adjoining to the church of saint Nicholas, and make thy story known to him, as far as thou thinkest meet: he will not fail to inform the princess, who is the mother of all that want her assistance. Farewell: it is not seemly for me to hold farther converse with a man at this unwonted hour.[7] May the saints guard thee, gracious lady! replied the peasant – but oh, if a poor and worthless stranger might presume to beg a minute's audience farther – am I so happy? – the casement is not shut – might I venture to ask – Speak quickly, said Matilda; the morning dawns apace:[8] should the labourers come into the fields and perceive us – What wouldst thou ask? – I know not how – I know not if I dare, said the young stranger faltering – yet the humanity with which you have spoken to me emboldens – Lady! dare I trust you? – Heavens! said Matilda, what dost thou mean? with what wouldst thou trust me? – Speak boldly, if thy secret is fit to be entrusted to a virtuous breast. – I would ask, said the peasant, recollecting himself, whether what I have heard from the domestics is true, that the princess is missing from the castle? What imports it to thee to know? replied Matilda. Thy first words bespoke a prudent and becoming gravity. Dost thou come hither to pry into the secrets of Manfred? Adieu. I have been mistaken in thee. – Saying these words, she shut the casement hastily, without giving the young man time to reply. I had acted more wisely, said the princess to Bianca with some sharpness, if I had let thee converse with this peasant: his inquisitiveness seems of a piece with thy own. It is not fit for me to argue with your highness, replied Bianca; but perhaps the questions I should have put to him, would have been more to the purpose, than those you have been pleased to ask him. Oh, no doubt, said Matilda; you are a very discreet personage! May I know what you would have asked him? A by-stander often sees more of the game than those that play, answered Bianca. Does your highness think, madam, that his question about my lady Isabella was the result of mere curiosity? No, no, madam; there is more in it than you great folks are aware of. Lopez told me, that all the servants believe this young fellow contrived my lady Isabella's escape – Now, pray, madam, observe — You and I both know that my lady Isabella never much fancied the prince your brother. – Well! he is killed just in the critical minute – I accuse nobody. A helmet falls from the moon – so my lord your father says; but Lopez and all the servants say that this young spark[9] is a magician, and stole it from Alfonso's tomb. – Have done with this rhapsody of impertinence, said Matilda. Nay, madam, as you please, cried Bianca – yet it is very particular though, that my lady Isabella should be missing the very same day, and that this young sorcerer should be found at the mouth of the trap-door – I accuse nobody – but if my young lord came honestly by his death – Dare not on thy duty, said Matilda, to breathe a suspicion on the purity of my dear Isabella's fame. – Purity, or not purity, said Bianca, gone she is: a stranger is found that nobody knows: you question him yourself: he tells you he is in love, or unhappy, it is the same thing – nay, he owned he was unhappy about others; and is any body unhappy about another, unless they are in love with them? And at the very next word he asks innocently, poor soul! if my lady Isabella is missing. – To be sure, said Matilda, thy observations are not totally without foundation – Isabella's flight amazes me: the curiosity of this stranger is very particular – yet

41

Isabella never concealed a thought from me. – So she told you, said Bianca, to fish out your secrets – but who knows, madam, but this stranger may be some prince in disguise? – Do, madam, let me open the window, and ask him a few questions. No, replied Matilda, I will ask him myself, if he knows aught of Isabella: he is not worthy that I should converse farther with him. She was going to open the casement, when they heard the bell ring at the postern-gate[10] of the castle, which is on the right hand of the tower, where Matilda lay. This prevented the princess from renewing the conversation with the stranger.

After continuing silent for some time; I am persuaded, said she to Bianca, that whatever be the cause of Isabella's flight, it had no unworthy motive. If this stranger was accessary to it, she must be satisfied of his fidelity and worth. I observed, did not you, Bianca? that his words were tinctured with an uncommon effusion of piety. It was no ruffian's speech: his phrases were becoming a man of gentle birth. I told you, madam, said Bianca, that I was sure he was some prince in disguise. – Yet, said Matilda, if he was privy to her escape, how will you account for his not accompanying her in her flight? Why expose himself unnecessarily and rashly to my father's resentment? As for that, madam, replied she, if he could get from under the helmet, he will find ways of eluding your father's anger. I do not doubt but he has some talisman or other about him. – You resolve every thing into magic, said Matilda – but a man who has any intercourse with infernal spirits does not dare to make use of those tremendous and holy words which he uttered. Didst thou not observe with what fervour he vowed to remember *me* to heaven in his prayers? Yes, Isabella was undoubtedly convinced of his piety. – Commend me to the piety of a young fellow and a damsel that consult to elope! said Bianca. No, no, madam; my lady Isabella is of another-guess mould[11] than you take her for. She used indeed to sigh and lift up her eyes in your company, because she knows you are a saint – but when your back was turned – You wrong her, said Matilda; Isabella is no hypocrite: she has a due sense of devotion, but never affected a call she has not. On the contrary, she always combated my inclination for the cloister: and though I own the mystery she has made to me of her flight confounds me; though it seems inconsistent with the friendship between us; I cannot forget the disinterested warmth with which she always opposed my taking the veil: she wished to see me married, though my dower would have been a loss to her and my brother's children. For her sake I will believe well of this young peasant. Then you do think there is some liking between them? said Bianca. – While she was speaking, a servant came hastily into the chamber, and told the princess that the lady Isabella was found. Where? said Matilda. She has taken sanctuary in saint Nicholas's church, replied the servant: father Jerome has brought the news himself: he is below with his highness. Where is my mother? said Matilda. She is in her own chamber, madam, and has asked for you.

Manfred had risen at the first dawn of light, and gone to Hippolita's apartment, to enquire if she knew ought[12] of Isabella. While he was questioning her, word was brought that Jerome demanded to speak with him. Manfred, little suspecting the cause of the friar's arrival, and knowing he was employed by Hippolita in her charities, ordered him to be admitted, intending to leave them together, while he pursued his search after Isabella. Is your business with me or the princess? said Manfred. With both, replied the holy man. The lady Isabella – What of her? interrupted Manfred eagerly – is at saint Nicholas's altar, replied Jerome. That is no business of Hippolita, said Manfred with confusion: let us retire to my chamber, father; and inform me how she came thither. No, my lord, replied the good man with an air of firmness and authority that daunted even the resolute Manfred, who could not help revering the saint-like virtues of Jerome: my commission is to both; and, with your highness's good-liking,[13] in the presence of both I shall deliver it – But first, my lord, I must interrogate the princess, whether she is acquainted with the cause of the lady Isabella's retirement from your castle. – No, on my soul, said Hippolita; does Isabella charge me with being privy to it? – Father, interrupted Manfred, I pay due reverence to your holy profession; but I am sovereign here, and will allow no meddling priest to interfere in the affairs of my domestic. If you have aught to say, attend me to my chamber – I do not use to let my Wife be acquainted with the secret affairs of my state; they are not within a woman's province. My lord; said the holy man, I am no intruder into the secrets of families. My office is to promote peace, to heal divisions, to preach repentance, and teach mankind to curb their headstrong passions. I forgive your highness's uncharitable apostrophe: I know my duty, and am the minister of a mightier prince than Manfred. Hearken to him who speaks through my organs.[14] Manfred trembled with rage and shame. Hippolita's countenance declared her astonishment, and impatience to know where this would end: her silence more strongly spoke her observance of Manfred.

The lady Isabella, resumed Jerome, commends herself to both your highnesses; she thanks both for the kindness with which she has been treated in your castle: she deplores the loss of your son, and her own misfortune in not becoming the daughter of such wise and noble princes, whom she shall always respect as *parents*: she prays for uninterrupted union and felicity between you: [Manfred's colour[15] changed] but as it is no longer possible for her to be allied to you, she entreats your consent to remain in sanctuary till she can learn news of her father; or, by the certainty of his death, be at liberty, with the approbation of her guardians, to dispose of herself in suitable marriage. I shall give no such consent, said the prince; but insist on her return to the castle without delay: I am answerable for her person to her guardians, and will not brook her being in any hands but my own. Your highness will recollect whether that can any longer be proper, replied the friar. I want no monitor, said Manfred colouring. Isabella's conduct leaves room for strange suspicions – and that young villain, who was at least the accomplice of her flight, if not the cause of it – The cause! interrupted Jerome; was a *young* man the cause? This is not to be borne! cried Manfred. Am I to be bearded[16] in my own palace by an insolent monk? Thou art privy, I guess, to their amours. I would pray to heaven to clear up your uncharitable surmises, said Jerome, if your highness were not satisfied in your conscience how unjustly you accuse me. I do pray to heaven to pardon that uncharitableness: and I implore your highness to leave the princess at peace in that holy place, where she is not liable to be disturbed by such vain and worldly fantasies as discourses of love from any man. Cant[17] not to me, said Manfred, but return, and bring the princess to her duty. It is my duty to prevent her return hither, said Jerome. She is where orphans and virgins are safest from the snares and wiles of this world; and nothing but a parent's authority shall take her thence. I am her parent, cried Manfred, and demand her. She wished to have you for her parent, said the friar; but heaven, that forbad that connexion, has for ever dissolved all ties betwixt you: and I announce to your highness – Stop! audacious man, said Manfred, and dread my displeasure. Holy father, said Hippolita, it is your office to be no respecter of persons: you must speak as your duty prescribes: but it is my duty to hear nothing that it pleases not my lord I should hear. I will retire to my oratory, and pray to the blessed Virgin to inspire you with her holy counsels, and to restore the heart of my gracious lord to its wonted peace and gentleness. Excellent woman! said the friar. – My lord, I attend your pleasure.

Manfred, accompanied by the friar, passed to his own apartment; where shutting the door, I perceive, father, said he, that Isabella has acquainted you with my purpose. Now hear my resolve, and obey. Reasons of state, most urgent reasons, my own and the safety of my people, demand that I should have a son. It is in vain to expect an heir from Hippolita. I have made choice of Isabella. You must bring her back; and you must do more. I know the influence you have with Hippolita: her conscience is in your hands. She is, I allow, a faultless woman: her soul is set on heaven, and scorns the little grandeur of this world: you can withdraw her from it entirely. Persuade her to consent to the dissolution of our marriage, and to retire into a monastery – she shall endow one if she will; and she shall have the means of being as liberal to your order as she or you can wish. Thus you will divert the calamities that are hanging over our heads, and have the merit of saving the principality of Otranto from destruction. You are a prudent man; and though the warmth of my temper betrayed me into some unbecoming expressions, I honour your virtue, and wish to be indebted to you for the repose of my life and the preservation of my family.

The will of heaven be done! said the friar. I am but its worthless instrument. It makes use of my tongue to tell thee, prince, of thy unwarrantable designs. The injuries of the virtuous Hippolita have mounted to the throne of pity. By me thou art reprimanded for thy adulterous intention of repudiating her: by me thou art warned not to pursue the incestuous design on thy contracted daughter. Heaven, that delivered her from thy fury, when the judgments so recently fallen on thy house ought to have inspired thee with other thoughts, will continue to watch over her. Even I, a poor and despised friar, am able to protect her from thy violence. – I, sinner as I am, and uncharitably reviled by your highness as an accomplice of I know not what amours, scorn the allurements with which it has pleased thee to tempt mine honesty. I love my order; I honour devout souls; I respect the piety of thy princess – but I will not betray the confidence she reposes in me, nor serve even the cause of religion by foul and sinful compliances – But forsooth! the welfare of the state depends on your highness having a son. Heaven mocks the short-sighted views of man. But yester-morn, whose house was so great, so flourishing as Manfred's? – Where is young Conrad now? – My lord, I respect your tears – but I mean not to check them – Let them flow, prince! they will weigh more with heaven towards the welfare of thy subjects, than a marriage, which, founded on lust or policy, could never prosper. The sceptre, which passed from the race of Alfonso to thine, cannot be preserved by a match which the church will never allow. If it is the will of the Most High that Manfred's name must perish, resign yourself, my lord, to its decrees; and thus deserve a crown that can never pass away.[18] – Come, my lord, I like this sorrow – Let us return to the princess: she is not apprized of your cruel intentions; nor did I mean more than to alarm you. You saw with what gentle patience, with what efforts of love, she heard, she rejected hearing the extent of your guilt. I know she longs to fold you in her arms, and assure you of her unalterable affection. Father, said the prince, you mistake my compunction: true, I honour Hippolita's virtues; I think her a saint; and wish it were for my soul's health to tie faster the knot that has united us. – But alas! father, you know not the bitterest of my pangs! It is some time that I have had scruples on the legality of our union: Hippolita is related to me in the fourth degree[19] – It is true, we had a dispensation;[20] but I have been informed that she had also been contracted to another. This it is that sits heavy at my heart: to this state of unlawful wedlock I impute the visitation that has fallen on me in the death of Conrad! – Ease my conscience of this burden; dissolve our marriage, and accomplish the work of godliness which your divine exhortations have commenced in my soul.

How cutting was the anguish which the good man felt, when he perceived this turn in the wily prince! He trembled for Hippolita, whose ruin he saw was determined; and he feared, if Manfred had no hope of recovering Isabella, that his impatience for a son would direct him to some other object, who might not be equally proof against the temptation of Manfred's rank. For some time the holy man remained absorbed in thought. At length, conceiving some hope from delay, he thought the wisest conduct would be to prevent the prince from despairing of recovering Isabella. Her the friar knew he could dispose, from her affection to Hippolita, and from the aversion she had expressed to him for Manfred's addresses, to second his views, till the censures of the church could be fulminated[21] against a divorce. With this intention, as if struck with the prince's scruples, he at length said, My lord, I have been pondering on what your highness has said; and if in truth it is delicacy of conscience that is the real motive of your repugnance to your virtuous lady, far be it from me to endeavour to harden your heart! The church is an indulgent mother; unfold your griefs to her: she alone can administer comfort to your soul, either by satisfying your conscience, or, upon examination of your scruples, by setting you at liberty, and indulging you in the lawful means of continuing your lineage. In the latter case, if the lady Isabella can be brought to consent — Manfred, who concluded that he had either over-reached[22] the good man, or that his first warmth had been but a tribute paid to appearance, was overjoyed at this sudden turn, and repeated the most magnificent promises, if he should succeed by the friar's mediation. The well-meaning priest suffered him to deceive himself, fully determined to traverse[23] his views, instead of seconding them.

Since we now understand one another, resumed the prince, I expect, father, that you satisfy me in one point. Who is the youth that we found in the vault? He must have been privy to Isabella's flight: tell me truly; is he her lover? or is he an agent for another's passion? I have often suspected Isabella's indifference to my son: a thousand circumstances crowd on my mind that confirm that suspicion. She herself was so conscious of it, that, while I discoursed her in the gallery, she outran my suspicions, and endeavoured to justify herself from coolness to Conrad. The friar, who knew nothing of the youth but what he had learnt occasionally from the princess, ignorant what was become of him, and not sufficiently reflecting on the impetuosity of Manfred's temper, conceived that it might not be amiss to sow the seeds of jealousy in his mind: they might be turned to some use hereafter, either by prejudicing the prince against Isabella, if he persisted in that union; or, by diverting his attention to a wrong scent, and employing his thoughts on a visionary intrigue, prevent his engaging in any new pursuit. With this unhappy policy, he answered in a manner to confirm Manfred in the belief of some connection between Isabella and the youth. The prince, whose passions wanted little fuel to throw them into a blaze, fell into a rage at the idea of what the friar suggested. I will fathom to the bottom of this intrigue, cried he; and quitting Jerome abruptly, with a command to remain there till his return, he hastened to the great hall of the castle, and ordered the peasant to be brought before him.

Thou hardened young impostor! said the prince, as soon as he saw the youth; what becomes of thy boasted veracity now? It was Providence, was it, and the light of the moon, that discovered the lock of the trap-door to thee? Tell me, audacious boy, who thou art, and how long thou hast been acquainted with the princess – and take care to answer with less equivocation than thou didst last night, or tortures shall wring the truth from thee. The young man, perceiving that his share in the flight of the princess was discovered, and concluding that any thing he should say could no longer be of service or detriment to her, replied, I am no impostor, my lord; nor have I deserved opprobrious language. I answered to every question your highness put to me last night with the same veracity that I shall speak now: and that will not be from fear of your tortures, but because my soul abhors a falsehood. Please to repeat your questions, my lord; I am ready to give you all the satisfaction in my power. You know my questions, replied the prince, and only want time to prepare an evasion. Speak directly; who art thou? and how long hast thou been known to the princess? I am a labourer at the next village, said the peasant; my name is Theodore. The princess found me in the vault last night: before that hour I never was in her presence. – I may believe as much or as little as I please of this, said Manfred; but I will hear thy own story, before I examine into the truth of it. Tell me, what reason did the princess give thee for making her escape? Thy life depends on thy answer. She told me, replied Theodore, that she was on the brink of destruction; and that, if she could not escape from the castle, she was in danger in a few moments of being made miserable for ever. And on this slight foundation, on a silly girl's report, said Manfred, thou didst hazard my displeasure? I fear no man's displeasure, said Theodore, when a woman in distress puts herself under my protection. – During this examination, Matilda was going to the apartment of Hippolita. At the upper end of the hall, where Manfred sat, was a boarded²⁴ gallery with latticed windows, through which Matilda and Bianca were to pass. Hearing her father's voice, and seeing the servants assembled round him, she stopped to learn the occasion. The prisoner soon drew her attention: the steady and composed manner in which he answered, and the gallantry of his last reply, which were the first words she heard distinctly, interested her in his favour. His person was noble, handsome and commanding, even in that situation: but his countenance soon engrossed her whole care. Heavens! Bianca, said the princess softly, do I dream? or is not that youth the exact resemblance of Alfonso's picture in the gallery? She could say no more, for her father's voice grew louder at every word. This bravado, said he, surpasses all thy former insolence. Thou shalt experience the wrath with which thou darest to trifle. Seize him, continued Manfred, and bind him – the first news the princess hears of her champion shall be, that he has lost his head for her sake. The injustice of which thou art guilty towards me, said Theodore, convinces me that I have done a good deed in delivering the princess from thy tyranny. May she be happy, whatever becomes of me! – This is a lover! cried Manfred in a rage: a peasant within sight of death is not animated by such sentiments. Tell me, tell me, rash boy, who thou art, or the rack shall force thy secret from thee. Thou hast threatened me with death already, said the youth, for the truth I have told thee: if that is all the encouragement I am to expect for sincerity, I am not tempted to indulge thy vain curiosity farther. Then thou wilt not speak? said Manfred. I will not, replied he. Bear him away into the court-yard, said Manfred; I will see his head this instant severed from his body. – Matilda fainted at hearing those words. Bianca shrieked, and cried, Help! help! the princess is dead! Manfred started at this ejaculation, and demanded what was the matter. The young peasant, who heard it too, was struck with horror, and asked eagerly the same question; but Manfred ordered him to be hurried into the court, and kept there for execution, till he had informed himself of the cause of Bianca's shrieks. When he learned the meaning, he treated it as a womanish panic; and ordering Matilda to be carried to her apartment, he rushed into the court, and, calling for one of his guards, bade Theodore kneel down and prepare to receive the fatal blow.

The undaunted youth received the bitter sentence with a resignation that touched every heart but Manfred's. He wished earnestly to know the meaning of the words he had heard relating to the princess; but, fearing to exasperate the tyrant more against her, he desisted. The only boon[25] he deigned to ask was, that he might be permitted to have a confessor, and make his peace with heaven. Manfred, who hoped by the confessor's means to come at the youth's history, readily granted his request: and being convinced that father Jerome was now in his interest, he ordered him to be called and shrieve[26] the prisoner. The holy man, who had little foreseen the catastrophe that his imprudence occasioned, fell on his knees to the prince, and adjured him in the most solemn manner not to shed innocent blood. He accused himself in the bitterest terms for his indiscretion, endeavoured to disculpate the youth, and left no method untried to soften the tyrant's rage. Manfred, more incensed than appeased by Jerome's intercession, whose retractation now made him suspect he had been imposed upon by both, commanded the friar to do his duty, telling him he would not allow the prisoner many minutes for confession. Nor do I ask many, my lord, said the unhappy young man. My sins, thank heaven! have not been numerous; nor exceed what might be expected at my years. Dry your tears, good father, and let us dispatch: this is a bad world; nor have I had cause to leave it with regret. Oh! wretched youth! said Jerome; how canst thou bear the sight of me with patience? I am thy murderer! It is I have brought this dismal hour upon thee! – I forgive thee from my soul, said the youth, as I hope heaven will pardon me. Hear my confession, father; and give me thy blessing. How can I prepare thee for thy passage, as I ought? said Jerome. Thou canst not be saved without pardoning thy foes – and canst thou forgive that impious man there? I can, said Theodore; I do. – And does not this touch thee, cruel prince? said the friar. I sent for thee to confess him, said Manfred sternly; not to plead for him. Thou didst first incense me against him – his blood be on thy head! – It will! it will! said the good man in an agony of sorrow. Thou and I must never hope to go where this blessed youth is going. – Dispatch! said Manfred: I am no more to be moved by the whining of priests, than by the shrieks of women. What! said the youth, is it possible that my fate could have occasioned what I heard? Is the princess then again in thy power? – Thou dost but remember me of thy wrath, said Manfred: prepare thee, for this moment is thy last. The youth, who felt his indignation rise, and who was touched with the sorrow which he saw he had infused into all the spectators, as well as into the friar, suppressed his emotions, and, putting off his doublet and unbuttoning his collar, knelt down to his prayers. As he stooped, his shirt slipped down below his shoulder, and discovered the mark of a bloody arrow. Gracious heaven! cried the holy man starting, what do I see! It is my child! my Theodore!

The passions that ensued must be conceived; they cannot be painted. The tears of the assistants were suspended by wonder, rather than stopped by joy. They seemed to enquire in the eyes of their lord what they ought to feel. Surprise, doubt, tenderness, respect, succeeded each other in the countenance of the youth. He received with modest submission the effusion of the old man's tears and embraces: yet afraid of giving a loose to hope, and suspecting from what had passed the inflexibility of Manfred's temper, he cast a glance towards the prince, as if to say, Canst thou be unmoved at such a scene as this?

Manfred's heart was capable of being touched. He forgot his anger in his astonishment; yet his pride forbad his owning himself affected. He even doubted whether this discovery was not a contrivance of the friar to save the youth. What may this mean? said he. How can he be thy son? Is it consistent with thy profession or reputed sanctity to avow a peasant's offspring for the fruit of thy irregular amours? – Oh God! said the holy man, dost thou question his being mine? Could I feel the anguish I do, if I were not his father? Spare him! good prince, spare him! and revile me as thou pleasest. – Spare him! spare him! cried the attendants, for this good man's sake! – Peace! said Manfred sternly: I must know more, ere I am disposed to pardon. A saint's bastard may be no saint himself. – Injurious lord! said Theodore: add not insult to cruelty. If I am this venerable man's son, though no prince as thou art, know, the blood that flows in my veins – Yes, said the friar, interrupting him, his blood is noble: nor is he that abject thing, my lord, you speak him. He is my lawful son; and Sicily can boast of few houses more ancient than that of Falconara – But alas! my lord, what is blood? what is nobility? We are all reptiles, miserable sinful creatures. It is piety alone that can distinguish us from the dust whence we sprung, and whither we must return. – Truce to your sermon, said Manfred; you forget you are no longer friar Jerome, but the count of Falconara. Let me know your history; you will have time to moralize hereafter, if you should not happen to obtain the grace of that sturdy criminal there. Mother of God! said the friar, is it possible my lord can refuse a father the life of his only, his long lost child? Trample me, my lord, scorn, afflict me, accept my life for his, but spare my son! – Thou canst feel then, said Manfred, what it is to lose an only son? A little hour ago thou didst preach up resignation to me: *my* house, if fate so pleased, must perish – but the count of Falconara – Alas! my lord, said Jerome, I confess I have offended; but aggravate not an old man's sufferings. I boast not of my family, nor think of such vanities – it is nature that pleads for this boy; it is the memory of the dear woman that bore him – Is she, Theodore, is she dead? – Her soul has long been with the blessed, said Theodore. Oh how? cried Jerome, tell me – No – she is happy! Thou art all my care now! – Most dread lord! will you – will you grant me my poor boy's life? Return to thy convent, answered Manfred; conduct the princess hither; obey me in what else thou knowest; and I promise thee the life of thy son. – Oh! my lord, said Jerome, is my honesty the price I must pay for this dear youth's safety? – For me! cried Theodore: let me die a thousand deaths, rather than stain thy conscience. What is it the tyrant would exact of thee? Is the princess safe from his power? Protect her, thou venerable old man! and let all his wrath fall on me. Jerome endeavoured to check the impetuosity of the youth; and ere Manfred could reply, the trampling of horses was heard, and a brazen[27] trumpet, which hung without the gate of the castle, was suddenly sounded. At the same instant the sable plumes on the enchanted helmet, which still remained at the other end of the court, were tempestuously agitated, and nodded thrice, as if bowed by some invisible wearer.

CHAPTER 3

Manfred's heart misgave him when he beheld the plumage on the miraculous casque shaken in concert with the sounding of the brazen trumpet. Father! said he to Jerome, whom he now ceased to treat as count of Falconara, what mean these portents? If I have offended – [the plumes were shaken with greater violence than before] Unhappy prince that I am! cried Manfred – Holy father! will you not assist me with your prayers? – My lord, replied Jerome, heaven is no doubt displeased with your mockery of its servants. Submit yourself to the church; and cease to persecute her ministers. Dismiss this innocent youth; and learn to respect the holy character I wear: heaven will not be trifled with: you see – [the trumpet sounded again] I acknowledge I have been too hasty, said Manfred. Father, do you go to the wicket, and demand who is at the gate. Do you grant me the life of Theodore? replied the friar. I do, said Manfred; but enquire who is without.

Jerome, falling on the neck of his son, discharged a flood of tears, that spoke the fullness of his soul. You promised to go to the gate, said Manfred. I thought, replied the friar, your highness would excuse my thanking you first in this tribute of my heart. Go, dearest sir, said Theodore, obey the prince; I do not deserve that you should delay his satisfaction for me.

Jerome, enquiring who was without, was answered, A herald.[1] From whom? said he. From the knight of the gigantic sabre, said the herald: and I must speak with the usurper of Otranto. Jerome returned to the prince, and did not fail to repeat the message in the very words it had been uttered. The first sounds struck Manfred with terror; but when he heard himself styled usurper, his rage rekindled, and all his courage

54

revived. Usurper! – Insolent villain! cried he, who dares to question my title? Retire, father; this is no business for monks: I will meet this presumptuous man myself. Go to your convent, and prepare the princess's return: your son shall be a hostage for your fidelity: his life depends on your obedience. – Good heaven! my lord, cried Jerome, your highness did but this instant freely pardon my child – have you so soon forgot the interposition[2] of heaven? – Heaven, replied Manfred, does not send heralds to question the title of a lawful prince – I doubt whether it even notifies its will through friars – but that is your affair, not mine. At present you know my pleasure; and it is not a saucy herald that shall save your son, if you do not return with the princess.

It was in vain for the holy man to reply. Manfred commanded him to be conducted to the postern-gate, and shut out from the castle: and he ordered some of his attendants to carry Theodore to the top of the black tower, and guard him strictly; scarce permitting the father and son to exchange a hasty embrace at parting. He then withdrew to the hall, and, seating himself in princely state, ordered the herald to be admitted to his presence.

Well, thou insolent! said the prince, what wouldst thou with me? I come, replied he, to thee, Manfred, usurper of the principality of Otranto, from the renowned and invincible knight, the knight of the gigantic sabre: in the name of his lord, Frederic marquis of Vicenza, he demands the lady Isabella, daughter of that prince, whom thou hast basely and traiterously got into thy power, by bribing her false guardians during his absence: and he requires thee to resign the principality of Otranto, which thou hast usurped from the said lord Frederic, the nearest of blood to the last rightful lord Alfonso the Good. If thou dost not instantly comply with these just demands, he defies thee to single combat to the last extremity. And so saying, the herald cast down his warder.[3]

And where is this braggart, who sends thee? said Manfred. At the distance of a league, said the herald: he comes to make good his lord's claim against thee, as he is a true knight, and thou an usurper and ravisher.

Injurious as this challenge was, Manfred reflected that it was not his interest to provoke the marquis. He knew how well-founded the claim of Frederic was; nor was this the first time he had heard of it. Frederic's ancestors had assumed the style of princes of Otranto, from the death of Alfonso the Good without issue:[4] but Manfred, his father, and grandfather, had been too powerful for the house of Vicenza to dispossess them. Frederic, a martial and amorous young prince, had married a beautiful young lady, of whom he was enamoured, and who had died in childbed of Isabella. Her death affected him so much, that he had taken the cross and gone to the Holy Land, where he was wounded in an engagement against the infidels, made prisoner, and reported to be dead. When the news reached Manfred's ears, he bribed the guardians of the lady Isabella to deliver her up to him as a bride for his son Conrad; by which alliance he had purposed to unite the claims of the two houses. This motive, on Conrad's death, had co-operated to make him so suddenly resolve on espousing her himself; and the same reflection determined him now to endeavour at obtaining the consent of Frederic to this marriage. A like policy inspired him with the thought of inviting Frederic's champion into his castle, lest he should be informed of Isabella's flight, which he strictly enjoined his domestics not to disclose to any of the knight's retinue.

Herald, said Manfred, as soon as he had digested these reflections, return to thy master, and tell him, ere we liquidate our differences by the sword, Manfred would hold some converse with him. Bid him welcome to my castle, where, by my faith, as I am a true knight, he shall have courteous reception, and full security for himself and followers. If we cannot adjust our quarrel by amicable means, I swear he shall depart in safety, and shall have full satisfaction according to the laws of arms: so help me God and his holy Trinity! – The herald made three obeisances, and retired.

During this interview Jerome's mind was agitated by a thousand contrary passions. He trembled for the life of his son, and his first idea was to persuade Isabella to return to the castle. Yet he was scarce less alarmed at the thought of her union with Manfred. He dreaded Hippolita's unbounded submission to the will of her lord: and though he did not doubt but he could alarm her piety not to consent to a divorce, if he could get access to her; yet should Manfred discover that the obstruction came from him, it might be equally fatal to Theodore.

He was impatient to know whence came the herald, who with so little management[5] had questioned the title of Manfred: yet he did not dare absent himself from the convent, lest Isabella should leave it, and her flight be imputed to him. He returned disconsolately to the monastery, uncertain on what conduct to resolve. A monk, who met him in the porch and observed his melancholy air, said, Alas! brother, is it then true that we have lost our excellent princess Hippolita? The holy man started, and cried, What meanest thou, brother? I come this instant from the castle, and left her in perfect health. Martelli, replied the other friar, passed by the convent but a quarter of an hour ago on his way from the castle, and reported that her highness was dead. All our brethren are gone to the chapel to pray for her happy transit to a better life, and willed me to wait thy arrival. They know thy holy attachment to that good lady, and are anxious for the affliction it will cause in thee – Indeed we have all reason to weep; she was a mother to our house – But this life is but a pilgrimage; we must not murmur – we shall all follow her; may our end be like hers! – Good brother, thou dreamest, said Jerome: I tell thee I come from the castle, and left the princess well – Where is the lady Isabella? – Poor gentlewoman! replied the friar; I told her the sad news, and offered her spiritual comfort; I reminded her of the transitory condition of mortality, and advised her to take the veil: I quoted the example of the holy princess Sanchia of Arragon.[6] – Thy zeal was laudable, said Jerome impatiently; but at present it was unnecessary: Hippolita is well – at least I trust in the Lord she is; I heard nothing to the contrary – Yet methinks, the prince's earnestness – Well, brother, but where is the lady Isabella? I know not, said the friar: she wept much, and said she would retire to her chamber. Jerome left his comrade abruptly, and hasted[7] to the princess, but she was not in her chamber. He enquired of the domestics of the convent, but could learn no news of her. He searched in vain throughout the monastery and the church, and dispatched messengers round the neighbourhood, to get intelligence if she had been seen; but to no purpose. Nothing could equal the good man's perplexity. He judged that Isabella, suspecting Manfred of having precipitated his wife's death, had taken the alarm, and withdrawn herself to some more secret place of concealment. This new flight would probably carry the prince's fury to the height. The report of Hippolita's death, though it seemed almost incredible, increased his consternation; and though Isabella's escape bespoke her aversion of Manfred for a husband, Jerome could feel no comfort from it, while it endangered the life of his son. He determined to return to the castle, and made several of his brethren accompany him to attest his innocence to Manfred, and, if necessary, join their intercession with his for Theodore.

The prince, in the mean time, had passed into the court, and ordered the gates of the castle to be flung open for the reception of the stranger knight and his train. In a few minutes the cavalcade arrived. First came two harbingers[8] with wands. Next a herald, followed by two pages and two trumpets. Then an hundred foot-guards. These were attended by as many horse. After them fifty footmen, clothed in scarlet and black, the colours of the knight. Then a led horse. Two heralds on each side of a gentleman on horseback bearing a banner with the arms of Vicenza and Otranto quarterly[9] – a circumstance that much offended Manfred – but he stifled his resentment. Two more pages. The knight's confessor telling his beads. Fifty more footmen, clad as before. Two knights habited in complete armour, their beavers[10] down, comrades to the principal knight. The 'squires of the two knights, carrying their shields and devices. The knight's own 'squire. An hundred gentlemen bearing an enormous sword, and seeming to faint under the weight of it. The knight himself on a chestnut steed, in complete armour, his lance in the rest, his face entirely concealed by his vizor, which was surmounted by a large plume of scarlet and black feathers. Fifty foot-guards with drums and trumpets closed the procession, which wheeled off to the right and left to make room for the principal knight.

As soon as he approached the gate, he stopped; and the herald advancing, read again the words of the challenge. Manfred's eyes were fixed on the gigantic sword, and he scarce seemed to attend to the cartel:[11] but his attention was soon diverted by a tempest of wind that rose behind him. He turned and beheld the plumes of the enchanted helmet agitated in the same extraordinary manner as before. It required intrepidity like Manfred's not to sink under a concurrence of circumstances that seemed to announce his fate. Yet scorning in the presence of strangers to betray the courage he had always manifested, he said boldly, Sir knight, whoever thou art, I bid thee welcome. If thou art of mortal mould, thy valour shall meet its equal: and if thou art a true knight, thou wilt scorn to employ sorcery to carry thy point. Be these omens from heaven or hell, Manfred trusts to the righteousness of his cause and to the aid of saint Nicholas, who has ever protected his house. Alight, sir knight, and repose thyself. To-morrow thou shalt have a fair field; and heaven befriend the juster side!

The knight made no reply, but, dismounting, was conducted by Manfred to the great hall of the castle. As they traversed the court, the knight stopped to gaze at the miraculous casque; and, kneeling down, seemed to pray inwardly for some minutes. Rising, he made a sign to the prince to lead on. As soon as they entered the hall, Manfred proposed to the stranger to disarm; but the knight shook his head in token of refusal. Sir knight, said Manfred, this is not courteous; but by my good faith I will not cross thee! nor shalt thou have cause to complain of the prince of Otranto. No treachery is designed on my part: I hope none is intended on thine. Here take my gage:[12] [giving him his ring] your friends and you shall enjoy the laws of hospitality. Rest here until refreshments are brought: I will but give orders for the accommodation of your train, and return to you. The three knights bowed, as accepting his courtesy. Manfred directed the stranger's retinue to be conducted to an adjacent hospital,[13] founded by the princess Hippolita for the reception of pilgrims. As they made the circuit of the court to return towards the gate, the gigantic sword burst from the supporters, and, falling to the ground opposite to the helmet, remained immoveable. Manfred, almost hardened to preternatural appearances, surmounted the shock of this new prodigy; and returning to the hall, where by this time the feast was ready, he invited his silent guests to take their places. Manfred, however ill his heart was at ease, endeavoured to inspire the company with mirth. He put several questions to them, but was answered only by signs. They raised their vizors but sufficiently to feed themselves, and that sparingly. Sirs, said the prince, ye are the first guests I ever treated within these walls, who scorned to hold any intercourse with me: nor has it oft been customary, I ween,[14] for princes to hazard their state and dignity against strangers and mutes. You say you come in the name of Frederic of Vicenza: I

59

have ever heard that he was a gallant and courteous knight; nor would he, I am bold to say, think it beneath him to mix in social converse with a prince that is his equal, and not unknown by deeds in arms. – Still ye are silent – Well! be it as it may – by the laws of hospitality and chivalry ye are masters under this roof: ye shall do your pleasure – but come, give me a goblet of wine; ye will not refuse to pledge me to the healths of your fair mistresses. The principal knight sighed and crossed himself, and was rising from the board – Sir knight, said Manfred, what I said was but in sport: I shall constrain you in nothing: use your good liking. Since mirth is not your mood, let us be sad. Business may hit your fancies better: let us withdraw; and hear if what I have to unfold may be better relished than the vain efforts I have made for your pastime.

Manfred, then, conducting the three knights into an inner chamber, shut the door, and, inviting them to be seated, began thus, addressing himself to the chief personage:

You come, sir knight, as I understand, in the name of the marquis of Vicenza, to re-demand the lady Isabella his daughter, who has been contracted in the face of holy church to my son, by the consent of her legal guardians; and to require me to resign my dominions to your lord, who gives himself for the nearest of blood to prince Alfonso, whose soul God rest! I shall speak to the latter article of your demands first. You must know, your lord knows, that I enjoy the principality of Otranto from my father Don Manuel, as he received it from his father Don Ricardo. Alfonso, their predecessor, dying childless in the Holy Land, bequeathed his estates to my grandfather Don Ricardo, in consideration of his faithful services – [The stranger shook his head] – Sir knight, said Manfred warmly, Ricardo was a valiant and upright man; he was a pious man; witness his munificent foundation of the adjoining church and two convents. He was peculiarly patronized by saint Nicholas – My grandfather was incapable – I say, sir, Don Ricardo was incapable – Excuse me, your interruption has disordered me – I venerate the memory of my grandfather – Well, sirs! he held this estate; he held it by his good sword, and by the favour of saint Nicholas – so did my father; and so, sirs, will I, come what come will. – But Frederic, your lord, is nearest in blood – I have consented to put my title to the issue of the sword – does that imply a vitious[15] title? I might have asked, where is Frederic, your lord? Report speaks him dead in captivity. You say, your actions say, he lives – I question it not – I might, sirs, I might – but I do not. Other princes would bid Frederic take his inheritance by force, if he can: they would not stake their dignity on a single combat: they would not submit it to the decision of unknown mutes! Pardon me, gentlemen, I am too warm: but suppose yourselves in my situation: as ye are stout knights, would it not move your choler[16] to have your own and the honour of your ancestors called in question? – But to the point. Ye require me to deliver up the lady Isabella – Sirs, I must ask if ye are authorized to receive her? [The knight nodded.] Receive her – continued Manfred: Well! you are authorized to receive her – But, gentle knight, may I ask if you have full powers? [The knight nodded.] 'Tis well, said Manfred: then hear what I have to offer – Ye see, gentlemen, before you the most unhappy of men! [he began to weep] afford me your compassion; I am entitled to it; indeed I am. Know, I have lost my only hope, my joy, the support of my house – Conrad died yester-morning. [The knights discovered signs of surprise.] Yes, sirs, fate has disposed of my son. Isabella is at liberty. – Do you then restore her, cried the chief knight, breaking silence. Afford me your patience, said Manfred. I rejoice to find, by this testimony of your good-will, that this matter may be adjusted[17] without blood. It is no interest of mine dictates what little I have farther to say. Ye behold in me a man disgusted with the world: the loss of my son has weaned me from earthly cares. Power and greatness have no longer any charms in my eyes. I wished to transmit the sceptre I had received from my ancestors with honour to my son – but that is over! Life itself is so indifferent to me, that I accepted your defiance with joy: a good knight cannot go to the grave with more satisfaction than when falling in his vocation. Whatever is the will of heaven, I submit; for, alas! sirs, I am a man of many sorrows. Manfred is no object of envy – but no doubt you are acquainted with my story. [The knight made signs of ignorance, and seemed curious to have Manfred proceed.] Is it possible, sirs, continued the prince, that my story should be a secret to you? Have you heard nothing relating to me and the princess Hippolita? [They shook their heads] – No! Thus then, sirs, it is.

You think me ambitious: ambition, alas, is composed of more rugged materials. If I were ambitious, I should not for so many years, have been a prey to all the hell of conscientious scruples – But I weary your patience: I will be brief. Know then, that I have long been troubled in mind on my union with the princess Hippolita. – Oh! sirs, if ye were acquainted with that excellent woman! if ye knew that I adore her like a mistress, and cherish her as a friend – But man was not born for perfect happiness! She shares my scruples, and with her consent I have brought this matter before the church, for we are related within the forbidden degrees. I expect every hour the definitive sentence that must separate us forever. I am sure you feel for me – I see you do – Pardon these tears! [The knights gazed on each other, wondering where this would end.] Manfred continued: The death of my son betiding while my soul was under this anxiety, I thought of nothing but resigning my dominions, and retiring forever from the sight of mankind. My only difficulty was to fix on a successor, who would be tender of my people, and to dispose of the lady Isabella, who is dear to me as my own blood. I was willing to restore the line of Alfonso, even in his most distant kindred: and though, pardon me, I am satisfied it was his will that Ricardo's lineage should take place of his own relations; yet, where was I to search for those relations? I knew of none but Frederic, your lord: he was a captive to the infidels, or dead; and were he living, and at home, would he quit the flourishing state of Vicenza for the inconsiderable principality of Otranto? If he would not, could I bear the thought of seeing a hard unfeeling viceroy[18] set over my poor faithful people? – for, sirs, I love my people, and thank heaven am beloved by them. – But ye will ask, Whither tends this long discourse? Briefly then, thus, sirs. Heaven in your arrival seems to point out a remedy for these difficulties and my misfortunes. The lady Isabella is at liberty: I shall soon be so. I would submit to any thing for the good of my people – Were it not the best, the only way to extinguish the feuds between our families, if I was to take the lady Isabella to wife? – You start – But though Hippolita's virtues will ever be dear to me, a prince must not consider himself; he is born for his people. – A servant at that instant entering the chamber, apprized Manfred that Jerome and several of his brethren demanded immediate access to him.

The prince, provoked at this interruption, and fearing that the friar would discover to the strangers that Isabella had taken sanctuary, was going to forbid Jerome's entrance. But recollecting that he was certainly arrived to notify the princess's return, Manfred began to excuse himself to the knights for leaving them for a few moments, but was prevented by the arrival of the friars. Manfred angrily reprimanded them for their intrusion, and would have forced them back from the chamber; but Jerome was too much agitated to be repulsed. He declared aloud the flight of Isabella, with protestations of his own innocence. Manfred, distracted at the news, and not less at its coming to the knowledge of the strangers, uttered nothing but incoherent sentences, now upbraiding the friar, now apologizing to the knights, earnest to know what was become of Isabella, yet equally afraid of their knowing, impatient to pursue her, yet dreading to have them join in the pursuit. He offered to dispatch messengers in quest of her: – but the chief knight, no longer keeping silence, reproached Manfred in bitter terms for his dark and ambiguous dealing, and demanded the cause of Isabella's first absence from the castle. Manfred, casting a stern look at Jerome, implying a command of silence, pretended that on Conrad's death he had placed her in sanctuary until he could determine how to dispose of her. Jerome, who trembled for his son's life, did not dare contradict this falsehood; but one of his brethren, not under the same anxiety, declared frankly that she had fled to their church in the preceding night. The prince in vain endeavoured to stop this discovery, which overwhelmed him with shame and confusion. The principal stranger, amazed at the contradictions he heard, and more than half persuaded that Manfred had secreted the princess, notwithstanding the concern he expressed at her flight, rushing to the door, said, Thou traitor-prince! Isabella shall be found. Manfred endeavoured to hold him; but the other knights assisting their comrade, he broke from the prince, and hastened into the court, demanding his attendants. Manfred, finding it vain to divert him from the pursuit, offered to accompany him; and summoning his attendants, and taking Jerome and some of the friars to guide them, they issued from the castle; Manfred privately giving orders to have the knight's company secured, while to the knight he affected to dispatch a messenger to require their assistance.

The company had no sooner quitted the castle, than Matilda, who felt herself deeply interested for the young peasant, since she had seen him condemned to death in the hall, and whose thoughts had been taken up with concerting measures to save him, was informed by some of the female attendants that Manfred had dispatched all his men various ways in pursuit of Isabella. He had in his hurry given this order in general terms, not meaning to extend it to the guard he had set upon Theodore, but forgetting it. The domestics, officious to obey so peremptory a prince, and urged by their own curiosity and love of novelty to join in any precipitate chace, had to a man left the castle. Matilda disengaged herself from her women, stole up to the black tower, and, unbolting the door, presented herself to the astonished Theodore. Young man, said she, though filial duty and womanly modesty condemn the step I am taking, yet holy charity, surmounting all other ties, justifies this act. Fly; the doors of thy prison are open: my father and his domestics are absent; but they may soon return: begone in safety; and may the angels of heaven direct thy course! – Thou art surely one of those angels! said the enraptured Theodore: none but a blessed saint could speak, could act, could look like thee! – May I not know the name of my divine protectress? Methought thou namedst thy father: is it possible? can Manfred's blood feel holy pity? – Lovely lady, thou answerest not – But how art thou here thyself? Why dost thou neglect thy own safety, and waste a thought on a wretch like Theodore? Let us fly together: the life thou bestowest shall be dedicated to thy defence. Alas! thou mistakest, said Matilda sighing: I am Manfred's daughter, but no dangers await me. Amazement! said Theodore: but last night I blessed myself for yielding thee the service thy gracious compassion so charitably returns me now. Still thou art in an error, said the princess; but this is no time for explanation. Fly, virtuous youth, while it is in my power to save thee: should my father return, thou and I both should indeed have cause to tremble. How? said Theodore: thinkest thou, charming maid, that I will accept of life at the hazard of aught calamitous to thee? Better I endured a thousand deaths — I run no risk, said Matilda, but by thy delay. Depart: it cannot be known that I assisted thy flight. Swear by the saints above, said Theodore, that thou canst not be suspected; else here I vow to await whatever can befall me. Oh! thou art too generous, said Matilda; but rest assured that no suspicion can alight on me. Give me thy beauteous hand in token that thou dost not deceive me, said Theodore; and let me bathe it with the warm tears of gratitude. – Forbear, said the princess: this must not be. – Alas! said Theodore, I have never known but calamity until this hour – perhaps shall never know other fortune again: suffer the chaste raptures of holy gratitude: 'tis my soul would print its effusions on thy hand. – Forbear, and begone, said Matilda: how would Isabella approve of seeing thee at my feet? Who is Isabella? said the young man with surprise. Ah me! I fear, said the princess, I am serving a deceitful one! Hast thou forgot thy curiosity this morning? – Thy looks, thy actions, all thy beauteous self seems an emanation of divinity, said Theodore, but thy words are dark and mysterious — Speak, lady, speak to thy servant's comprehension. – Thou understandest but too well, said Matilda: but once more I command thee to be gone: thy blood, which, I may preserve, will be on my head, if I waste the time in vain discourse. I go, lady, said Theodore, because it is thy will, and because I would not bring the grey hairs of my father with sorrow to the grave. Say but, adored lady, that I have thy gentle pity. – Stay, said Matilda; I will conduct thee to the subterraneous vault by which Isabella escaped; it will lead thee to the church of saint Nicholas, where thou mayst take sanctuary. – What! said Theodore, was it another, and not thy lovely self, that I assisted to find the subterraneous passage? It was, said Matilda: but ask no more; I tremble to see thee still abide here: fly to the sanctuary. – To sanctuary! said Theodore: No, princess; sanctuaries are for helpless damsels, or for criminals. Theodore's soul is free from guilt, nor will wear the appearance of it. Give me a sword, lady, and thy father shall learn that Theodore scorns an ignominious flight. Rash youth! said Matilda, thou wouldst not dare to lift thy presumptuous arm against the prince of Otranto? Not against *thy* father; indeed I dare not, said Theodore: excuse me, lady; I had forgotten – but could I gaze on thee, and remember thou art sprung from the tyrant Manfred? – But he is thy father, and from this moment my injuries are buried in oblivion. A deep and hollow groan, which seemed to come from above, startled the princess and Theodore. Good heaven! we are overheard! said the princess. They listened; but perceiving no farther noise, they both concluded it the effect of pent-up vapours:[19] and the princess, preceding Theodore softly, carried him to her father's armoury; where equipping him with a complete suit, he was conducted by Matilda to the postern-gate. Avoid the town, said the princess, and all the western side of the castle: 'tis there the search must be making by Manfred and the strangers: but hie thee to the opposite quarter. Yonder, behind that forest to the east is a chain of rocks, hollowed into a labyrinth of caverns that reach to the sea-coast. There thou mayst lie concealed, till thou canst make signs to some vessel to put on shore and take thee off. Go! heaven be thy guide! – and sometimes in thy prayers remember – Matilda! – Theodore flung himself at her feet, and seizing her lily hand, which with struggles she suffered him to kiss, he vowed on the earliest opportunity to get himself knighted, and fervently entreated her permission to swear himself eternally her knight. – Ere the princess could reply, a clap of thunder was suddenly heard, that shook the battlements. Theodore, regardless[20] of the tempest, would have urged his suit; but the princess, dismayed, retreated hastily into the castle, and commanded the youth to be gone, with an air that would not be disobeyed. He sighed, and retired, but with eyes fixed on the gate, until Matilda closing it put an end to an interview, in which the hearts of both had drunk so deeply of a passion which both now tasted for the first time.

Theodore went pensively to the convent, to acquaint his father with his deliverance. There he learned the absence of Jerome, and the pursuit that was making after the lady Isabella, with some particulars of whose story he now first became acquainted. The generous gallantry of his nature prompted him to wish to assist her; but the monks could lend him no lights to guess at the route she had taken. He was not tempted to wander far in search of her; for the idea of Matilda had imprinted itself so strongly on his heart, that he could not bear to absent himself at much distance from her abode. The tenderness Jerome had expressed for him concurred to confirm this reluctance; and he even persuaded himself that filial affection was the chief cause of his hovering between the castle and monastery. Until Jerome should return at night, Theodore at length determined to repair to the forest that Matilda had pointed out to him. Arriving there, he sought the gloomiest shades, as best suited to the pleasing melancholy that reigned in his mind. In this mood he roved insensibly to the caves which had formerly served as a retreat to hermits, and were now reported round the country to be haunted by evil spirits. He recollected to have heard this tradition; and being of a brave and adventurous disposition, he willingly indulged his curiosity in exploring the secret recesses of this labyrinth. He had not penetrated far before he thought he heard the steps of some person who seemed to retreat before him. Theodore, though firmly grounded in all our holy faith enjoins to be believed, had no apprehension that good men were abandoned without cause to the malice of the powers of darkness. He thought the place more likely to be infested by robbers, than by those infernal agents who are reported to molest and bewilder travellers. He had long burned with impatience to approve[21] his valour. Drawing his sabre, he marched sedately onwards, still directing his steps as the imperfect rustling sound before him led the way. The armour he wore was a like indication to the person who avoided him. Theodore, now convinced that he was not mistaken, redoubled his pace, and evidently gained on the person that fled; whose haste increasing, Theodore came up just as a woman fell breathless before him. He hasted to raise her; but her terror was so great, that he apprehended she would faint in his arms. He used every gentle word to dispel her alarms, and assured her that, far from injuring, he would defend her at the peril of his life. The lady recovering her spirits from his courteous demeanour, and gazing on her protector, said, Sure I have heard that voice before? – Not to my knowledge, replied Theodore, unless, as I conjecture, thou art the lady Isabella. – Merciful heaven! cried she, thou art not sent in quest of me, art thou? And saying those words she threw herself at his feet, and besought him not to deliver her up to Manfred. To Manfred! cried Theodore – No, lady: I have once already delivered thee from his tyranny, and it shall fare hard with me now, but I will place thee out of the reach of his daring. Is it possible, said she, that thou shouldst be the generous unknown whom I met last night in the vault of the castle? Sure thou art not a mortal, but my guardian angel: on my knees let me thank – Hold, gentle princess, said Theodore, nor demean thyself before a poor and friendless young man. If heaven has selected me for thy deliverer, it will accomplish its work, and strengthen my arm in thy cause. But come, lady, we are too near the mouth of the cavern; let us seek its inmost recesses: I can have no tranquillity till I have placed thee beyond the reach of danger. – Alas! what mean you, sir? said she. Though all your actions are noble, though your sentiments speak the purity of your soul, is it fitting that I should accompany you alone into these perplexed retreats? Should we be found together, what would a censorious world think of my conduct? – I respect your virtuous delicacy, said Theodore; nor do you harbour a suspicion that wounds my honour. I meant to conduct you into the most private cavity of these rocks; and then, at the hazard of my life, to guard their entrance against every living thing. Besides, lady, continued he, drawing a deep sigh, beauteous and all perfect as your form is, and though my wishes are not guiltless of aspiring, know, my soul is dedicated to another; and although – A sudden noise prevented Theodore from proceeding. They soon distinguished these sounds, Isabella! What ho! Isabella! – The trembling princess relapsed into her former agony of fear. Theodore endeavoured to encourage her, but in vain. He assured her he would die rather than suffer her to return under Manfred's power; and begging her to remain concealed, he went forth to prevent the person in search of her from approaching.

At the mouth of the cavern he found an armed knight discoursing with a peasant, who assured him he had seen a lady enter the passes of the rock. The knight was preparing to seek her, when Theodore, placing himself in his way, with his sword drawn, sternly forbad him at his peril to advance. And who art thou who darest to cross my way? said the knight haughtily. One who does not dare more than he will perform, said Theodore. I seek the lady Isabella, said the knight; and understand she has taken refuge among these rocks. Impede me not, or thou wilt repent having provoked my resentment. – Thy purpose is as odious as thy resentment is contemptible, said Theodore. Return whence thou camest, or we shall soon know whose resentment is most terrible. – The stranger, who was the principal knight that had arrived from the marquis of Vicenza, had galloped from Manfred as he was busied in getting information of the princess, and giving various orders to prevent her falling into the power of the three knights. Their chief had suspected Manfred of being privy to the princess's absconding; and this insult from a man who he concluded was stationed by that prince to secrete her, confirming his suspicions, he made no reply, but, discharging a blow with his sabre at Theodore, would soon have removed all obstruction, if Theodore, who took him for one of Manfred's captains, and who had no sooner given the provocation than prepared to support it, had not received the stroke on his shield. The valour that had so long been smothered in his breast, broke forth at once: he rushed impetuously on the knight, whose pride and wrath were not less powerful incentives to hardy deeds. The combat was furious, but not long. Theodore wounded the knight in three several places, and at last disarmed him as he fainted with the loss of blood. The peasant, who had fled on the first onset, had given the alarm to some of Manfred's domestics, who by his orders were dispersed through the forest in pursuit of Isabella. They came up as the knight fell, whom they soon discovered to be the noble stranger. Theodore, notwithstanding his hatred to Manfred, could not behold the victory he had gained without emotions of pity and generosity: but he was more touched, when he learned the quality of his adversary, and was informed that he was no retainer, but an enemy of Manfred. He assisted the servants of the latter in disarming the knight, and in endeavouring to staunch the blood that flowed from his wounds. The knight, recovering his speech, said in a faint and faltering voice, Generous foe, we have both been in an error: I took thee for an instrument of the tyrant; I perceive thou hast made the like mistake – It is too late for excuses – I faint. – If Isabella is at hand, call her – I have important secrets to – He is dying! said one of the attendants; has nobody a crucifix about them? Andrea, do thou pray over him. – Fetch some water, said Theodore, and pour it down his throat, while I hasten to the princess. Saying this, he flew to Isabella; and in few words told her modestly, that he had been so unfortunate by mistake as to wound a gentleman from her father's court, who wished ere he died to impart something of consequence to her. The princess, who had been transported at hearing the voice of Theodore as he called to her to come forth, was astonished at what she heard. Suffering herself to be conducted by Theodore, the new proof of whose valour recalled her dispersed spirits, she came where the bleeding knight lay speechless on the ground – but her fears returned when she beheld the domestics of Manfred. She would again have fled, if Theodore had not made her observe that they were unarmed, and had not threatened them with instant death, if they should dare to seize the princess. The stranger, opening his eyes, and beholding a woman, said, Art thou – pray tell me truly – art thou Isabella of Vicenza? I am, said she; good heaven restore thee! – Then thou – then thou – said the knight, struggling for utterance – seest – thy father! – Give me one –– Oh! amazement! horror! what do I hear! what do I see! cried Isabella. My father! You my father! How came you here, sir? For heaven's sake speak! – Oh! run for help, or he will expire! – 'Tis most true, said the wounded knight, exerting all his force; I am Frederic thy father – Yes, I came to deliver thee – It will not be – Give me a parting kiss, and take –– Sir, said Theodore, do not exhaust yourself: suffer us to convey you to the castle. – To the castle! said Isabella: Is there no help nearer than the castle? Would you expose my father to the tyrant? If he goes thither, I dare not accompany him. – And yet, can I leave him? – My child, said Frederic, it matters not for me whither I am carried: a few minutes will place me beyond danger: but while I have eyes to doat on thee, forsake me not, dear Isabella! This brave knight – I know not who he is – will protect thy innocence. Sir, you will not abandon my child, will you? – Theodore, shedding tears over his victim, and vowing to guard the princess at the expence of his life, persuaded Frederic to suffer himself to be conducted to the castle. They placed him on a horse belonging to one of the domestics, after binding up his wounds as well as they were able. Theodore marched by his side; and the afflicted Isabella, who could not bear to quit him, followed mournfully behind.

CHAPTER 4

The sorrowful troop no sooner arrived at the castle, than they were met by Hippolita and Matilda, whom Isabella had sent one of the domestics before to advertise of their approach. The ladies, causing Frederic to be conveyed into the nearest chamber, retired, while the surgeons examined his wounds. Matilda blushed at seeing Theodore and Isabella together; but endeavoured to conceal it by embracing the latter, and condoling with her on her father's mischance. The surgeons soon came to acquaint Hippolita that none of the marquis's wounds were dangerous; and that he was desirous of seeing his daughter and the princesses. Theodore, under pretence of expressing his joy at being freed from his apprehensions of the combat being fatal to Frederic, could not resist the impulse of following Matilda. Her eyes were so often cast down on meeting his, that Isabella, who regarded Theodore as attentively as he gazed on Matilda, soon devined who the object was that he had told her in the cave engaged his affections. While this mute scene passed, Hippolita demanded of Frederic the cause of his having taken that mysterious course for reclaiming his daughter; and threw in various apologies to excuse her lord for the match contracted between their children. Frederic, however incensed against Manfred, was not insensible to the courtesy and benevolence of Hippolita: but he was still more struck with the lovely form of Matilda. Wishing to detain them by his bed-side, he informed Hippolita of his story. He told her, that, while prisoner to the infidels, he had dreamed that his daughter, of whom he had learned no news since his captivity, was detained in a castle, where she was in danger of the most dreadful misfortunes; and that if he obtained his liberty, and repaired to a wood near Joppa,[1] he would learn more. Alarmed at this dream, and incapable of obeying the direction given by it, his chains became more grievous than ever. But while his thoughts were occupied on the means of obtaining his liberty, he received the agreeable news that the confederate princes, who were warring in Palestine, had paid his ransom. He instantly set out for the wood that had been marked in his dream. For three days he and his attendants had wandered in the forest without seeing a human form: but on the evening of the third they came to a cell, in which they found a venerable hermit in the agonies of death. Applying rich cordials, they brought the saint-like man to his speech. My sons, said he, I am bounden to your charity – but it is in vain – I am going to my eternal rest – yet I die with the satisfaction of performing the will of heaven. When first I repaired to this solitude, after seeing my country become a prey to unbelievers [it is, alas! above fifty years since I was witness to that dreadful scene!] saint Nicholas appeared to me, and revealed a secret, which he bade me never disclose to mortal man, but on my death-bed. This is that tremendous hour, and ye are no doubt the chosen warriors to whom I was ordered to reveal my trust. As soon as ye have done the last offices to this wretched corse, dig under the seventh tree on the left hand of this poor cave, and your pains will – Oh! good heaven receive my soul! With those words the devout man breathed his last. By break of day, continued Frederic, when we had committed the holy relics to earth, we dug according to direction – But what was our astonishment, when about the depth of six feet we discovered an enormous sabre – the very weapon yonder in the court! On the blade, which was then partly out of the scabbard, though since closed by our efforts in removing it, were written the following lines — No; excuse me, madam, added the marquis, turning to Hippolita, if I forbear to repeat them: I respect your sex and rank, and would not be guilty of offending your ear with sounds injurious to aught that is dear to you. – He paused. Hippolita trembled. She did not doubt but Frederic was destined by heaven to accomplish the fate that seemed to threaten her house. Looking with anxious fondness at Matilda, a silent tear stole down her cheek; but recollecting herself, she said, Proceed, my lord; heaven does nothing in vain: mortals must receive its divine behests with lowliness and submission.[2] It is our part to deprecate its wrath, or bow to its decrees. Repeat the sentence, my lord: we listen resigned. – Frederic was grieved that he had proceeded so far. The dignity and patient firmness of Hippolita penetrated him with respect, and the tender silent affection, with which the princess and her daughter regarded each other, melted him almost to tears. Yet apprehensive that his forbearance to obey would be more alarming, he repeated in a faltering and low voice the following lines:

> Where'er a casque that suits this sword is found,
> With perils is thy daughter compass'd round:
> Alfonso's blood alone can save the maid,
> And quiet a long-restless prince's shade.

What is there in these lines, said Theodore impatiently, that affects these princesses? Why were they to be shocked by a mysterious delicacy, that has so little foundation? Your words are rude, young man, said the marquis; and though fortune has favoured you once – My honoured lord, said Isabella, who resented Theodore's warmth, which she perceived was dictated by his sentiments for Matilda, discompose not yourself for the glosing[3] of a peasant's son: he forgets the reverence he owes you; but he is not accustomed – Hippolita, concerned at the heat that had arisen, checked Theodore for his boldness, but with an air acknowledging his zeal; and, changing the conversation, demanded of Frederic where he had left her lord? As the marquis was going to reply, they heard a noise without; and rising to enquire the cause, Manfred, Jerome, and part of the troop, who had met an imperfect rumour of what had happened, entered the chamber. Manfred advanced hastily towards Frederic's bed to condole with him on his misfortune, and to learn the circumstances of the combat; when starting in an agony of terror and amazement, he cried, Ha! what art thou, thou dreadful spectre! Is my hour come? – My dearest, gracious lord, cried Hippolita, clasping him in her arms, what is it you see? Why do you fix your eye-balls thus?[4] – What! cried Manfred breathless – dost thou see nothing, Hippolita? Is this ghastly phantom sent to me alone – to me, who did not — For mercy's sweetest self, my lord, said Hippolita, resume your soul, command your reason. There is none here but we, your friends. – What, is not that Alfonso? cried Manfred: dost thou not see him? Can it be my brain's delirium? – This! my lord, said Hippolita; this is Theodore, the youth who has been so unfortunate – Theodore! said Manfred mournfully, and striking his forehead – Theodore, or a phantom, he has unhinged the soul of Manfred. – But how comes he here? and how comes he in armour? I believe he went in search of Isabella, said Hippolita. Of Isabella? said Manfred, relapsing into rage – Yes, yes, that is not doubtful – But how did he escape from durance in which I left him? Was it Isabella, or this hypocritical old friar, that procured his enlargement? – And would a parent be criminal, my lord, said Theodore, if he meditated the deliverance of his child? Jerome, amazed to hear himself in a manner accused by his son, and without foundation, knew not what to think. He could not comprehend how Theodore had escaped, how he came to be armed, and to encounter Frederic. Still he would not venture to ask any questions that might tend to inflame Manfred's wrath against his son. Jerome's silence convinced Manfred that he had contrived Theodore's release. – And is it thus, thou ungrateful old man, said the prince, addressing himself to the friar, that thou repayest mine and Hippolita's bounties? And not content with traversing my heart's nearest wishes, thou armest thy bastard, and bringest him into my own castle to insult me! My lord, said Theodore, you wrong my father: nor he nor I is capable of harbouring a thought against your peace. Is it insolence thus to surrender myself to your highness's pleasure? added he, laying his sword respectfully at Manfred's feet. Behold my bosom; strike, my lord, if you suspect that a disloyal thought is lodged there. There is not a sentiment engraven on my heart, that does not venerate you and yours. The grace and fervour with which Theodore uttered these words, interested every person present in his favour. Even Manfred was touched – yet still possessed with his resemblance to Alfonso, his admiration was dashed with secret horror. Rise, said he; thy life is not my present purpose. – But tell me thy history, and how thou camest connected with this old traitor here. My lord! said Jerome eagerly. – Peace, impostor! said Manfred; I will not have him prompted. My lord, said Theodore, I want no assistance; my story is very brief. I was carried at five years of age to Algiers with my mother, who had been taken by corsairs[5] from the coast of Sicily. She died of grief in less than a twelvemonth. – The tears gushed from Jerome's eyes, on whose countenance a thousand anxious passions stood expressed. Before she died, continued Theodore, she bound a writing about my arm under my garments, which told me I was the son of the Count Falconara. – It is most true, said Jerome; I am that wretched father. – Again I enjoin thee silence, said Manfred: proceed. I remained in slavery, said Theodore, until within these two years, when attending on my master in his cruizes, I was delivered by a christian vessel, which overpowered the pirate; and discovering myself to the captain, he generously put me on shore in Sicily. But alas! instead of finding a father, I learned that his estate, which was situated on the coast, had during his absence been laid waste by the rover[6] who had carried my mother and me into captivity: that his castle had been burnt to the ground: and that my father on his return had sold what remained, and was retired into religion in the kingdom of Naples, but where, no man could inform me. Destitute and friendless, hopeless almost of attaining the transport of a parent's embrace, I took the first opportunity of setting sail for Naples; from whence within these six days I wandered into this province, still supporting myself by the labour of my hands; nor till yester-morn did I believe that heaven had reserved any lot for me but peace of mind and contented poverty. This, my lord, is Theodore's story. I am blessed beyond my hope in finding a father; I am unfortunate beyond my desert in having incurred your highness's displeasure. He ceased. A murmur of approbation gently arose from the audience. This is not all; said Frederic; I am bound in honour to add what he suppresses. Though he is modest, I must be generous – he is one of the bravest youths on christian ground. He is warm too; and from the short knowledge I have of him, I will pledge myself for his veracity: if what he reports of himself were not true, he would not utter it – and for me, youth, I honour a frankness which becomes thy birth. But now, and thou didst offend me; yet the noble blood which flows in thy veins may well be allowed to boil out, when it has so recently traced itself to its source. Come, my lord, [turning to Manfred] if I can pardon him, surely you may: it is not the youth's fault, if you took him for a spectre. This bitter taunt galled the soul of Manfred. If beings from another world, replied he haughtily, have power to impress my mind with awe, it is more than living man can do; nor could a stripling's arm – My lord, interrupted Hippolita, your guest has occasion for repose; shall we not leave him to his rest? Saying this, and taking Manfred by the hand, she took leave of Frederic, and led the company forth. The prince, not sorry to quit a conversation which recalled to mind the discovery he had made of his most secret sensations, suffered himself to be conducted to his own apartment, after permitting Theodore, though under engagement to return to the castle on the morrow, [a condition the young man gladly accepted] to retire with his father to the convent. Matilda and Isabella were too much occupied with their own reflections, and too little content with each other, to wish for farther converse that night. They separated each to her chamber, with more expressions of ceremony, and fewer of affection, than had passed between them since their childhood.

If they parted with small cordiality, they did but meet with greater impatience as soon as the sun was risen. Their minds were in a situation that excluded sleep, and each recollected a thousand questions which she wished she had put to the other overnight. Matilda reflected that Isabella had been twice delivered by Theodore in very critical situations, which she could not believe accidental. His eyes, it was true, had been fixed on her in Frederic's chamber; but that might have been to disguise his passion for Isabella from the fathers of both. It were better to clear this up. She wished to know the truth, lest she should wrong her friend by entertaining a passion for Isabella's lover. Thus jealousy prompted, and at the same time borrowed an excuse from friendship to justify its curiosity.

Isabella, not less restless, had better foundation for her suspicions. Both Theodore's tongue and eyes had told her his heart was engaged, it was true – yet perhaps Matilda might not correspond to his passion – She had ever appeared insensible to love; all her thoughts were set on heaven – Why did I dissuade her? said Isabella to herself; I am punished for my generosity – But when did they meet? where? – It cannot be; I have deceived myself – Perhaps last night was the first time they ever beheld each other – it must be some other object that has prepossessed his affections – If it is, I am not so unhappy as I thought; if it is not my friend Matilda – How! can I stoop to wish for the affection of a man, who rudely and unnecessarily acquainted me with his indifference? and that at the very moment in which common courtesy demanded at least expressions of civility. I will go to my dear Matilda, who will confirm me in this becoming pride – Man is false – I will advise with her on taking the veil: she will rejoice to find me in this disposition; and I will acquaint her that I no longer oppose her inclination for the cloister. In this frame of mind, and determined to open her heart entirely to Matilda, she went to that princess's chamber, whom she found already dressed, and leaning pensively on her arm. This attitude,[7] so correspondent to what she felt herself, revived Isabella's suspicions, and destroyed the confidence she had purposed to place in her friend. They blushed at meeting, and were too much novices to disguise their sensations with address. After some unmeaning questions and replies, Matilda demanded of Isabella the cause of her flight. The latter, who had almost forgotten Manfred's passion, so entirely was she occupied by her own, concluding that Matilda referred to her last escape from the convent, which had occasioned the events of the preceding evening, replied, Martelli brought word to the convent that your mother was dead. – Oh! said Matilda interrupting her, Bianca has explained that mistake to me: on seeing me faint, she cried out, The princess is dead! and Martelli, who had come for the usual dole[8] to the castle — and what made you faint? said Isabella, indifferent to the rest. Matilda blushed, and stammered – My father – he was sitting in judgment on a criminal. – What criminal? said Isabella eagerly. — A young man, said Matilda – I believe – I think it was that young man that – What, Theodore? said Isabella. Yes, answered she; I never saw him before; I do not know how he had offended my father – but, as he has been of service to you, I am glad my lord has pardoned him. Served me? replied Isabella: do you term it serving me, to wound my father, and almost occasion his death? Though it is but since yesterday that I am blessed with knowing a parent, I hope Matilda does not think I am such a stranger to filial tenderness as not to resent the boldness of that audacious youth, and that it is impossible for me ever to feel any affection for one who dared to lift his arm against the author of my being. No, Matilda, my heart abhors him; and if you still retain the friendship for me that you have vowed from your infancy, you will detest a man who has been on the point of making me miserable for ever. Matilda held down her head, and replied, I hope my dearest Isabella does not doubt her Matilda's friendship: I never beheld that youth until yesterday; he is almost a stranger to me: but as the surgeons have pronounced your father out of danger, you ought not to harbour uncharitable resentment against one who I am persuaded did not know the marquis was related to you. You plead his cause very pathetically, said Isabella, considering he is so much a stranger to you! I am mistaken, or he returns your charity. What mean you? said Matilda. Nothing, said Isabella; repenting that she had given Matilda a hint of Theodore's inclination for her. Then changing the discourse, she asked Matilda what occasioned Manfred to take Theodore for a spectre? Bless me, said Matilda, did not you observe his extreme resemblance to the portrait of Alfonso in the gallery? I took notice of it to Bianca even before I saw him in armour; but with the helmet on, he is the very image of that picture. I do not much observe pictures, said Isabella; much less have I examined this young man so attentively as you seem to have done. — Ah! Matilda, your heart is in danger – but let me warn you as a friend – He has owned to me that he is in love: it cannot be with you, for yesterday was the first time you ever met – was it not? Certainly, replied Matilda. But why does my dearest Isabella conclude from any thing I have said, that – She paused – then continuing, He saw you first, and I am far from having the vanity to think that my little portion of charms could engage a heart devoted to you. May you be happy, Isabella, whatever is the fate of Matilda! – My lovely friend, said Isabella, whose heart was too honest to resist a kind expression, it is you that Theodore admires; I saw it; I am persuaded of it; nor shall a thought of my own happiness suffer me to interfere with yours. This frankness drew tears from the gentle Matilda; and jealousy, that for a moment had raised a coolness between these amiable maidens, soon gave way to the natural sincerity and candour of their souls. Each confessed to the other the impression that Theodore had made on her; and this confidence was followed by a struggle of generosity, each insisting on yielding her claim to her friend. At length, the dignity of Isabella's virtue reminding her of the preference which Theodore had almost declared for her rival, made her determine to conquer her passion, and cede the beloved object to her friend.

During this contest of amity, Hippolita entered her daughter's chamber. Madam, said she to Isabella, you have so much tenderness for Matilda, and interest yourself so kindly in whatever affects our wretched house, that I can have no secrets with my child, which are not proper for you to hear. The princesses were all attention and anxiety. Know then, madam, continued Hippolita, and you, my dearest Matilda, that being convinced by all the events of these two last ominous days, that heaven purposes the sceptre of Otranto should pass from Manfred's hands into those of the marquis Frederic, I have been perhaps inspired with the thought of averting our total destruction by the union of our rival houses. With this view I have been proposing to Manfred my lord to tender this dear dear child to Frederic your father – Me to lord Frederic! cried Matilda – Good heavens! my gracious mother – and have you named it to my father? I have, said Hippolita: he listened benignly to my proposal, and is gone to break it to the marquis. Ah! wretched princess! cried Isabella, what hast thou done? What ruin has thy inadvertent goodness been preparing for thyself, for me, and for Matilda! Ruin from me to you and to my child! said Hippolita: What can this mean? Alas! said Isabella, the purity of your own heart prevents your seeing the depravity of others. Manfred, your lord, that impious man — Hold, said Hippolita; you must not in my presence, young lady, mention Manfred with disrespect: he is my lord and husband, and – Will not long be so, said Isabella, if his wicked purposes can be carried into execution. This language amazes me, said Hippolita. Your feeling, Isabella, is warm; but until this hour I never knew it betray you into intemperance. What deed of Manfred authorizes you to treat him as a murderer, an assassin? Thou virtuous, and too credulous princess! replied Isabella; it is not thy life he aims at – it is to separate himself from thee! to divorce thee! To – to divorce me! To divorce my mother! cried Hippolita and Matilda at once. – Yes, said Isabella; and to complete his crime, he meditates – I cannot speak it! What can surpass what thou hast already uttered? said Matilda. Hippolita was silent. Grief choked her speech: and the recollection of Manfred's late ambiguous discourses confirmed what she heard. Excellent, dear lady! madam! mother! cried Isabella, flinging herself at Hippolita's feet in a transport of passion; trust me, believe me, I will die a thousand deaths sooner than consent to injure you, than yield to so odious – oh! – This is too much! cried Hippolita: what crimes does one crime suggest! Rise, dear Isabella; I do not doubt your virtue. Oh! Matilda, this stroke is too heavy for thee! Weep not, my child; and not a murmur, I charge thee. Remember, he is *thy* father still. – But you are my mother too, said Matilda fervently; and *you* are virtuous, *you* are guiltless! – Oh! must not I, must not I complain? You must not, said Hippolita – Come, all will yet be well. Manfred, in the agony for the loss of thy brother, knew not what he said: perhaps Isabella misunderstood him: his heart is good – and, my child, thou knowest not all. There is a destiny hangs over us; the hand of Providence is stretched out – Oh! could I but save thee from the wreck! – Yes, continued she in a firmer tone, perhaps the sacrifice of myself may atone for all —— I will go and offer myself to this divorce – it boots not what becomes of me. I will withdraw into the neighbouring monastery, and waste the remainder of life in prayers and tears for my child and – the prince! Thou art as much too good for this world, said Isabella, as Manfred is execrable – But think not, lady, that thy weakness shall determine for me. I swear – hear me, all ye angels —— Stop, I adjure thee, cried Hippolita; remember, thou dost not depend on thyself; thou hast a father. – My father is too pious, too noble, interrupted Isabella, to command an impious deed. But should he command it; can a father enjoin[9] a cursed act? I was contracted to the son; can I wed the father? – No, madam, no; force should not drag me to Manfred's hated bed. I loathe him, I abhor him: divine and human laws forbid. – And my friend, my dearest Matilda! would I wound her tender soul by injuring her adored mother? my own mother – I never have known another. —— Oh! she is the mother of both! cried Matilda. Can we, can we, Isabella, adore her too much? My lovely children, said the touched Hippolita, your tenderness overpowers me – but I must not give way to it. It is not ours to make election for ourselves; heaven, our fathers, and our husbands, must decide for us. Have patience until you hear what Manfred and Frederic have determined. If the marquis accepts Matilda's hand, I know she will readily obey. Heaven may interpose and prevent the rest. What means my child? continued she, seeing Matilda fall at her feet with a flood of speechless tears – But no; answer me not, my daughter; I must not hear a word against the pleasure of thy father. Oh! doubt not my obedience, my dreadful obedience to him and to you! said Matilda. But can I, most respected of women, can I experience all this tenderness, this world of goodness, and conceal a thought from the best of mothers? What art thou going to utter? said Isabella trembling. Recollect thyself, Matilda. No, Isabella, said the princess, I should not deserve this incomparable parent, if the inmost recesses of my soul harboured a thought without her permission – Nay, I have offended her; I have suffered a passion to enter my heart without her avowal – But here I disclaim it; here I vow to heaven and her — My child! my child! said Hippolita, what words are these? What new calamities has fate in store for us? Thou a passion! thou, in this hour of destruction — Oh! I see all my guilt! said Matilda. I abhor myself, if I cost my mother a pang. She is the dearest thing I have on earth – Oh! I will never, never behold him more! Isabella, said Hippolita, thou art conscious to this unhappy secret, whatever it is. Speak – What! cried Matilda, have I so forfeited my mother's love that she will not permit me even to speak my own guilt? Oh! wretched, wretched Matilda! – Thou art too cruel, said Isabella to Hippolita: canst thou behold this anguish of a virtuous mind, and not commiserate it? Not pity my child! said Hippolita, catching Matilda in her arms – Oh! I know she is good, she is all virtue, all tenderness, and duty. I do forgive thee, my excellent, my only hope! The princesses then revealed to Hippolita their mutual inclination for Theodore, and the purpose of Isabella to resign him to Matilda. Hippolita blamed their imprudence, and shewed them the improbability that either father would consent to bestow his heiress on so poor a man, though nobly born. Some comfort it gave her to find their passion of so recent a date, and that Theodore had but little cause to suspect it in either. She strictly enjoined them to avoid all correspondence with him. This Matilda fervently promised: but Isabella, who flattered herself that she meant no more than to promote his union with her friend, could not determine to avoid him; and made no reply. I will go to the convent, said Hippolita, and order new masses to be said for a deliverance from these calamities. – Oh! my mother, said Matilda, you mean to quit us: you mean to take sanctuary, and to give my father an opportunity of pursuing his fatal intention. Alas! on my knees I supplicate you to forbear – Will you leave me a prey to Frederic? I will follow you to the convent. – Be at peace, my child, said Hippolita: I will return instantly. I will never abandon thee, until I know it is the will of heaven, and for thy benefit. Do not deceive me, said Matilda. I will not marry Frederic until thou commandest it. Alas! what will become of me? – Why that exclamation? said Hippolita. I have promised thee to return. – Ah! my mother, replied Matilda, stay and save me from myself. A frown from thee can do more than all my father's severity. I have given away my heart, and you alone can make me recall it. No more, said Hippolita: thou must not relapse, Matilda. I can quit Theodore, said she, but must I wed another? Let me attend thee to the altar, and shut myself from the world forever. Thy fate depends on thy father, said Hippolita: I have ill bestowed my tenderness, if it has taught thee to revere aught beyond him. Adieu, my child! I go to pray for thee.

Hippolita's real purpose was to demand of Jerome, whether in conscience she might not consent to the divorce. She had oft urged Manfred to resign the principality, which the delicacy of her conscience rendered an hourly burthen to her. These scruples concurred to make the separation from her husband appear less dreadful to her than it would have seemed in any other situation.

Jerome, at quitting the castle overnight, had questioned Theodore severely why he had accused him to Manfred of being privy to his escape. Theodore owned it had been with design to prevent Manfred's suspicion from alighting on Matilda; and added, the holiness of Jerome's life and character secured him from the tyrant's wrath. Jerome was heartily grieved to discover his son's inclination for that princess; and, leaving him to his rest, promised in the morning to acquaint him with important reasons for conquering his passion. Theodore, like Isabella, was too recently acquainted with parental authority to submit to its decisions against the impulse of his heart. He had little curiosity to learn the friar's reasons, and less disposition to obey them. The lovely Matilda had made stronger impressions on him than filial affection. All night he pleased himself with visions of love; and it was not till late after the morning-office, that he recollected the friar's commands to attend him at Alfonso's tomb.

Young man, said Jerome, when he saw him, this tardiness does not please me. Have a father's commands already so little weight? Theodore made awkward excuses, and attributed his delay to having overslept himself. And on whom were thy dreams employed? said the friar sternly. His son blushed. Come, come, resumed the friar, inconsiderate youth, this must not be; eradicate this guilty passion from thy breast. – Guilty passion! cried Theodore: can guilt dwell with innocent beauty and virtuous modesty? It is sinful, replied the friar, to cherish those whom heaven has doomed to destruction. A tyrant's race must be swept from the earth to the third and fourth generation. Will heaven visit the innocent for the crimes of the guilty? said Theodore. The fair Matilda has virtues enough – To undo thee, interrupted Jerome. Hast thou so soon forgotten that twice the savage Manfred has pronounced thy sentence? Nor have I forgotten, sir, said Theodore, that the charity of his daughter delivered me from his power. I can forget injuries, but never benefits. The injuries thou hast received from Manfred's race, said the friar, are beyond what thou canst conceive. – Reply not, but view this holy image! Beneath this marble monument rest the ashes of the good Alfonso; a prince adorned with every virtue: the father of his people! the delight of mankind! Kneel, head-strong boy, and list, while a father unfolds a state of horror, that will expel every sentiment from thy soul, but sensations of sacred vengeance.[10] – Alfonso! much injured prince! let thy unsatisfied shade sit awful on the troubled air, while these trembling lips – Ha! who comes there? – The most wretched of women, said Hippolita, entering the choir. Good father, art thou at leisure? – But why this kneeling youth? what means the horror imprinted on each countenance? why at this venerable tomb – Alas! hast thou seen aught? We were pouring forth our orisons to heaven, replied the friar with some confusion, to put an end to the woes of this deplorable province. Join with us, lady! thy spotless soul may obtain an exemption from the judgments which the portents of these days but too speakingly denounce against thy house. I pray fervently to heaven to divert them, said the pious princess. Thou knowest it has been the occupation of my life to wrest a blessing for my lord and my harmless children – One, alas! is taken from me! Would heaven but hear me for my poor Matilda! Father, intercede for her! – Every heart will bless her, cried Theodore with rapture. – Be dumb, rash youth! said Jerome. And thou, fond princess, contend not with the powers above! The Lord giveth, and the Lord taketh away:[11] bless his holy name, and submit to his decrees. I do most devoutly, said Hippolita: but will he not spare my only comfort? must Matilda perish too? – Ah! father, I came – But dismiss thy son. No ear but thine must hear what I have to utter. May heaven grant thy every wish, most excellent princess! said Theodore retiring. Jerome frowned.

Hippolita then acquainted the friar with the proposal she had suggested to Manfred, his approbation of it, and the tender of Matilda that he was gone to make to Frederic. Jerome could not conceal his dislike of the motion, which he covered under pretence of the improbability that Frederic, the nearest of blood to Alfonso, and who was come to claim his succession, would yield to an alliance with the usurper of his right. But nothing could equal the perplexity of the friar, when Hippolita confessed her readiness not to oppose the separation, and demanded his opinion on the legality of her acquiescence. The friar catched eagerly at her request of his advice; and without explaining his aversion to the proposed marriage of Manfred and Isabella, he painted to Hippolita in the most alarming colours the sinfulness of her consent, denounced judgments against her if she complied, and enjoined her in the severest terms to treat any such proposition with every mark of indignation and refusal.

Manfred, in the mean time, had broken his purpose to Frederic, and proposed the double marriage. That weak prince, who had been struck with the charms of Matilda, listened but too eagerly to the offer. He forgot his enmity to Manfred, whom he saw but little hope of dispossessing by force; and flattering himself that no issue might succeed from the union of his daughter with the tyrant, he looked upon his own succession to the principality as facilitated by wedding Matilda. He made faint opposition to the proposal; affecting, for form only, not to acquiesce unless Hippolita should consent to the divorce. Manfred took that upon himself. Transported with his success, and impatient to see himself in a situation to expect sons, he hastened to his wife's apartment, determined to extort her compliance. He learned with indignation that she was absent at the convent. His guilt suggested to him that she had probably been informed by Isabella of his purpose. He doubted whether her retirement to the convent did not import an intention of remaining there, until she could raise obstacles to their divorce; and the suspicions he had already entertained of Jerome, made him apprehend that the friar would not only traverse his views, but might have inspired Hippolita with the resolution of taking sanctuary. Impatient to unravel this clue, and to defeat its success, Manfred hastened to the convent, and arrived there as the friar was earnestly exhorting the princess never to yield to the divorce.

Madam, said Manfred, what business drew you hither? Why did not you await my return from the marquis? I came to implore a blessing on your councils, replied Hippolita. My councils do not need a friar's intervention, said Manfred – and of all men living is that hoary traitor the only one whom you delight to confer with? Profane prince! said Jerome: is it at the altar that thou choosest to insult the servants of the altar? – But, Manfred, thy impious schemes are known. Heaven and this virtuous lady know them. Nay, frown not, prince. The church despises thy menaces. Her thunders will be heard above thy wrath. Dare to proceed in thy curst purpose of a divorce, until her sentence be known, and here I lance her anathema[12] at thy head. Audacious rebel! said Manfred, endeavouring to conceal the awe with which the friar's words inspired him; dost thou presume to threaten thy lawful prince? Thou art no lawful prince, said Jerome; thou art no prince – Go, discuss thy claim with Frederic; and when that is done – It is done, replied Manfred: Frederic accepts Matilda's hand, and is content to wave his claim, unless I have no male issue. – As he spoke those words three drops of blood fell from the nose of Alfonso's statue. Manfred turned pale, and the princess sunk on her knees. Behold! said the friar: mark this miraculous indication that the blood of Alfonso will never mix with that of Manfred! My gracious lord, said Hippolita, let us submit ourselves to heaven. Think not thy ever obedient wife rebels against thy authority. I have no will but that of my lord and the church. To that revered tribunal let us appeal. It does not depend on us to burst the bonds that unite us. If the church shall approve the dissolution of our marriage, be it so – I have but few years, and those of sorrow, to pass. Where can they be worn away so well as at the foot of this altar, in prayers for thine and Matilda's safety? – But thou shalt not remain here until then, said Manfred. Repair with me to the castle, and there I will advise on the proper measures for a divorce. – But this meddling friar[13] comes not thither; my hospitable roof shall never more harbour a traitor – and for thy reverence's offspring, continued he, I banish him from my dominions. He, I ween, is no sacred personage, nor under the protection of the church. Whoever weds Isabella, it shall not be father Falconara's started-up son. They start up, said the friar, who are suddenly beheld in the seat of lawful princes; but they wither away like the grass,[14] and their place knows them no more. Manfred, casting a look of scorn at the friar, led Hippolita forth; but at the door of the church whispered one of his attendants to remain concealed about the convent, and bring him instant notice, if any one from the castle should repair thither.

CHAPTER 5

Every reflection which Manfred made on the friar's behaviour, conspired to persuade him that Jerome was privy to an amour between Isabella and Theodore. But Jerome's new presumption, so dissonant from his former meekness, suggested still deeper apprehensions. The prince even suspected that the friar depended on some secret support from Frederic, whose arrival coinciding with the novel appearance of Theodore seemed to bespeak a correspondence. Still more was he troubled with the resemblance of Theodore to Alfonso's portrait. The latter he knew had unquestionably died without issue. Frederic had consented to bestow Isabella on him. These contradictions agitated his mind with numberless pangs. He saw but two methods of extricating himself from his difficulties. The one was to resign his dominions to the marquis. – Pride, ambition, and his reliance on ancient prophecies, which had pointed out a possibility of his preserving them to his posterity, combated that thought. The other was to press his marriage with Isabella. After long ruminating on these anxious thoughts, as he marched silently with Hippolita to the castle, he at last discoursed with that princess on the subject of his disquiet, and used every insinuating and plausible argument to extract her consent to, even her promise of promoting, the divorce. Hippolita needed little persuasion to bend her to his pleasure. She endeavoured to win him over to the measure of resigning his dominions; but finding her exhortations fruitless, she assured him, that as far as her conscience would allow, she would raise no opposition to a separation, though, without better founded scruples than what he yet alleged, she would not engage to be active in demanding it.

This compliance, though inadequate, was sufficient to raise Manfred's hopes. He trusted that his power and wealth would easily advance his suit at the court of Rome, whither he resolved to engage Frederic to take a journey on purpose. That prince had discovered so much passion for Matilda, that Manfred hoped to obtain all he wished by holding out or withdrawing his daughter's charms, according as the marquis should appear more or less disposed to co-operate in his views. Even the absence of Frederic would be a material point gained, until he could take farther measures for his security.

Dismissing Hippolita to her apartment, he repaired to that of the marquis; but crossing the great hall through which he was to pass, he met Bianca. That damsel he knew was in the confidence of both the young ladies. It immediately occurred to him to sift her on the subject of Isabella and Theodore. Calling her aside into the recess of the oriel window[1] of the hall, and soothing her with many fair words and promises, he demanded of her whether she knew aught of the state of Isabella's affections. I! my lord? No, my lord – Yes, my lord – Poor lady! she is wonderfully alarmed about her father's wounds; but I tell her he will do well; don't your highness think so? I do not ask you, replied Manfred, what she thinks about her father: but you are in her secrets: come, be a good girl and tell me, is there any young man – ha? – you understand me. Lord bless me! understand your highness? No, not I: I told her a few vulnerary[2] herbs and repose — I am not talking, replied the prince impatiently, about her father: I know he will do well. Bless me, I rejoice to hear your highness say so; for though I thought it not right to let my young lady despond, methought his greatness had a wan look, and a something – I remember when young Ferdinand was wounded by the Venetian. Thou answerest from the point, interrupted Manfred; but here, take this jewel, perhaps that may fix thy attention – Nay, no reverences; my favour shall not stop here – Come, tell me truly; how stands Isabella's heart? Well! your highness has such a way, said Bianca – to be sure – but can your highness keep a secret? If it should ever come out of your lips — It shall not, it shall not, cried Manfred. Nay, but swear, your highness – by my halidame,[3] if it should ever be known that I said it – Why, truth is truth, I do not think my lady Isabella ever much affectioned my young lord, your son: yet he was a sweet youth as one should see. I am sure if I had been a princess – But bless me! I must attend my lady Matilda; she will marvel what is become of me. – Stay, cried Manfred, thou hast not satisfied my question. Hast thou ever carried any message, any letter? – I! Good gracious! cried Bianca: I carry a letter? I would not to be a queen. I hope your highness thinks, though I am poor, I am honest. Did your highness never hear what Count Marsigli offered me, when he came a-wooing to my lady Matilda? – I have not leisure, said Manfred, to listen to thy tales. I do not question thy honesty; but it is thy duty to conceal nothing from me. How long has Isabella been acquainted with Theodore? – Nay, there is nothing can escape your highness, said Bianca – not that I know any thing of the matter. Theodore, to be sure, is a proper young man, and, as my lady Matilda says, the very image of good Alfonso: Has not your highness remarked it? Yes, yes – No – thou torturest me, said Manfred: Where did they meet? when? – Who, my lady Matilda? said Bianca. No, no, not Matilda; Isabella: When did Isabella first become acquainted with this Theodore? – Virgin Mary! said Bianca, how should I know? Thou dost know, said Manfred; and I must know; I will. – Lord! your highness is not jealous of young Theodore? said Bianca. – Jealous! No, no: why should I be jealous? – Perhaps I mean to unite them – if I was sure Isabella would have no repugnance. – Repugnance! No, I'll warrant her, said Bianca: he is as comely a youth as ever trod on christian ground: we are all in love with him: there is not a soul in the castle but would be rejoiced to have him for our prince – I mean, when it shall please heaven to call your highness to itself. – Indeed! said Manfred: has it gone so far? Oh! this cursed friar! – But I must not lose time – Go, Bianca, attend Isabella; but I charge thee, not a word of what has passed. Find out how she is affected towards Theodore; bring me good news, and that ring has a companion. Wait at the foot of the winding staircase: I am going to visit the marquis, and will talk farther with thee at my return.

Manfred, after some general conversation, desired Frederic to dismiss the two knights his companions, having to talk with him on urgent affairs. As soon as they were alone, he began in artful guise to sound the marquis on the subject of Matilda; and finding him disposed to his wish, he let drop hints on the difficulties that would attend the celebration of their marriage, unless — At that instant Bianca burst into the room, with a wildness in her look and gestures that spoke the utmost terror. Oh! my lord, my lord! cried she, we are all undone! It is come again! it is come again! – What is come again? cried Manfred amazed. – Oh! the hand! the giant! the hand! – Support me! I am terrified out of my senses, cried Bianca: I will not sleep in the castle to-night. Where shall I go? My things may come after me to-morrow. – Would I had been content to wed Francesco! This comes of ambition! – What has terrified thee thus, young woman? said the marquis: thou art safe here; be not alarmed. Oh! your greatness is wonderful good, said Bianca, but I dare not – No, pray let me go – I had rather leave every thing behind me, than stay another hour under this roof. Go to, thou hast lost thy senses, said Manfred. Interrupt us not; we were communing on important matters. – My lord, this wench is subject to fits – Come with me, Bianca. – Oh! the saints! No, said Bianca – for certain it comes to warn your highness; why should it appear to me else? I say my prayers morning and evening – Oh! if your highness had believed Diego! 'Tis the same hand that he saw the foot to in the gallery-chamber – Father Jerome has often told us the prophecy would be out one of these days – Bianca, said he, mark my words. – Thou ravest, said Manfred in a rage: Begone, and keep these fooleries to frighten thy companions. – What! my lord, cried Bianca, do you think I have seen nothing? Go to the foot of the great stairs yourself – As I live I saw it. Saw what? Tell us, fair maid, what thou hast seen, said Frederic. Can your highness listen, said Manfred, to the delirium of a silly wench, who has heard stories of apparitions until she believes them? This is more than fancy, said the marquis; her terror is too natural and too strongly impressed to be the work of imagination. Tell us, fair maiden, what it is has moved thee thus. Yes, my lord, thank your greatness, said Bianca – I believe I look very pale; I shall be better when I have recovered myself. – I was going to my lady Isabella's chamber by his highness's order – We do not want the circumstances, interrupted Manfred: since his highness will have it so, proceed; but be brief. – Lord, your highness thwarts one so! replied Bianca – I fear my hair – I am sure I never in my life – Well! as I was telling your greatness, I was going by his highness's order to my lady Isabella's chamber: she lies in the watchet-coloured[4] chamber, on the right-hand, one pair of stairs: so when I came to the great stairs – I was looking on his highness's present here. Grant me patience! said Manfred, will this wench never come to the point? What imports it to the marquis, that I gave thee a bawble for thy faithful attendance on my daughter? We want to know what thou sawest. I was going to tell your highness, said Bianca, if you would permit me. – So, as I was rubbing the ring – I am sure I had not gone up three steps, but I heard the rattling of armour; for all the world such a clatter, as Diego says he heard when the giant turned him about in the gallery-chamber. – What does she mean, my lord? said the marquis. Is your castle haunted by giants and goblins? – Lord, what, has not your greatness heard the story of the giant in the gallery-chamber? cried Bianca. I marvel his highness has not told you – mayhap you do not know there is a prophecy – This trifling is intolerable, interrupted Manfred. Let us dismiss this silly wench, my lord: we have more important affairs to discuss. By your favour, said Frederic, these are no trifles: the enormous sabre I was directed to in the wood; yon casque, its fellow – are these visions of this poor maiden's brain? – So Jaquez thinks, may it please your greatness, said Bianca. He says this moon will not be out without our seeing some strange revolution. For my part, I should not be surprised if it was to happen to-morrow; for, as I was saying, when I heard the clattering of armour, I was all in a cold sweat – I looked up, and, if your greatness will believe me, I saw upon the uppermost banister of the great stairs a hand in armour as big, as big – I thought I should have swooned – I never stopped until I came hither – Would I were well out of this castle! My lady Matilda told me but yester-morning that her highness Hippolita knows something – Thou art an insolent! cried Manfred – Lord marquis, it much misgives me that this scene is concerted to affront me. Are my own domestics suborned[5] to spread tales injurious to my honour? Pursue your claim by manly daring; or let us bury our feuds, as was proposed, by the intermarriage of our children: but trust me, it ill becomes a prince of your bearing to practice on mercenary wenches. – I scorn your imputation, said Frederic; until this hour I never set eyes on this damsel: I have given her no jewel! – My lord, my lord, your conscience, your guilt accuses you, and would throw the suspicion on me – But keep your daughter, and think no more of Isabella: the judgments already fallen on your house forbid my matching into it.

Manfred, alarmed at the resolute tone in which Frederic delivered these words, endeavoured to pacify him. Dismissing Bianca, he made such submissions to the marquis, and threw in such artful encomiums on Matilda, that Frederic was once more staggered. However, as his passion was of so recent a date, it could not at once surmount the scruples he had conceived. He had gathered enough from Bianca's discourse to persuade him that heaven declared itself against Manfred. The proposed marriages too removed his claim to a distance: and the principality of Otranto was a stronger temptation, than the contingent reversion of it with Matilda. Still he would not absolutely recede from his engagements; but purposing to gain time, he demanded of Manfred if it was true in fact that Hippolita consented to the divorce. The prince, transported to find no other obstacle, and depending on his influence over his wife, assured the marquis it was so, and that he might satisfy himself of the truth from her own mouth.

As they were thus discoursing, word was brought that the banquet was prepared. Manfred conducted Frederic to the great hall, where they were received by Hippolita and the young princesses. Manfred placed the marquis next to Matilda, and seated himself between his wife and Isabella. Hippolita comported herself with an easy gravity; but the young ladies were silent and melancholy. Manfred, who was determined to pursue his point with the marquis in the remainder of the evening, pushed on the feast until it waxed late; affecting unrestrained gaiety, and plying Frederic with repeated goblets of wine. The latter, more upon his guard than Manfred wished, declined his frequent challenges, on pretence of his late loss of blood; while the prince, to raise his own disordered spirits, and to counterfeit unconcern, indulged himself in plentiful draughts, though not to the intoxication of his senses.

The evening being far advanced, the banquet concluded. Manfred would have withdrawn with Frederic; but the latter, pleading weakness and want of repose, retired to his chamber, gallantly telling the prince, that his daughter should amuse his highness until himself could attend him. Manfred accepted the party; and, to the no small grief of Isabella, accompanied her to her apartment. Matilda waited on her mother, to enjoy the freshness of the evening on the ramparts of the castle.

Soon as the company was dispersed their several ways, Frederic, quitting his chamber, enquired if Hippolita was alone; and was told by one of her attendants, who had not noticed her going forth, that at that hour she generally withdrew to her oratory,[6] where he probably would find her. The marquis during the repast had beheld Matilda with increase of passion. He now wished to find Hippolita in the disposition her lord had promised. The portents that had alarmed him were forgotten in his desires. Stealing softly and unobserved to the apartment of Hippolita, he entered it with a resolution to encourage her acquiescence to the divorce, having perceived that Manfred was resolved to make the possession of Isabella an unalterable condition, before he would grant Matilda to his wishes.

The marquis was not surprised at the silence that reigned in the princess's apartment. Concluding her, as he had been advertised,[7] in her oratory, he passed on. The door was a-jar; the evening gloomy and overcast. Pushing open the door gently, he saw a person kneeling before the altar. As he approached nearer, it seemed not a woman, but one in a long woollen weed, whose back was towards him. The person seemed absorbed in prayer. The marquis was about to return, when the figure rising, stood some moments fixed in meditation, without regarding him. The marquis, expecting the holy person to come forth, and meaning to excuse his uncivil interruption, said, Reverend father, I sought the lady Hippolita. – Hippolita! replied a hollow voice: camest thou to this castle to seek Hippolita? – And then the figure, turning slowly round, discovered to Frederic the fleshless jaws and empty sockets of a skeleton, wrapt in a hermit's cowl. Angels of grace, protect me![8] cried Frederic recoiling. Deserve their protection, said the spectre. Frederic, falling on his knees, adjured the phantom to take pity on him. Dost thou not remember me? said the apparition. Remember the wood of Joppa! Art thou that holy hermit? cried Frederic trembling – can I do aught for thy eternal peace? – Wast thou delivered from bondage, said the spectre, to pursue carnal delights? Hast thou

forgotten the buried sabre, and the behest of heaven engraven on it? –
I have not, I have not, said Frederic – But say, blest spirit, what is thy
errand to me? what remains to be done? To forget Matilda! said the
apparition – and vanished.

Frederic's blood froze in his veins. For some minutes he remained
motionless. Then falling prostrate on his face before the altar, he
besought the intercession of every saint for pardon. A flood of tears
succeeded to this transport; and the image of the beauteous Matilda
rushing in spite of him on his thoughts, he lay on the ground in a
conflict of penitence and passion. Ere he could recover from this agony
of his spirits, the princess Hippolita, with a taper in her hand, entered
the oratory alone. Seeing a man without motion on the floor, she gave
a shriek, concluding him dead. Her fright brought Frederic to himself.
Rising suddenly, his face bedewed with tears, he would have rushed
from her presence; but Hippolita, stopping him, conjured him in the
most plaintive accents to explain the cause of his disorder, and by what
strange chance she had found him there in that posture. Ah! virtuous
princess! said the marquis, penetrated with grief – and stopped. For
the love of heaven, my lord, said Hippolita, disclose the cause of this
transport! What mean these doleful sounds, this alarming exclamation
on my name? What woes has heaven still in store for the wretched
Hippolita? – Yet silent? – By every pitying angel, I adjure thee, noble
prince, continued she, falling at his feet, to disclose the purport of what
lies at thy heart – I see thou feelest for me; thou feelest the sharp pangs
that thou inflictest – Speak, for pity! – Does aught thou knowest
concern my child? – I cannot speak, cried Frederic, bursting from her
– Oh! Matilda!

Quitting the princess thus abruptly, he hastened to his own apartment. At the door of it he was accosted by Manfred, who, flushed by
wine and love, had come to seek him, and to propose to waste some
hours of the night in music and revelling. Frederic, offended at an
invitation so dissonant from the mood of his soul, pushed him rudely
aside, and, entering his chamber, flung the door intemperately against
Manfred, and bolted it inwards. The haughty prince, enraged at this
unaccountable behaviour, withdrew in a frame of mind capable of the
most fatal excesses. As he crossed the court, he was met by the domestic

CHAPTER 5

whom he had planted at the convent as a spy on Jerome and Theodore. This man, almost breathless with the haste he had made, informed his lord, that Theodore and some lady from the castle were at that instant in private conference at the tomb of Alfonso in St. Nicholas's church. He had dogged Theodore thither, but the gloominess of the night had prevented his discovering who the woman was.

Manfred, whose spirits were inflamed, and whom Isabella had driven from her on his urging his passion with too little reserve, did not doubt but the inquietude she had expressed had been occasioned by her impatience to meet Theodore. Provoked by this conjecture, and enraged at her father, he hastened secretly to the great church. Gliding softly between the aisles, and guided by an imperfect gleam of moonshine that shone faintly through the illuminated windows, he stole towards the tomb of Alfonso, to which he was directed by indistinct whispers of the persons he sought. The first sounds he could distinguish were – Does it, alas, depend on me? Manfred will never permit our union. – No, this shall prevent it! cried the tyrant, drawing his dagger, and plunging it over her shoulder into the bosom of the person that spoke – Ah me, I am slain! cried Matilda sinking: Good heaven, receive my soul! – Savage, inhuman monster! what hast thou done? cried Theodore, rushing on him, and wrenching his dagger from him. – Stop, stop thy impious hand, cried Matilda; it is my father! – Manfred, waking as from a trance, beat his breast, twisted his hands in his locks, and endeavoured to recover his dagger from Theodore to dispatch himself. Theodore, scarce less distracted, and only mastering the transports of his grief to assist Matilda, had now by his cries drawn some of the monks to his aid. While part of them endeavoured in concert with the afflicted Theodore to stop the blood of the dying princess, the rest prevented Manfred from laying violent hands on himself.

Matilda, resigning herself patiently to her fate, acknowledged with looks of grateful love the zeal of Theodore. Yet oft as her faintness would permit her speech its way, she begged the assistants to comfort her father. Jerome by this time had learnt the fatal news, and reached the church. His looks seemed to reproach Theodore; but turning to Manfred, he said, Now, tyrant! behold the completion of woe fulfilled

95

on thy impious and devoted head! The blood of Alfonso cried to heaven for vengeance; and heaven has permitted its altar to be polluted by assassination, that thou mightest shed thy own blood at the foot of that prince's sepulchre! – Cruel man! cried Matilda, to aggravate the woes of a parent! May heaven bless my father, and forgive him as I do! My lord, my gracious sire, dost thou forgive thy child? Indeed I came not hither to meet Theodore! I found him praying at this tomb, whither my mother sent me to intercede for thee, for her – Dearest father, bless your child, and say you forgive her. – Forgive thee! Murderous monster! cried Manfred – can assassins forgive? I took thee for Isabella; but heaven directed my bloody hand to the heart of my child! – Oh! Matilda – I cannot utter it – canst thou forgive the blindness of my rage? – I can, I do, and may heaven confirm it! said Matilda – But while I have life to ask it – oh, my mother! what will she feel! – Will you comfort her, my lord? Will you not put her away? Indeed she loves you – Oh, I am faint! bear me to the castle – can I live to have her close my eyes?

Theodore and the monks besought her earnestly to suffer herself to be borne into the convent; but her instances were so pressing to be carried to the castle, that, placing her on a litter,[9] they conveyed her thither as she requested. Theodore supporting her head with his arm, and hanging over her in an agony of despairing love, still endeavoured to inspire her with hopes of life. Jerome on the other side comforted her with discourses of heaven, and holding a crucifix before her, which she bathed with innocent tears, prepared her for her passage to immortality. Manfred, plunged in the deepest affliction, followed the litter in despair.

Ere they reached the castle, Hippolita, informed of the dreadful catastrophe, had flown to meet her murdered child; but when she saw the afflicted procession, the mightiness of her grief deprived her of her senses, and she fell lifeless to the earth in a swoon. Isabella and Frederic, who attended her, were overwhelmed in almost equal sorrow. Matilda alone seemed insensible to her own situation: every thought was lost in tenderness for her mother. Ordering the litter to stop, as soon as Hippolita was brought to herself, she asked for her father. He approached, unable to speak. Matilda, seizing his hand and her mother's, locked them in her own, and then clasped them to her heart. Manfred could not support this act of pathetic piety. He dashed himself on the ground, and cursed the day he was born. Isabella, apprehensive that these struggles of passion were more than Matilda could support, took upon herself to order Manfred to be borne to his apartment, while she caused Matilda to be conveyed to the nearest chamber. Hippolita, scarce more alive than her daughter, was regardless of every thing but her: but when the tender Isabella's care would have likewise removed her, while the surgeons examined Matilda's wound, she cried, Remove me? Never! never! I lived but in her, and will expire with her. Matilda raised her eyes at her mother's voice, but closed them again without speaking. Her sinking pulse, and the damp coldness of her hand, soon dispelled all hopes of recovery. Theodore followed the surgeons into the outer chamber, and heard them pronounce the fatal sentence with a transport equal to phrensy – Since she cannot live mine, cried he, at least she shall be mine in death! – Father! Jerome! will you not join our hands? cried he to the friar, who with the marquis had accompanied the surgeons. What means thy distracted rashness? said Jerome: is this an hour for marriage? It is, it is, cried Theodore: alas, there is no other! Young man, thou art too unadvised,[10] said Frederic: dost thou think we are to listen to thy fond transports in this hour of fate? What pretensions hast thou to the princess? Those of a prince, said Theodore; of the sovereign of Otranto. This reverend man, my father, has informed me who I am. Thou ravest, said the marquis: there is no prince of Otranto but myself, now Manfred by murder, by sacrilegious murder, has forfeited all pretensions. My lord, said Jerome, assuming an air of command, he tells you true. It was not my purpose the secret should have been divulged so soon; but fate presses onward to its work. What his hot-headed passion has revealed, my tongue confirms. Know, prince, that when Alfonso set sail for the Holy Land – Is this a season for explanations? cried Theodore. Father, come and unite me to the princess: she shall be mine – in every other thing I will dutifully obey you. My life! my adored Matilda! continued Theodore, rushing back into the inner chamber, will you not be mine? will you not bless your — Isabella made signs to him to be silent, apprehending the princess was near her end. What, is she dead? cried Theodore: is it possible?

The violence of his exclamations brought Matilda to herself. Lifting up her eyes she looked round for her mother – Life of my soul! I am here, cried Hippolita: think not I will quit thee! – Oh! you are too good, said Matilda – but weep not for me, my mother! I am going where sorrow never dwells. – Isabella, thou hast loved me; wot thou not supply my fondness to this dear, dear woman? Indeed I am faint! – Oh! my child! my child! said Hippolita in a flood of tears, can I not withhold thee a moment? – It will not be, said Matilda – Commend me to heaven – Where is my father? Forgive him, dearest mother – forgive him my death; it was an error – Oh! I had forgotten – Dearest mother, I vowed never to see Theodore more – Perhaps that has drawn down this calamity – but it was not intentional – can you pardon me? – Oh! wound not my agonizing soul! said Hippolita; thou never couldst offend me. – Alas, she faints! Help! help! – I would say something more, said Matilda struggling, but it wonnot[11] be – Isabella – Theodore – for my sake – oh! – She expired. Isabella and her women tore Hippolita from the corse; but Theodore threatened destruction to all who attempted to remove him from it. He printed a thousand kisses on her clay-cold hands, and uttered every expression that despairing love could dictate.

Isabella, in the mean time, was accompanying the afflicted Hippolita to her apartment; but in the middle of the court they were met by Manfred, who, distracted with his own thoughts, and anxious once more to behold his daughter, was advancing to the chamber where she lay. As the moon was now at its height, he read in the countenances of this unhappy company the event he dreaded. What! is she dead? cried he in wild confusion – A clap of thunder at that instant shook the castle to its foundations; the earth rocked, and the clank of more than mortal armour was heard behind. Frederic and Jerome thought the last day was at hand. The latter, forcing Theodore along with them, rushed into the court. The moment Theodore appeared, the walls of the castle behind Manfred were thrown down with a mighty force, and the form of Alfonso, dilated to an immense magnitude, appeared in the centre of the ruins. Behold in Theodore, the true heir of Alfonso! said the vision: and having pronounced those words, accompanied by a clap of thunder, it ascended solemnly towards heaven, where the clouds parting asunder, the form of saint Nicholas was seen; and receiving Alfonso's shade, they were soon wrapt from mortal eyes in a blaze of glory.

The beholders fell prostrate on their faces, acknowledging the divine will. The first that broke silence was Hippolita. My lord, said she to the desponding Manfred, behold the vanity of human greatness! Conrad is gone! Matilda is no more! in Theodore we view the true prince of Otranto. By what miracle he is so, I know not – suffice it to us, our doom is pronounced! Shall we not, can we but dedicate the few deplorable hours we have to live, in deprecating the farther wrath of heaven? Heaven ejects us – whither can we fly, but to yon holy cells that yet offer us a retreat? – Thou guileless but unhappy woman! unhappy by my crimes! replied Manfred, my heart at last is open to thy devout admonitions. Oh! could – but it cannot be – ye are lost in wonder – let me at last do justice on myself! To heap shame on my own head is all the satisfaction I have left to offer to offended heaven. My story has drawn down these judgments: let my confession atone – But ah! what can atone for usurpation and a murdered child? a child murdered in a consecrated place! — List, sirs, and may this bloody record be a warning to future tyrants!

Alfonso, ye all know, died in the Holy Land – Ye would interrupt me; ye would say he came not fairly to his end – It is most true – why else this bitter cup which Manfred must drink to the dregs? Ricardo, my grandfather, was his chamberlain[12] – I would draw a veil over my ancestor's crimes – but it is in vain: Alfonso died by poison. A fictitious will declared Ricardo his heir. His crimes pursued him – yet he lost no Conrad, no Matilda! I pay the price of usurpation for all! A storm overtook him. Haunted by his guilt, he vowed to saint Nicholas to found a church and two convents if he lived to reach Otranto. The sacrifice was accepted: the saint appeared to him in a dream, and promised that Ricardo's posterity should reign in Otranto until the rightful owner should be grown too large to inhabit the castle, and as long as issue-male from Ricardo's loins should remain to enjoy it. – Alas! alas! nor male nor female, except myself, remains of all his wretched race! – I have done – the woes of these three days speak the rest. How this young man can be Alfonso's heir I know not – yet I do not doubt it. His are these dominions; I resign them – yet I knew not Alfonso had an heir – I question not the will of heaven – poverty and prayer must fill up the woeful space, until Manfred shall be summoned to Ricardo.

What remains is my part to declare, said Jerome. When Alfonso set sail for the Holy Land, he was driven by a storm to the coast of Sicily. The other vessel, which bore Ricardo and his train, as your *lordship* must have heard, was separated from him. It is most true, said Manfred; and the title you give me is more than an out-cast can claim – Well, be it so – proceed. Jerome blushed, and continued. For three months lord Alfonso was wind-bound in Sicily. There he became enamoured of a fair virgin named Victoria. He was too pious to tempt her to forbidden pleasures. They were married. Yet deeming this amour incongruous with the holy vow of arms by which he was bound, he was determined to conceal their nuptials until his return from the crusado, when he purposed to seek and acknowledge her for his lawful wife. He left her pregnant. During his absence she was delivered of a daughter: but scarce had she felt a mother's pangs, ere she heard the fatal rumour of her lord's death, and the succession of Ricardo. What could a friendless, helpless woman do? would her testimony avail? – Yet, my lord, I have an authentic writing. – It needs not, said Manfred; the horrors of these days, the vision we have but now seen, all corroborate thy evidence beyond a thousand parchments. Matilda's death and my expulsion – Be composed, my lord, said Hippolita; this holy man did not mean to recall your griefs. Jerome proceeded.

I shall not dwell on what is needless. The daughter of which Victoria was delivered, was at her maturity bestowed in marriage on me. Victoria died; and the secret remained locked in my breast. Theodore's narrative has told the rest.

The friar ceased. The disconsolate company retired to the remaining part of the castle. In the morning Manfred signed his abdication of the principality, with the approbation of Hippolita, and each took on them the habit of religion in the neighbouring convents.[13] Frederic offered his daughter to the new prince, which Hippolita's tenderness for Isabella concurred to promote: but Theodore's grief was too fresh to admit the thought of another love; and it was not till after frequent discourses with Isabella, of his dear Matilda, that he was persuaded he could know no happiness but in the society of one with whom he could forever indulge the melancholy that had taken possession of his soul.

NOTES

1. *WILLIAM MARSHALL*: It is likely that Walpole chose the name 'William Marshall' unconsciously, since, just before finishing the novel, he received a letter from William Cole dated 2 August 1764 mentioning an engraver of the same name. See *Correspondence*, Vol. 1, p. 71.

2. *ONUPHRIO MURALTO*: As with 'William Marshall', 'Onuphrio Muralto' appears to have been chosen by Walpole unconsciously. A likely source is an unidentified musician named Onofrio, who was part of a party attended by Walpole thrown by Miss Pelham in mid-May of 1763. See Walpole's letter to George Montagu, 17 May 1763, in *Correspondence*, Vol. 10, p. 73. For a different hypothesis about the origin of the name, see *Notes and Queries*, 3rd series 12 (1867), p. 305, which, via a suggestion from Sir Walter Scott, turns Onuphrio into Horace.

3. *St. NICHOLAS*: Most likely Walpole means Saint Nicholas I, Pope from the year 858 to 867. His reign was marked by a struggle with King Lothair of Lorraine, who sought to divorce his wife Theutberga on charges of incest. Theutberga appealed to Nicholas in 862 when King Lothair obtained permission to remarry; this permission was confirmed at the synod of Metz in 863 through Nicholas's legatees, the archbishops Günther of Cologne and Theutgaud of Trier. When these legatees arrived in Rome with their decree from Metz, Nicholas overruled the proceedings against Theutberga and deposed the archbishops.

NOTES

TITLE-PAGE OF THE SECOND EDITION

1. *Figentur species . . . Reddantur formæ*: The epigraph is taken from Horace, *Ars Poetica*, ll. 7–9. It was added by Walpole to the second edition of 1765 in order to call attention to his claims about *Otranto* as a new kind of romance. The original Latin of Horace reads '*vanæ/ Fingentur species, ut nec pes nec caput uni/reddantur formæ*' ['Idle fancies shall be shaped (like a sick man's dream) so that neither foot nor head can be assigned to a single shape']. As W. S. Lewis has demonstrated, Walpole's alterations reverse the meaning of these lines so that they say 'nevertheless head and foot are assigned to a single shape'. The lines call attention both to *Otranto*'s plot (where, as the story progresses, various parts of Alfonso the Good's are sighted in gigantic form until they are finally assembled to form a single body) and to Walpole's claims concerning ancient and modern romance in the Preface to his second edition. The suggestion here is that for all its supposed violations of literary propriety *The Castle of Otranto* nevertheless possesses an aesthetic and artistic coherence.

PREFACE TO THE FIRST EDITION

1. *ancient catholic family in the north of England*: Part of Walpole's ruse of presenting *The Castle of Otranto* as a 'found' text rests on a logic of centres and margins. The strangeness of *Otranto*'s subject matter and the circumstances of its 'discovery' are here registered by the geographic and religious remoteness of its discoverers. The manuscript has been discovered in the library of an ancient (as opposed to modern) family who is Catholic (as opposed to Protestant) in the north of England (as opposed to London, or the south of England).

2. *It was printed at Naples*: Walpole's choice of Naples as the setting for *The Castle of Otranto* extends the geographical logic of the sentence. Just as the manuscript is found in 'the north of England', so it originates from the southernmost part of Italy. As E. J. Clery has noted (see Further Reading), Walpole originated the tradition of setting Gothic stories in Italy rather than in northern Europe; his decision to call *Otranto* 'A Gothic Story' on the title-page of its second edition shows him using the word 'Gothic' as a historical and cultural adjective rather than a racial one, meaning 'medieval' and 'barbaric' rather than 'of the Goths'.

3. *black letter*: Gothic typeface, or the similarly thick typeface used by early printers around 1600, distinguished from Roman type, which subsequently prevailed.

4. *in the year 1529*: Walpole's choice of 1529 as the fictitious date of *The Castle of Otranto*'s composition is part of his desire to locate his romance in the immediate aftermath of the Reformation.

5. *The style is the purest Italian*: As Jerrold Hogle has noted (see Further Reading), these lines resemble Hamlet's description of *The Murder of Gonzago*, a 'story . . . extant, and written in very choice Italian' (*Hamlet*, III.ii.256–7). (All references to Shakespeare's plays are based on the text of *The Riverside Shakespeare*, 2nd edition (Boston and New York: Houghton Mifflin, 1997)).

6. *between 1095 . . . and 1243*: The Crusades were a series of military expeditions undertaken by European nobility against the Muslim control of Jerusalem. At Clermont in 1095, Pope Urban II called for a Christian army to aid Byzantine emperor Alexius I Comnenus, whose capital at Constantinople was under threat by the Seljuq Turks. The First Crusade succeeded in capturing Antioch in 1098 and Jerusalem in 1099. The Muslim capture of Edessa in 1144 caused Pope Eugenius III to call for a Second Crusade, which was forced to retreat from Damascus in 1154. Jerusalem was then retaken by Muslim forces in 1187, the news of which inspired a Third Crusade led by Emperor Frederick Barbarossa. Several more crusades followed between 1189 and 1270, when King Louis IX of France and most of his army died of disease in North Africa. Walpole's reference to the year 1243 refers to the Sixth Crusade, which succeeded in capturing Jerusalem in 1244 but failed in Egypt.

7. *the names of the actors are evidently fictitious*: As E. J. Clery has noted, the action of *The Castle of Otranto* resembles the events that defined the final years of the House of Hohenstaufen, which not only ruled the Kingdom of Sicily (an area including Naples, Otranto and other parts of southern Italy) but also presided over the Holy Roman Empire from 1138 to 1208 and from 1212 to 1254. Early in the thirteenth century Frederick II established a secular kingdom in Sicily, and as emperor his reign was characterized by a series of conflicts with the papacy over control of Italy. In spite of his excommunication in 1227, he led the diplomatically successful Fifth Crusade (1228–9) before returning to face a series of intrigues and rebellions at home, including that of his son Henry in 1234–5. In 1237, after imprisoning Henry, Frederick made his second son Conrad king of Germany. With Frederick's death in 1250, Conrad succeeded to the empire and to the Sicilian kingdom, Frederick's will decreeing that his other, illegitimate son, Manfred of Taranto, serve as viceroy of Sicily in the event Conrad chose to remain in Germany. When Conrad died in Italy in 1258, Manfred exploited rumours of the death of Conrad's heir, Conradin, so as to declare himself king of Sicily. He was eventually defeated and killed at the Battle of Benevuto by Charles of Anjou in 1266. See Clery's edition of *The Castle of Otranto* (Oxford and New York: Oxford University Press, 1996), pp. 116–17.

8. *Arragonian kings in Naples*: Aragonian claims to Naples exist from the thirteenth century, and originated in a series of marriages into the House of Hohenstaufen. In 1209 Constance, the sister of King Peter of Aragon, married Frederick II, and in 1262 James I of Aragon married Constance, daughter and heir to Manfred of Taranto. When Manfred was overthrown by the Angevins in 1266, James opposed their rule but could do little about it. As Alan Ryder notes, 'The situation changed when the execution of Conradin (October 1268) left James's daughter-in-law Constance the best-placed champion of the Hohenstaufen cause. After . . . the accession of her devoted husband Peter [of Aragon] . . . the rising of the Vespers in March 1282 came spontaneously from the Sicilians themselves, and it was they who invited Peter to be their defender and king. Thus Aragon set foot in Sicily as the champion of rebels against the rightful king and suzerain, Charles I and Pope Martin IV' (*The Kingdom of Naples under Alfonso the Magnanimous: The Making of a Modern State* (Oxford: Clarendon Press, 1976), p. 21). The Aragonian kings were not able to extend their Italian holdings by conquering Naples, however, until Alfonso V conquered it on 6 June 1442.

9. *Luther*: Martin Luther (1483–1546), German preacher, reformer, and author of the *Ninety-five Theses*, which he famously nailed to the door of All Saints' Church in Wittenburg on 1 November 1517. Though written in Latin, the *Theses* were quickly translated into German, circulated throughout Germany and the rest of Europe, and sparked the Reformation in northern Europe. Luther was a prolific writer of 'books of controversy'; his translation of the Bible into vernacular German was a foundational contribution to German literature. Walpole's own references to Luther in his *Correspondence* are lively and often flippant, and show a consistent suspicion of organized religion. In a letter from Walpole to George Montagu dated 23 August 1765, 'Luther' functions as a short-hand term for radical Protestantism generally and Methodism particularly: 'If I don't make haste, the Reformation in France will demolish half that I want to see. I tremble for the Val de Grace and St-Cyr. The devil take Luther for putting it into the heads of his Methodists to pull down churches! I believe in twenty years there will not be a convent left in Europe but this at Strawberry' (Vol. 10, pp. 167–8). Walpole's 12 October 1771 letter to William Cole, on the other hand, describes Luther with similar wit but more positively: 'I hope the satire on Henry VIII will make you excuse the compliment to Luther, which like most poetic compliments does not come from my heart – I only like him better than Henry, Calvin, and the Church of Rome, who were bloody persecutors. Calvin was an execrable villain and the worst of all, for he copied those whom he pretended to correct. Luther was as jovial as Wilkes, and served the cause of liberty, without canting' (Vol. 1, p. 241).

NOTES

10. *flowers*: Embellishments or ornaments in speech or writing, choice phrases.
11. *rules of the drama*: Referring to the doctrine that drama should be governed by 'unities' of action, time and place – that is, that a drama should be comprised of a coherent series of events, that it should occur within a finite period (at most twenty-four hours), and that it take place in a single setting. The doctrine of the unities is usually ascribed to Aristotle (384–322 BC), and is the product of the energetic reading and interpretation of the *Poetics* that occurred in Europe after 1500. See especially Section 5.4 of the *Poetics*: 'the plot, as the imitation of an action, should imitate a single unified action – and ... the structure of the various sections of the events must be such that the transposition or removal of any one section dislocates and changes the whole'. Since 1500 the doctrine of the unities has been embraced by a number of British literary critics, including Sir Philip Sidney and Matthew Arnold. Walpole's association of Aristotle with such 'rules', and his sense of their artificiality, is best shown in his 28 June 1760 letter to Sir David Dalrymple, responding to the publication of James Macpherson's *Fragments of Ancient Poetry* (Edinburgh, 1760). There, he disagrees with Hugh Blair (1718–1800) over the fragments' status as part of an epic poem and questions the ability of an ancient poet unacquainted with the *Poetics* to write according to its principles: 'I should not expect a *bard* to write by the rules of Aristotle' (*Correspondence*, Vol. 15, p. 69).
12. *passions*: Strong and fundamental emotions of the mind, such as Love, Hatred, Anger and Fear. In seventeenth-century Britain, the word possessed a technical and philosophical sense, as in Thomas Wright's *The Passions of the Minde in Generall* (London, 1601), Robert Burton's *Anatomy of Melancholy* (London, 1621) and René Descartes's *The Passions of the Soul* (first English translation: London, 1650). Most often associated with the literature of sensibility in the second half of the eighteenth century, the term receives its fullest treatment in Joanna Baillie's *A Series of Plays ... on the Passions*, 3 vols. (London, 1798–1812), a work owing much to Walpole's *The Castle of Otranto* and *The Mysterious Mother*.
13. *the sins of fathers are visited on their children to the third and fourth generation*: See Exodus 20.5 and 34.7; Numbers 14.18; and Deuteronomy 5.9.
14. *the censure to which romances are but too liable*: Romance was attacked fairly consistently throughout the eighteenth century as a literary form capable of deluding and debauching young, uneducated, inexperienced and (most relentlessly) female readers by inviting them to accept romantic fantasy as reality. One sees cautionary examples of such readers in characters like Daniel Defoe's Arina Donna Quixota (in *Mist's Magazine*, 1720), Charlotte Lennox's Arabella (in *The Female Quixote*, 1752) and Jane Austen's Catherine Moreland (in *Northanger Abbey*, 1818). For a useful anthology of responses to romance

in the eighteenth century, see Ioan Williams, ed., *Novel and Romance 1700–1800: A Documentary Record* (New York: Barnes & Noble, 1970).

15. *The scene is undoubtedly laid in some real castle*: Walpole's model was his own Strawberry Hill, and parts of Cambridge University (especially Trinity College). See Walpole's 27 January 1775 letter to Madame du Deffand (*Correspondence*, Vol. 6, p. 145); and W. S. Lewis, 'The Genesis of Strawberry Hill', *Metropolitan Museum Studies* 5 (1934–6), pp. 57–92.

PREFACE TO THE SECOND EDITION

1. *The favourable manner . . . received by the public*: Walpole here most likely refers to sales rather than critical reception. Lownds's first edition of 500 copies sold out in four months, and on 11 April 1765 a second edition of 500 copies was published. The initial reviews of *The Castle of Otranto* were mixed, and are included in the Appendix to this edition. See also the Introduction to this edition (pp. xiii–xviii).

2. *rules of probability*: In eighteenth-century criticism, usually referring to the idea that a reader or viewer of fiction must be able to suspend disbelief to gain pleasure or instruction from it. Walpole here argues for the psychological realism of his text and its verisimilitude of character. His earlier claims concerning 'the rules of the drama' derive from similar assumptions about the relation between readerly belief and readerly pleasure.

3. *My rule was nature*: Walpole's friend and fellow antiquarian, William Cole, wrote to him on 17 March 1765 in a similar vein: 'I, who know your facility and ease in composing, am not so much surprised at the shortness of the time you completed your volume in, as at the insight you have expressed in the nature and language, both of the male and female domestics. Their dialogues, especially the latter, are inimitable and very Nature itself' (*Correspondence*, Vol. 1, p. 92). Cole's letter likely reached Walpole while he was composing the second Preface, and may have encouraged him to expand upon his use of Shakespeare as a model for representing the domestics in the novel.

4. *affections*: An affecting or moving of the mind, especially of the emotions or feelings, brought about by influence.

5. *sublime*: Of lofty bearing or aspect; noble and grand; of high intellectual, moral or spiritual level.

6. *vested in heroics*: Walpole here refers to *Hamlet*, II.ii and V.i; and *Julius Caesar*, I.i.

7. *Voltaire*: The pen-name of François-Marie Arouet (1694–1778), voluminous writer and central figure of the French Enlightenment. Voltaire's familiarity

with English literature and drama stemmed chiefly from his three-year residence in England between 1726 and 1728. While there he met Pope and Swift and regularly went to the theatre. His *Letters Concerning the English Nation* (1733; published in French as *Lettres philosophiques*) effectively introduced the writing of Locke, Newton, Shakespeare and Swift into French culture. His opinion of Shakespeare's plays, characterized by excessive praise and censure, is best captured in Letter XVIII of the *Letters*, which describes Shakespeare as 'a strong, fruitful genius . . . natural and sublime, but [he] had not so much as a single Spark of good Taste, or knew one Rule of the Drama . . . the great Merit of this Dramatic Poet has been the Ruin of the English Stage'. By the 1770s, Shakespeare's reputation in France had grown so markedly as to become an embarrassment to Voltaire; see Walpole's letter to Horace Mann, 1 December 1776: 'Voltaire, who first brought us into fashion in France, is stark mad at his own success. Out of envy to writers of his own nation, he cried up Shakespeare; and now is distracted at the just encomiums bestowed on that first genius of the world in the new translation. He sent to the French Academy an invective that bears all the marks of passionate dotage. Mrs. Montagu happened to be present when it was read' (*Correspondence*, Vol. 24, p. 267).

8. *Corneille*: Pierre Corneille (1606–84), French poet and dramatist, considered the creator of French classical tragedy. *Le Cid* (1637), *Horace* (1640), *Cinna* (1641) and *Polyeucte* (1643) are his best-known plays. Voltaire's criticisms of Shakespeare's habit of mixing coarse jokes into his tragedies occurs in his 'Remarques sur *Le Cid*', which prefaced his edition of that play. See *The Complete Works of Voltaire*, ed. Theodore Besterman et al. (Geneva: Institut et musée Voltaire; Buffalo and Toronto: University of Toronto Press, 1968). For Voltaire's thoughts on the relative merits of Corneille, Racine and Shakespeare, see his *Appel à toutes les nations de l'Europe, des jugemens d'un écrivain anglais* (1761), p. 39; and his *Le Théâtre de Pierre Corneille, avec des commentaires* (1764), in the *Complete Works*, Vol. 54, pp. 38–9. Commenting upon Shakespeare's *King John*, IV.i.48–9, in his own 'Book of Materials 1771', Walpole wrote: 'Is there an incident in all Racine, Corneille, Voltaire, Addison or Otway, so natural, so pathetic, so sublime, as Prince Arthur's reminding Hubert of his having bound a handkerchief wrought by a Princess on the jailer's temples? It is that contrast between royalty and the keeper of a prison that exalts both, and augments the compassion for Arthur.'

9. Walpole's Note: 'The following remark is foreign to the present question, yet excusable in an Englishman, who is willing to think that the severe criticisms of so masterly a writer as Voltaire on our immortal countryman, may have been the effusions of wit and precipitation, rather than the result of judgment and attention. May not the critic's skill in the force and powers of our language

have been as incorrect and incompetent as his knowledge of our history? Of the latter his own pen has dropped glaring evidence. In his preface to Thomas Corneille's Earl of Essex, monsieur de Voltaire allows that the truth of history has been grossly perverted in that piece. In excuse he pleads, that when Corneille wrote, the noblesse of France were much unread in English story; but now, says the commentator, that they study it, such misrepresentation would not be suffered – Yet forgetting that the period of ignorance is lapsed, and that it is not very necessary to instruct the knowing, he undertakes from the overflowing of his own reading to give the nobility of his own country a detail of queen Elizabeth's favourites – of whom, says he, Robert Dudley was the first, and the earl of Leicester the second. – Could one have believed that it could be necessary to inform monsieur de Voltaire himself, that Robert Dudley and the earl of Leicester were the same person?'

10. *twice translated the same speech in Hamlet*: Walpole refers to Shakespeare's *Hamlet*, III.i.55–86, the soliloquy beginning 'To be or not to be.' Voltaire first translated it in Letter XVIII of his *Letters Concerning the English Nation*, and later in *Appel à toutes les nations de l'Europe, des jugemens d'un écrivain anglais*, pp. 34–9.

11. *On y voit . . . le mieux traité*: 'One sees there a mix of seriousness and jesting, of the comical and the touching; often even a single episode produces all these contrasts. Nothing is so common than a house in which a father is in a tirade while the daughter, occupied by her own passion, weeps. The son makes fun of the two, some relatives take different sides, etc. We do not infer from this that all comedy must have scenes of buffoonery and tenderness: there are many very good plays in which nothing reigns but gaiety; others entirely serious; others mixed: others where tenderness brings us to the point of tears: it is not necessary to exclude any type: and if one were to ask me which kind is the best, I would answer, that which is the best treated.' See *Œvres Complètes de Voltaire*, ed. Louis Moland (Paris: Garnier Frères, Libraires-Éditeurs, 1883), Vol. 3, p. 443. Walpole's quotation truncates the passage and takes liberties with its punctuation. Its first sentences, for example, should read '*On y voit un melange de serieux et de plaisanterie, de comique et de touchant. C'est ainsi que la vie des hommes est bigarrée;* souvent même une seule avanture *produit tous ces contrastes.*' (My thanks to Daniel White for his assistance in translating this passage and that in n. 14 below.)

12. *the same person*: Walpole is correct in assuming that Voltaire had written the Preface to *L'Enfant prodigue*.

13. *Maffei, prefixed to his Merope*: Francesco Scipione Maffei (1675–1755), Italian dramatist. His verse tragedy *Merope*, which introduced French classical taste into Italian drama, was published in 1713 and met with immediate success.

NOTES

Voltaire wrote a play engaging the same subject matter, prefixing it with an epistle discussing national differences in dramatic practice.

14. *Tous ces traits . . . espece de simplicité*: 'All these characteristics are naïve; all are appropriate to those you introduce into the scene, and to the morals that you give them. These natural familiarities would have been, I believe, well received in Athens; but Paris and our parterre wish for another species of simplicity.' See *Œvres Complètes de Voltaire*, Vol. 4, p. 188.

15. *parterre*: The part of the ground floor of the auditorioum behind the orchestra. Like the area called the 'pit' in eighteenth-century London theatres, the *parterre* traditionally was the area of the theatre where the critics and intelligentsia sat.

16. *difficiles nugæ*: Laboured nothings. See Martial, *Epigrams*, II.86.9.

17. *Racine*: Jean-Baptiste Racine (*c.* 1639–99), French poet and dramatist, best-known for his tragedies *Britannicus* (1669), *Bérénice* (1670), *Bajazet* (1672) and *Phèdre* (1677).

18. *De son . . . la reine*: Voltaire's defence of these lines occurs in his remarks on *Bérénice, tragédie*. See *Complete Works*, Vol. 55, p. 941.

19. *ichnography*: A ground-plan; the representation of the horizontal section of a building or of part of it.

SONNET

1. *Lady Mary Coke*: Lady Mary Campbell (1727–1811), who married Edward Coke in 1747; her *Journals* were edited by J. A. Home (Edinburgh, 1889–96). As is noted in the *Correspondence*, she was the 'fourth daughter of John Duke of Argyll, and widow of Edward Lord Viscount Coke, only son of Thomas Earl of Leicester' (Vol. 23, p. 530n.). In a letter to Horace Mann dated 28 November 1773, Walpole describes her as 'though . . . greatly born, she has a frenzy for royalty . . . However, bating every English person's madness, for every English person must have their madness, Lady Mary . . . is noble, generous, high-spirited, undauntable, is most friendly, sincere, affectionate, and above any mean action' (ibid., pp. 530–31). In a letter to George Montagu written 23 December 1761 (ibid., Vol. 10, p. 413), Walpole transcribes other verses written by him to her.

CHAPTER I

1. *Alfonso the Good*: Walpole's Alfonso appears to be loosely based on the many Castilian and Aragonian kings of that name, most of whom were known by various titles, including Alfonso the Brave (Alfonso VI of Castile 1065–1109), Alfonso the Wise (Alfonso X of Castile, 1252–84), Alfonso the Liberal (Alfonso III of Aragon, 1285–91), Alfonso the Kind (Alfonso IV of Aragon, 1327–36), and Alfonso the Magnanimous (Alfonso V of Aragon, 1416–58). Of these, Alfonso V, the first Aragonian king of Naples, appears to be the primary model for Alfonso the Good. Known for his large nose and penetrating eyes, he was praised as a military conqueror and as a king remarkable for his evenness of temper, abstemiousness, piety, and rectitude in observing personal obligations. See Ryder, *Alfonso the Magnanimous*.

2. *gripe*: A now rare and obscure form of the word 'grip', sometimes carrying with it suggestions of tenaciousness.

3. *obeisance*: A bodily act or gesture expressing submission or respect, such as a bow or curtsy.

4. *poignarded*: Stabbed with a dagger.

5. *the portrait of his grandfather . . . heaved its breast*: See Walpole's letter to William Cole, dated 9 March 1765, in *Correspondence*, Vol. 1, p. 88: 'When you read of the picture quitting its panel, did not you recollect the portrait of Lord Falkland all in white in my gallery?' He makes the same attribution in *Description of the Villa of Strawberry Hill* in *Works of Horatio Walpole, Earl of Orford*, ed. Mary Berry, 9 vols. (London: John Murray, 1798–1825), Vol. 2, p. 466.

6. *I will follow . . . perdition*: This exclamation recalls Shakespeare's *As You Like It*, II.iii.69–70 and *Hamlet*, I.iv.79.

7. *essay*: Attempt or trial.

8. *disculpate*: To clear from blame or accusation.

9. *Providence*: That is, divine providence, the foreknowing and beneficent care of God, meaning divine direction, control or guidance. The exchange here is reminiscent of Shakespeare's *The Tempest*, I.ii.158–9.

10. *comprehensive*: Evidently a deliberate maloproprism for comic effect; Jaquez means 'apprehensive'.

11. *Sot!*: Obscure form meaning 'a foolish or stupid person; a fool, blockhead or dolt'.

12. *wont*: Accustomed, in the habit of (doing something).

13. *aught*: Anything, or anything of worth.

14. *part of his leg*: Anna Letitia Barbauld identifies 'Le Bélier' by Count

Anthony Hamilton as a possible source for Walpole's decision to represent the ghost as a series of glimpses of giant body parts. See Appendix, no. 11.

15. *revenue*: An obscure and rare use of the word, meaning 'return to a place'.

16. *pallet-bed*: A bed with a straw mattress, or simply a poor or modest bed.

CHAPTER 2

1. *moped*: To confine or shut up. Bianca's reference to Matilda's willingness to be 'moped' also connotes a secondary meaning for the word: 'yielding oneself to ennui'.

2. *orisons*: Prayers. As Kristina Bedford notes, the association of Matilda with 'orisons' recalls Hamlet's similar characterization of Ophelia; see Shakespeare, *Hamlet*, III.i.88. See also Further Reading, Bedford.

3. *saint by the almanack*: Almanacs had regularly carried calendars of ecclesiastical holidays and saints' days since the fifteenth century.

4. *If they are spirits . . . by questioning them*: See Shakespeare, *Hamlet*, I.i.130–32.

5. *let us sift him*: See Philip Massinger, *The Unnatural Combat* (1639), IV.i.168; and Shakespeare, *Hamlet*, II.ii.58.

6. *make a property of*: An obscure and rare form meaning 'to make a tool of', 'to use for one's own ends; to exploit'.

7. *it is not seemly . . . at this unwonted hour*: See Francis Beaumont and John Fletcher, *The Maid's Tragedy* (1619), IV.9.

8. *the morning dawns apace*: See Shakespeare, *Romeo and Juliet*, II.ii.176.

9. *spark*: A young man who affects smartness or display in dress and manners.

10. *postern-gate*: A back or side gate; any gate distinct from the main entrance.

11. *another-guess mould*: Another nature.

12. *ought*: A variant of 'aught', meaning 'anything' or 'anything of worth'.

13. *good-liking*: Approval; goodwill; satisfaction.

14. *Hearken to him who speaks through my organs*: See Exodus 15.26.

15. *colour*: Complexion.

16. *bearded*: Opposed openly and resolutely, with daring or with effrontery; defied, affronted or thwarted.

17. *Cant*: To speak in the jargon of a particular class or profession; to affect religious or pietistic phraseology, especially as a matter of fashion or profession.

18. *resign yourself . . . a crown that can never pass away*: See Daniel 7.14.

19. *degree*: A 'step' in direct line of descent; the number of such steps to a common ancestor, determining the proximity of blood of collateral descendants.

20. *dispensation*: The action of dispensing with a requirement; an arrangement made by the administrator of the laws or canons of the Church, granting, in special circumstances or in a particular case, an exemption from, or relaxation of, the penalty incurred by a breach of the law.

21. *fulminated*: Thundered; be made to strike like thunderbolts.

22. *over-reached*: Gotten the better of; outwitted; circumvented in dealing.

23. *traverse*: Cross; obstruct; thwart; sabotage.

24. *boarded*: Panelled with wood.

25. *boon*: A thing asked as a favour; a favour (asked for).

26. *shrieve*: An obscure form of 'shrive': 'to administer absolution upon', 'to hear the confession of'.

27. *brazen*: Brass.

CHAPTER 3

1. *herald*: An officer having the special duty of making royal or state proclamations, and of bearing ceremonial messages between princes or sovereign powers.

2. *interposition*: The act of placing something or oneself between; interference; intervention.

3. *warder*: A staff or wand carried as a sign of office or authority.

4. *issue*: Offspring; a child or children.

5. *management*: The use of contrivance, prudence or diplomacy.

6. *Sanchia of Arragon*: Walpole here appears to have mistaken King Sancho I of Aragon for Sancho I of Portugal. The daughter of the latter was St Sancha (*c*. 1180–1229), who helped the first Franciscan and Dominican foundations in Portugal and later joined the Cistercians at Cellas.

7. *hasted*: Acted with haste or expedition.

8. *harbingers*: Attendants who announce the arrival of another.

9. *the arms of Vicenza and Otranto quarterly*: That is, a coat of arms divided into four parts, with the arms of each house placed in quadrants diagonal to one another.

10. *beavers*: The lower portion of the face-guard of a helmet, often confounded with the upper portion, or visor.

11. *cartel*: A written challenge; a letter of defiance.

12. *gage*: Something of value deposited to ensure the performance of some action, and liable to forfeiture in case of non-performance; a pawn, pledge, or security.

13. *hospital*: A house or hostel for the reception and entertainment of pilgrims, travellers and strangers; a hospice.

14. *ween*: Think; surmise; suppose; believe.

15. *vitious*: A variant of 'vicious', used in this case in its legal sense, meaning 'marred or rendered void by some inherent fault or defect'; 'not satisfying legal requirements or conditions'; 'unlawful'.

16. *choler*: Bile; one of the 'four humours' of early physiology, supposed to cause anger and irascibility of temper.

17. *adjusted*: Composed; harmonized; settled.

18. *viceroy*: One who acts as governor of a country or province in the name and by the authority of the supreme ruler.

19. *pent-up vapours*: A sudden exhalation of trapped gas. This line appears to be an intentionally ridiculous moment in Walpole's text, illustrating the absurd lengths to which people will go to explain the supernatural through rational means.

20. *regardless*: Heedless; indifferent; without regard of.

21. *approve*: To show to be true; demonstrate; prove.

CHAPTER 4

1. *Joppa*: Also known as Jaffa, Joppa was an old Canaanite city that became capital of the Egyptian New Kingdom in the fifteenth century BC. It was later occupied, in turn, by Israelite kings David and Solomon, by Assyrian king Sennacherib, the Persians and the Ptolemies, and, again, the Syrians and Israelites before being conquered by Rome in AD 68. The crusaders captured it in 1126, lost it to Saladin in 1187, and, under Richard I, captured it again in 1191 before finally losing it in 1196. In 1950 the town was incorporated with Tel Aviv to form Tel Aviv-Yafo.

2. *mortals must . . . behests . . . lowliness and submission*: See Ephesians 4.2; 'behests' are commands; injunctions.

3. *glosing*: Variant of 'glozing', meaning 'the action of glossing, commenting, or interpreting', often carrying the pejorative sense of 'explaining away'.

4. *Why do you fix your eye-balls thus?*: These lines, and the scene more generally, are similar to the banquet scene (III.iv) of Shakespeare's *Macbeth*.

5. *corsairs*: The name in the languages of the Mediterranean for privateers; chiefly applied to the cruisers of Barbary. In English often treated as identical with 'pirate', though the Saracen and Turkish corsairs were authorized and recognized by their own governments as part of a settled policy towards Christendom.

6. *rover*: A sea-robber or pirate.

7. *attitude*: A posture of the body proper to, or implying, some action or mental state.

8. *dole*: Dealing out or distribution of gifts, especially of food or money given in charity.

9. *enjoin*: To impose a penalty, task, duty or obligation.

10. *while a father . . . sacred vengeance*: This speech strongly recalls Shakespeare's *Hamlet*, I.v.7 and I.v.25.

11. *The Lord giveth, and the Lord taketh away*: Proverbial.

12. *lance her anathema*: To fling or hurl a curse of excommunication and damnation.

13. *meddling friar*: See Shakespeare, *Measure for Measure*, V.i.127.

14. *but they wither away like the grass*: See Psalms 37.2; and James 1.10.

CHAPTER 5

1. *oriel window*: A window projecting from the outer face of the wall of a building, usually, in an upper story.

2. *vulnerary*: Used in healing wounds; having curative properties in respect of external injuries.

3. *by my halidame*: A common expression in seventeenth- and eighteenth-century drama. See, for example, Shakespeare, *Two Gentlemen of Verona*, IV.ii.135; or *Henry VIII*, V.i.116. A 'halidame' is a holy thing, a relic, or anything regarded as sacred.

4. *watchet-coloured*: Light blue or sky blue.

5. *suborned*: Bribed, or caused by other devious means, to give false testimony.

6. *oratory*: A place of prayer, usually a small chapel or shrine used for private worship.

7. *advertised*: Informed; notified; given notice.

8. *Angels of grace, protect me!*: See Shakespeare, *Hamlet*, I.iv.39.

9. *litter*: A vehicle containing a couch shut in by curtains, and carried on men's shoulders or by beasts; a framework supporting a bed or couch for the transport of the sick and wounded.

10. *thou art too unadvised*: See Shakespeare, *Romeo and Juliet*, II.ii.116–20.

11. *wonnot*: A form of 'will not'.

12. *chamberlain*: An officer charged with the management of the private chambers of a sovereign or nobleman.

13. *each took . . . in the neighbouring convents*: See Shakespeare, *As You Like It*, V.iv.179–81.

APPENDIX

Early Responses to *The Castle of Otranto*

1. Review of *The Castle of Otranto*,
Critical Review 19 (January 1765), pp. 50–51. Extract.

The ingenious translator of this very curious performance informs that it was found in the library of an ancient catholic family in the north of England: that it was printed at Naples, in the black letter, in the year 1529; and that the stile is of the purest Italian: he also conjectures, that if the story was written near the time it is supposed to have happened, it must have been between 1095, the æra of the first crusade, and 1243, the date of the last, or not long afterwards . . . [Reviewer continues to quote directly from the Preface.]

Such is the character of this work given us by its judicious translator; but whether he speaks seriously or ironically, we neither know nor care. The publication of any work, at this time, in England composed of such rotten materials, is a phœnomenon we cannot account for. That our readers may form some idea of the absurdity of its contents, we are to inform them that Manfred, prince of Otranto, had only one son, a youth of about fifteen years of age, who on the day appointed for his marriage was 'dashed to pieces, and almost buried under an enormous helmet, an hundred times more large than any casque ever made for human being, and shaded with proportionable quantity of black feathers.' This helmet, it seems, resembled that upon a statue of Alfonso the Good, one of the former princes of Otranto, whose dominions Manfred usurped; and therefore the helmet, or the resemblance of it, by way of poetical justice, dashed out his son's brains.

The above wonder is amongst the least of the wonderful things in this story. A picture comes out of its pannel, and stalks through the room, to dissuade Manfred from marrying the princess who had been betrothed to his son. It even utters deep sighs, and heaves its breasts. We cannot help thinking that this circumstance is some presumption that the castle of Otranto is a modern fabrick; for we doubt much whether pictures were fixed in pannels before the year 1243. We shall not affront our readers' understanding so much as to describe the other monstrosities of this story; but, excepting those absurdities, the characters are well marked, and the narrative kept up with surprising spirit and propriety. The catastrophe is most wretched. Manfred stabs his own daughter inadvertently, and she dies. The true heir of Alfonso's throne is discovered, whose name is Theodore. Manfred relents and repents, and at last the whole moral of the story turns out to, 'That the sins of the fathers are visited on their children to the third and fourth generation.'

2. Review of *The Castle of Otranto*,
Monthly Review 32 (February 1765), pp. 97–9. Extract.

Those who can digest the absurdities of Gothic fiction, and bear with the machinery of ghosts and goblins, may hope, at least, for considerable entertainment from the performance before us: for it is written with no common pen; the language is accurate and elegant; the characters are highly finished; and the disquisitions into human manners, passions, and pursuits, indicate the keenest penetration, and the most perfect knowledge of mankind. The Translator, in his Preface, informs us that the original 'was found in the library of an ancient catholic family in the North of England . . .' [The Reviewer continues to quote the Preface].

The natural prejudice which a translator [this is said on the supposition that the work really is a translation, as pretended] entertains in favour of his original, has not carried this gentleman beyond the bounds of truth; and his criticisms on his Author bear equal marks of taste and candour. The principal defect of this performance does not remain unnoticed. That unchristian doctrine of visiting the sins of the fathers upon the children, is certainly, under our present system, not only a very useless, but a very insupportable moral, and yet it is almost the only one deducible from this story. Nor is it at all rendered more tolerable through the insinuation that such evils might be diverted by devotion to St. Nicholas; for there the good canon was evidently preaching in favour of his own household. However, as a work of genius, evincing great dramatic powers, and exhibiting fine views of nature, the Castle of Otranto may still be read with pleasure. To give the Reader an analysis of the story, would be to introduce him to a company of skeletons; to refer him to the book will be to recommend him to an assemblage of beautiful pictures.

3. William Mason to Horace Walpole
(14 April 1765), *Correspondence*, Vol. 18, pp. 5–6.

Sir,

Though I neglected returning you my thanks for the present you made me of Lord Herbert's life, and of which, as you favoured me with a view of the proof sheets, I before gave you my sentiments, yet I will not omit thanking you for a more extraordinary thing in its kind, which though it comes not from your press, yet I have episcopal evidence is written by your hand. And indeed less than such evidence would scarce have contented me. For when a friend of mine to whom I had recommended *The Castle of Otranto* returned it me with some doubts of its originality, I laughed him to scorn, and wondered he could be so absurd as to think that anybody nowadays had imagination enough to invent such a story. He replied that his suspicion arose merely from some parts of familiar dialogue in it, which he thought of too modern a cast. Still sure of my point, I affirmed this objection, if there was anything in it, was merely owing to its not being translated a century ago. All this I make it a point of conscience to tell you, for though it proves me your dupe, I should be glad to be so duped again every year of my life. I have the honour to be, Sir,

Your much obliged and obedient servant,
W. Mason

4. Review of *The Castle of Otranto* (2nd edition),
Monthly Review 32 (May 1765), p. 394.

When this book was published as a translation from an old Italian romance, we had the pleasure of distinguishing in it the marks of genius, and many beautiful characteristic paintings; we were dubious, however, concerning the antiquity of the work upon several considerations, but being willing to find some excuse for the absurd and monstrous fictions it contained, we wished to acquiesce in the declaration of the title page, that it was really a translation from an ancient writer. While we considered it as such, we could readily excuse its preposterous phenomena, and consider them as sacrifices to a gross and unenlightened age. – But when, as in this edition, the Castle of Otranto is declared to be a modern performance, that indulgence we afforded to the foibles of a supposed antiquity, we can by no means extend to the singularity of a false taste in a cultivated period of learning. It is, indeed, more than strange, that an Author,[1] of a refined and polished genius, should be an advocate for re-establishing the barbarous superstitions of Gothic devilism! *Incredulus odi*[2] is, or ought to be a charm against all such infatuation. Under the same banner of singularity he attempts to defend all the trash of Shakespeare, and what that great genius evidently threw out as a necessary sacrifice to that idol the *cæcum vulgus*,[3] he would adopt in the worship of the true God of Poetry.

5. Review of *The Castle of Otranto* (2nd edition), *Critical Review* 19 (June 1765), p. 469.

We have already reviewed the *Castle of Otranto* and we then spoke of it in terms pretty near the character given by the author. He solves, by his preface to this edition, the phœnomenon for which we could not account, by his diffidence as to his success; and he asks pardon of his readers, for having offered it to them under the borrowed personage of a translator. He says that it is an attempt to blend the two kinds of romance, the ancient and the modern; and besides many ingenious reasons to justify his undertaking, he brings the authority of Shakespear's practice, who, in his *Hamlet* and *Julius Caesar*, (he might have added many other of his plays) has blended humour and clumsy jests with dignity and solemnity.

Notwithstanding the high opinion we have of this writer's acquaintance with whatever relates to his subject, we cannot but think if Shakespear had possessed the critical knowledge of modern times, he would have kept these two kinds of writing distinct, if the prepossessions and habits of the age could have suffered him.

We are pleased with the just freedom with which this writer has animadverted on Voltaire, who, while he is apologizing for the ignorance of the French noblesse in Corneille's time, makes Robert Dudley and the earl of Leicester, queen Elizabeth's favourite, different persons. We applaud the noble warmth against which our author has expressed in defence of Shakespear against Voltaire, who, he says, is a genius, but not of Shakespear's magnitude. We are sorry this ingenious gentleman has put those two names in the same sentence. Voltaire is so far from being a genius, that he is not a poet of the first magnitude, even in his own country, the most fruitful in poetry, but the most barren in genius (if we except Germany) of any perhaps under the sun.

We have thought this tribute of praise due to the noble spirit which Mr. W. has shewn in defence of the glory of this country, against a Frenchman, who, in poetry, never could arrive so high as even to rival the imperfections of that divine writer.

6. Voltaire [François-Marie Arouet] to Horace Walpole (15 July 1768).[1]
This translation appeared in the *Monthly Mirror* 19 (March 1805),
pp. 158–62. Extract.

After reading the preface to your 'History,' I read that of your Romance, (the Castle of Otranto). You jest a little with me: Frenchmen understand raillery; but I shall answer you gravely. – You have almost persuaded your nation that I undervalue Shakspeare. I am the first who has made Shakspeare known in France: I translated parts of him forty years since; also of Milton, Waller, Rochester, Dryden, and of Pope. I can assure you that previous to this Frenchmen knew nothing of English poetry. I was persecuted thirty years by a swarm of bigots, for having asserted that Locke[2] is the Hercules of metaphysics, who has prescribed the boundaries of the human understanding.

My ambition was always to be the first that should explain to my countrymen the discoveries of the great Newton, which some among us even yet call an hypothesis. I have been your apostle, and your martyr: in truth, the English complain of me unjustly. I have always said that if Shakspeare had lived in the time of Addison,[3] he would have united with his genius the elegance and purity that render Addison so estimable. I have said that his genius is his own praise, and his faults are to be attributed to the age in which he flourished. He resembles, in my mind, Lopez de Vega,[4] of Spain, and Caldéron.[5] There are the charms of nature, but rude and uncultivated; no regularity, no discrimination, no art; the despicable associated with the lofty – the ludicrous with the terrible: it is a chaos of tragedy in which there are a hundred rays of light.

The Italians, who restored tragedy an age before the English and the Spaniards, have not fallen into this error; they wisely imitated the Greeks. There are no buffoons in the Electra and the Œdipus of Sophocles.[6] I greatly suspect that this rude custom had its origin in our 'court fools.' We were all tinctured with barbarism on this side of the Alps: every noble had a fool in his establishment. Illiterate princes, the nurslings of ignorance, were incapable of appreciating the sublime pleasures of intellect; they degraded human nature even to the paying knaves for abusing them: hence came our *mère sotte*;[7] and till the time of Moliere[8] they had a court fool in nearly all their comedies. The practice is abominable.

I have said, it is true, Sir, as you relate it, that there are some serious comedies, such as the Misanthrope, which are masterpieces; that there are very humorous ones, like George Dandin;[9] that the comic, the serious, and the pathetic, may very rationally meet in the same play. I have said every style is good – except the drowsy; but grossness is not a style. I have never presumed that it was proper to introduce, in the same situation, Charles the Fifth and Don Joseph of Armenia, Augustus and a drunken sailor, Marcus Aurelius and a street buffoon. It appears to me that Horace thought so in the most refined of ages: – consult his Art of Poetry.[10] All Europe, enlightened, think so at this day, and Spain begins to escape from bad taste at the same time that it proscribes the inquisition; for good sense is alike hostile to both.

You so acutely perceive how greatly tragedy is debased by the mean and low, that you reproach Racine for making Antiochus say, in Berenice,

> Hither the emperor's apartments lay,
> And this to Berenice's leads the way.

These certainly are not lofty verses, but have the goodness to remember they form part of an expository scene, which ought to be simple. Here is no beauty of poetry, but there is the beauty of exactitude, which ascertains the situation of the characters, and at once fixes the attention of the spectator to the scene before him, while it informs him that all the persons will meet in a saloon, which is common to all the apartments; and without this intimation it would scarcely appear probable how Titus, Berenice, and Antiochus should always speak in the same chamber.

> Clear and determinate be the scenic ground,

says the judicious Boileau, the oracle of good taste, in his Art of Poetry,[11] equal at least to that of Horace. Our excellent Racine has scarcely ever violated this rule, and it is worth observing, that Athalia appears in the temple of the Jews, and in the same place where one has seen the high-priest, without any offence to probability. – You will rather pardon the illustrious Racine, Sir, when you reflect that the palace of Berenice was, in some measure, the history of Louis the Fourteenth, and your English princess, the sister of Charles the Second. They both lodged on the same floor of St. Germains, and a saloon alone divided their bed-chambers. [Voltaire continues making minute factual corrections about *Berenice*.]

You disregard, you *free Britons*, all the unities of place, time, and action. In truth, your works are not the better for it: probability ought surely to stand for something. The art is certainly the more difficult for them, but infinitely more praise and pleasure arise when those difficulties are successfully combated.

Permit me, altogether Englishman as you are, to take a little the part of my country. I have so often told her of her faults, that it is but fair to praise her when there is good reason. Yes, Sir, I have thought, I do think, and I shall think, that Paris is superior to Athens in the composition of tragedies and comedies. Moliere and even Regnard,[12] appear to my mind as much to surpass

Aristophanes, and Demosthenes[13] is superior to our bawling advocates. I tell you boldly that all the Greek tragedies appear to me the works of school-boys, compared with the sublime scenes of Corneille, and the perfect tragedies of Racine. It was so Boileau thought, admirer as he was of the ancients; he made no hesitation of writing under the portrait of Racine, that this great man had surpassed Euripides,[14] and equalled Corneille. Yes, I think it proved that there are more men of judgment in Paris than in Athens. We have more than thirty thousand admirers of the fine arts, and Athens had but six thousand in it. The lower class of Athens were never admitted to the spectacles, nor indeed with us, except when an exhibition is allowed them *gratis*, on some solemn or ridiculous occasion. Our continual intercourse with the other sex has imparted greater elegance to our sentiments, much refinement to our manners, and peculiar delicacy to our taste. Leave us, then, our theatre; leave the Italians their rustic fables, (*favole boscarecie*), you are still rich enough in better things.[15]

It must not be denied that wretched pieces, barbarously constructed and ignorantly written, have attained extraordinary success at Paris, supported by a cabal, the spirit of party, fashion, and the temporary protection of men looked up to. This was the intoxication of the moment, but in a few years the illusion vanished. Don Japhel of Armenia, and Jodolet, are returned to the vulgar, and the Siege of Calais[16] is esteemed only at Calais.

It is necessary I should say a few words on the subject of rhyme, with which you reproach us. Almost all Dryden's works are in rhyme,[17] and they are so much the more difficult. Those verses which are perpetually quoted from memory are in rhyme; and I maintain that the Cimna, Athalia, Phædra, and Iphigenia,[18] being all written in rhyme, whoever should endeavour to cast off the burden, in France, would be regarded as a feeble artist, unable to wield its power.

With the garrulous quality of an old man, I will relate to you an anecdote. I one day demanded of Pope[19] why Milton[20] had not written his 'Paradise Lost' in rhyme, while other poets used that style of poetry, in imitation of the Italians? His answer was, '*because he could not.*'

I have now, Sir, opened my heart to you; but I confess that I am guilty of a heinous fault in not remembering that the Earl of Leicester was originally called Dudley; but if you have an inclination to enter the house of peers, and change your title, I shall ever remember the name of Walpole with the highest respect.

Before the departure of my letter, I have had an opportunity of reading your 'Richard the Third.' You make an excellent *Attorney-General*; – you calculate all the probabilities, but it is evident you have a secret partiality for the hunch-back. You insist that he was a handsome, and, at the same time, a very gallant man. I am inclined to think, with you, that he was neither so ugly nor so cruel as he is reported; but I cannot say I should choose to have had any concern with him. Your *red rose* and your *white rose*[21] were terrible thorns to your nation:

> Those gracious kings are all a pack of rogues.

To say truth, when reading the history of York and Lancaster, and some others, one is tempted to think one is reading the history of robbers on the high-way. As to your Henry the Seventh, he was little better than a cut-purse.

Ferney, July 15, 1768

7. Clara Reeve, Preface to *The Old English Baron*, 2nd edition[1] (London, 1778).

As this Story is of a species which, tho' not new, is out of the common track, it has been thought necessary to point out some circumstances to the reader, which will elucidate the design, and, it is hoped, will induce him to form a favourable, as well as a right judgment of the work before him.

This Story is the literary offspring of the Castle of Otranto, written upon the same plan, with a design to unite the most attractive and interesting circumstances of the ancient Romance and the modern Novel, at the same time it assumes a character and manner of its own, that differs from both; it is distinguished by the appellation of a Gothic Story, being a picture of Gothic times and manners. Fictitious Stories have been the delight of all times and all countries, by oral tradition in barbarous, by writing in more civilized ones; and altho' some persons of wit and learning have condemned them indiscriminately, I would venture to affirm, that even those who so much affect to despise them under one form, will receive and embrace them under another.

Thus, for instance, a man shall admire and almost adore the Epic poems of the Ancients, and yet despise and execrate the ancient Romances, which are only Epics in prose.[2]

History represents human nature as it is in real life; – alas, too often a melancholy retrospect! – Romance displays only the amiable side of the picture; it shews the pleasing features, and throws a veil over the blemishes: Mankind are naturally pleased with what gratifies their vanity; and vanity, like all other passions of the human heart, may be rendered subservient to good and useful purposes.

I confess that it may be abused, and become an instrument to corrupt the manners and morals of mankind; so may poetry, so may plays, so may every kind of composition; but that will prove nothing more than the old saying lately revived by the philosophers the most in fashion, 'that every earthly thing has two handles.'

The business of Romance is, first, to excite the attention; and, secondly, to direct it to some useful, or at least innocent, end; Happy the writer who attains both these points, like Richardson! and not unfortunate, or undeserving praise, he who gains only the latter, and furnishes out an entertainment for the reader!

Having, in some degree, opened my design, I beg leave to conduct my reader back again, till he comes within view of the Castle of Otranto; a work which, as already had been observed, is an attempt to unite the various merits and graces of the ancient Romance and modern Novel. To attain this end, there is required a sufficient degree of the marvellous, to excite the attention; enough of the manners of real life, to give an air of probability to the work; and enough of the pathetic, to engage the heart in its behalf.

The book we have mentioned is excellent in the two last points, but has a redundancy in the first; the opening excites the attention very strongly; the conduct of the story is artful and judicious; the characters are admirably drawn and supported; the diction polished and elegant; yet, with all these brilliant advantages, it palls upon the mind (though it does not upon the ear); and the reason is obvious, the machinery is so violent, that it destroys the effect it is intended to excite. Had the story been kept within the utmost *verge* of probability, the effect had been preserved, without losing the least circumstance that excites or detains the attention.

For instance; we can conceive, and allow of, the appearance of a ghost; we can even dispense with an enchanted sword and helmet; but then they must keep within certain limits of credibility: A sword so large as to require an hundred men to lift it; a helmet that by its own weight forces a passage through a court-yard into an arched vault, big enough for a man to go through; a picture that walks out of its frame; a skeleton ghost in a hermit's cowl: – When your expectation is wound up to the highest pitch, these circumstances take it down with a witness, destroy the work of imagination, and, instead of attention, excite laughter. I was both surprised and vexed to find the enchantment dissolved, which I wished might continue to the end of the book; and several of its readers have confessed the same disappointment to me: The beauties are so numerous, that we cannot bear the defects, but want it to be perfect in all respects.

In the course of my observations upon this singular book, it seemed to me that it was possible to compose a work upon the same plan, wherein these defects might be avoided; and the *keeping*, as in *painting*,[3] might be preserved.

But I began to fear it might happen to me as to certain translators, and imitators of Shakespeare; the unities may be preserved, while the spirit is evaporated. However, I ventured to attempt it; I read the beginning to a circle of friends of approved judgment, and by their approbation was encouraged to proceed, and to finish it.

By the advice of the same friends I printed the first Edition in the country, where it circulated chiefly, very few copies being sent to London, and being thus encouraged, I have determined to offer a second Edition to that public which has so often rewarded the efforts of those, who have endeavoured to contribute to its entertainment.

The work has lately undergone a revision and correction, the former Edition being very incorrect; and by the earnest solicitation of several friends, for whose judgment I have the greatest deference, I have consented to a change of the title from the *Champion of Virtue* to the *Old English Baron*: – as that character is thought to be the principal one in the story.

I have also been prevailed upon, though with extreme reluctance, to suffer my name to appear in the title-page; and I do now, with the utmost respect and diffidence, submit the whole to the candour of the Public.

8. Review of Robert Jephson, *The Count of Narbonne*,
Critical Review 52 (December 1781), pp. 456–63. Extract.

This Tragedy, undoubtedly one of the best that has appeared for some years, is founded on Mr. Horace Walpole's celebrated novel, or romance, called the Castle of Otranto, from whence the ingenious Mr. Jephson has drawn almost all the interesting circumstances and events that compose his drama, very judiciously omitting the marvellous part of it, as well knowing that *nodding helmets, waving plumes*, and *walking pictures*, would have made but a ridiculous figure on an English stage. The Fable is artfully conducted throughout; the characters well sustained, and discriminated; the sentiments, for the most part, natural, unaffected, and suitable to the persons by whom they are delivered; the style and diction remarkably correct, elegant, and harmonious; sufficiently raised above vulgar language to become the dignity of the tragic muse, and at the same time without affectation, bombast, or puerility. The first, third, and fifth acts have some scenes that are masterly and pathetic, in which good actors may always appear to great advantage; the second and fourth are rather heavy and uninteresting: every picture however must have light and shade, and we do not recollect any modern tragedy which has fewer faults and imperfections than the Count of Narbonne.

The following extracts may serve to convince our readers that what we have said, with regard to Mr. Jephson's style and manner, in this applauded performance, is not more than he deserves; and will, we doubt not, invite them to a perusal of the whole drama. [Reviewer then quotes from Act I, scene vi and Act IV, scene iii.]

This tragedy, with all its beauties, which are numerous, has one capital and essential defect, viz. the want of a proper moral lesson resulting from the whole.

'I am not blind, (says Mr. Walpole, in his preface to the first edition of the Castle of Otranto) to my author's defects. I could wish he had grounded his plan on a more useful *moral* than this, that, *the sins of fathers are visited on their children to the third and fourth generations.* I doubt whether in his time any more than at present, ambition curbed its appetite of dominion from the dread of so remote a punishment.' – The same objection which Mr. Walpole made to his own novel, must every spectator and every reader make to Mr. Jephson's drama. The Count of Narbonne is judiciously painted by the author as passionate, ambitious, sensual, and revengeful, though guiltless of the intended murther of his daughter; and therefore we do not lament his fate: but what had the wronged mother and the innocent daughter done, that should involve them in the same punishment with the murtherous Alphonso, and the false, ambitious Narbonne? Why must all poetical justice be thus sacrificed to inculcate an idea that is shocking to truth and equity? Will such a notion, if universally received, operate towards rendering mankind more cautious of committing crimes that may be attended with such consequences? The effect, as Mr. Walpole properly observed, is much too remote, while the undeserved punishment of innocence is to the last degree offensive, and must tend to discourage men from the practice of virtue, not only so unjustly but severely chastised.

Our author's fable is liable also to this censure: the catastrophe, which he has founded on injustice, is produced by superstition; the accomplishment of a prophecy. What conclusion can be drawn from hence, but that oracles, divinations, and prophecies, should be believed, and must always be fulfilled? Such notions can only tend to enslave the mind, and bring us back to the long exploded errors of ignorance and barbarism. We wish therefore to see a tragedy of Mr. Jephson's free from those objections, and from which a better moral may be drawn than from the Count of Narbonne.

9. Ann Yearsley, 'To the Honourable H[orac]e W[alpol]e,
on Reading *The Castle of Otranto* (December 1784)',
Poems on Several Occasions (London: T. Cadell, 1785),
pp 87–96. Extract.

To praise thee, Walpole, asks a pen divine,
    And common sense to me is hardly given,
Bianca's Pen now owns the daring line,
    And who expects *her* muse should drop from Heaven.

*   *   *   *   *   *

The drowsy eye, half-closing to the lid,
    Stares on Otranto's walls; grim terrors rise,
The horrid helmet strikes my soul unbid,
    And with thy Conrad, lo! Bianca dies.   20

Funereal plumes now wave; Alphonso's ghost
    Frowns o'er my shoulder; silence aids the scene,
The taper's flame, in fancy'd blueness lost,
    Pale spectres shews, to Manfred only seen.

Ah! Manfred! thine are bitter draughts of woe,
    Strong gusts of passion hurl thee on thy fate;
Tho' eager to elude, thou meet'st the blow,
    And for Ricardo Manfred weeps in state.

By all the joys which treasur'd virtues yield,
    I feel thy agonies in Walpole's line;   30
Love, pride, revenge, by turns maintain the field,
    And hourly tortures rend my heart for thine.

Hail, magic pen, that strongly paint'st the soul,
    Where fell Ambition holds his wildest roar,
The whirlwind rages to the distant pole,
    And Virtue, stranded, pleads her cause no more.

Where's Manfred's refuge? Walpole, tell me where?
    Thy pen to great St. Nicholas points the eye,
E'en Manfred calls to guard Alphonso's heir,
    Tho' conscious shame oft gives his tongue the lie.   40

Matilda! ah, how soft thy yielding mind,
    When hard obedience cleaves thy timid heart!
How nobly strong, when love and virtue join'd
    To melt thy soul and take a lover's part!

Ah, rigid duties, which two souls divide!
    Whose iron talons rend the panting breast!
Pluck the dear image from the widow'd side,
    Where Love had lull'd its every care to rest.

Hypolita! fond, passive to excess,
    Her low submission suits not souls like mine;   50
Bianca might have lov'd her Manfred less,
    Not offer'd less at great Religion's shrine.

Implicit Faith, all hail! Imperial man
    Exacts submission; reason we resign;
Against our senses we adopt the plan
    Which Reverence, Fear, and Folly think divine.

*   *   *   *   *   *

But be it so, Bianca ne'er shall prate,
    Nor Isabella's equal powers reveal;
You Manfreds boast your power, and prize your state;
    We ladies our omnipotence conceal.   60

But whilst the Hermit does my soul affright,
    Love dies – Lo! in yon corner down he kneels;
I shudder, see the taper sinks in night,
    He rises, and his fleshless form reveals.

Hide me, thou parent Earth! see low I fall,
   My sins now meet me in the fainting hour;
Say, do thy Manes[1] for Heaven's vengeance call,
   Or can I free thee from an angry power?   80

Stella! if Walpole's spectres thus can scare,
   Then near the great Magician's walls ne'er tread,
He'll surely conjure many a spirit there,
   Till, fear-struck, thou art number'd with the dead.

Oh! with this noble Sorcerer ne'er converse,
   Fly, Stella, quickly from the magic storm;
Or, soon he'll close thee in some high-plum'd hearse,
   Then raise another Angel in thy form.

Trust not his art, for should he stop thy breath,
   And good Alphonso's ghost unbidden rise;   90
He'd vanish, leave thee in the jaws of death,
   And quite forget to close thy aching eyes.

But is Bianca safe in this slow vale?
   For should his Goblins stretch their dusky wing,
Would they not bruise me for the saucy tale,
   Would they not pinch me for the truths I sing?

Yet whisper not I've call'd him names, I fear
   His Ariel would my hapless sprite torment,
He'd cramp my bones,[2] and all my sinews tear,
   Should Stella blab the secret I'd prevent.   100

But hush, ye winds, ye crickets chirp no more,
   I'll shrink to bed, nor these sad omens hear,
An hideous rustling shakes the lattic'd door,
   His spirits hover in the sightless air.

Now, Morpheus,[3] shut each entrance of my mind,
   Sink, sink, Otranto, in this vacant hour;
To thee, Oh, balmy God! I'm all resign'd,
   To thee e'en Walpole's wand resigns its power.

10. Thomas James Mathias, *The Pursuits of Literature:*
A Satirical Poem in Four Dialogues (London: T. Beckett, 1798),
pp. 87–8, Dialogue IV, ll. 503–10.

Yet speak, the hour demands: Is Learning fled?
Spent all her vigour, all her spirit dead?
Have Gallic arms and unrelenting war
Borne all her trophies from Britannia far?
Shall nought but ghosts and trinkets be display'd,
Since Walpole[1] ply'd the virtuoso's trade,
Bade sober truth revers'd for fiction pass,
And mus'd o'er Gothic toys through Gothic glass?

11. Anna Letitia Barbauld, 'Horace Walpole',
The British Novelists, ed. A. L. Barbauld, 50 vols.
(London: F. C. & J. Rivington et al., 1810), Vol. 22, pp. i–iii.

The Castle of Otranto was written by The Honourable Horace Walpole, son of
Sir Robert Walpole, who at the close of his life became Earl of Orford. It was
printed at Strawberry Hill, and composed, the author tells us in one of his
letters, in eight days or rather evenings. Though a slight performance, it is
calculated to make a great impression on those who relish the fictions of the
Arabian Tales, and similar performances. It was one of the first of the modern
productions founded on appearances of terror.

Since this author's time, from the perusal of Mrs. Radcliffe's productions[1]
and some of the German tales, we may be said to have 'supped full with
horrors,'[2] but none of those compositions have a livelier play of fancy than *The
Castle of Otranto*. It is the sportive effusion of a man of genius, who throws the
reins loose upon the neck of his imagination. The large limbs of the gigantic
figure which inhabits the castle, and which are visible at intervals; the plumes
of the helmet, which rise and wave with ominous meaning; and the various
enchantments of the place, are imagined with the richness and wildness of
poetic fancy. A sufficient degree of interest is thrown into the novel part of the
story; but in the characters of some of the attendants there is an attempt at
humour which has not succeeded.

The works of Horace Walpole are well known. He was a gentleman author,
and wrote and printed for his own amusement, living in literary ease at his

elegant seat of Strawberry Hill, in the architecture and furniture of which he has also shown a predilection for the romantic ideas connected with gothic and chivalrous times. He always moved in the highest circles of company, and joined the man of fashion and man of wit to the elegant scholar. Mr. Walpole was fond of French literature, and few Englishmen have more imbibed the spirit and taste of the writers of that nation. His little jeu d'esprit upon Rousseau[3] is well known.

The Castle of Otranto is much in the spirit of the tales of Count Hamilton.[4] In one of those tales we meet with a vast leg of a giant, which probably suggested the prodigy of the former. Horace Walpole wrote, *A Catalogue of royal and noble Authors; Anecdotes of Painting, enlarged from Vertue; An Essay on modern Gardening*, in which there is a good deal of taste; and *The Mysterious Mother*, a tragedy. The last work was much spoken of while it was handed about with a certain air of secrecy, but sunk into neglect soon after it was published. Not but that there are some fine lines, and some strong moral sentiment in the piece; but no play could be expected to support itself under a subject so disgustingly repulsive. The story itself is in the *Gesta Romanorum*,[5] and in Taylor's *Cases of Conscience*;[6] and as in a play it never could be acted, it had better have remained in the form of a story.

Lord Orford's works have been published since his death, in a pompous edition, with his letters and some posthumous fragments, in both of which there is a good deal of light easy wit and entertaining court anecdote; but what is new in them has not been made very accessible to the public in general, as it is not to be had without purchasing works which they were long before in possession of.

12. Walter Scott, Introduction to *The Castle of Otranto* (Edinburgh: James Ballantyne, 1811), pp. iii–xxxvi. Extract.

The Castle of Otranto is remarkable not only for the wild interest of the story, but as the first modern attempt to found a tale of amusing fiction upon the basis of the ancient romances of chivalry. The neglect and discredit of these venerable legends commenced so early as the reign of Queen Elizabeth, when, as we learn from the criticism of the times, Spenser's fairy web[1] was rather approved on account of the mystic and allegorical interpretation, than the plain and obvious meaning of his chivalrous pageant. The drama, which shortly afterwards rose into splendour, and versions from the innumerable novelists of Italy, supplied to the higher class the amusement which their fathers received from the legends of Don Belianis[2] and the Mirror of Knighthood;[3] and the huge volumes which were once the pastime of nobles and princes, shorn of their ornaments, and shrunk into abridgments, were banished to the kitchen or nursery, or at best, to the hall-window of the old-fashioned country manor-house. Under Charles II the prevailing taste for French Literature dictated the introduction of those dullest of dull folios, the romances of Calprenede[4] and Scuderi,[5] works which hover between the ancient tale of chivalry and the modern novel. The alliance was so ill conceived, that they retained all the insufferable length and breadth of the prose volumes of chivalry, the same detailed account of reiterated and unvaried combats, the same unnatural and extravagant turn of incident, without the rich and sublime strokes of genius, and vigour of imagination, which often distinguished the early romance; while they exhibited all the sentimental langour and flat love-intrigue of the novel, without being enlivened by its variety of character, just traits of feeling, or acute views of life. Such an ill-imagined species of composition retained its ground longer than might have been expected, only because these romances were called works of entertainment, and that there was nothing better to supply their room. Even in the days of the Spectator, Clelia, Cleaopatra, and the Grand Cyrus, (as that precious folio is christened by its butcherly translator), were the favourite closet companions of the fair sex. But this unnatural taste began to give way early in the eighteenth century; and, about the middle of it, was entirely superseded by the works of Le Sage,[6] Richardson,[7] Fielding,[8] and Smollett;[9] so that even the very name of romance, now so venerable in the ear of antiquaries and book-collectors, was almost forgotten at the time the Castle of Otranto made its first appearance. [Scott then provides a general account of Walpole's life and social position.]

He loved, as a satirist has expressed it, 'to gaze on Gothic toys through Gothic glass';[10] and the villa at Strawberry-Hill, which he chose for his abode, gradually swelled into a feudal castle, by the addition of turrets, towers, galleries, and corridors, whose fretted roofs, carved pannels, and illuminated windows, were garnished with the appropriate furniture of scutcheons,[11] armorial bearings, shields, tilting lances, and all the panoply of chivalry. The Gothic order of architecture is now so generally, and, indeed, indiscriminately used, that we are rather surprised if the country-house of a tradesman retired from business does not exhibit lanceolated[12] windows, divided by stone shafts, and garnished by painted glass, a cupboard in the form of a cathedral-stall, and a pig-house with a front borrowed from the façade of an ancient chapel. But, in the middle of the eighteenth century, when Mr. Walpole began to exhibit specimens of the Gothic style, and to show how patterns, collected from cathedrals and monuments, might be applied to chimney-pieces, ceilings, windows, and balustrades, he did not comply with the dictates of a prevailing fashion, but pleased his own taste, and realised his own visions,[13] in the romantic cast of the mansion which he erected.[14]

Mr. Walpole's lighter studies were conducted upon the same principle which influenced his historical researches, and his taste in architecture. His extensive acquaintance with foreign literature, on which he justly prided himself, was subordinate to his pursuits as an English antiquary and genealogist, in which he gleaned subjects for poetry and for romantic fiction, as well as for historical controversy. These are studies, indeed, proverbially dull; but it is only when they are pursued by those whose fancies nothing can enliven. A Horace Walpole, or a Thomas Warton,[15] is not a mere collector of dry and minute facts, which the general historian passes over with disdain. He brings with him the torch of genius, to illuminate the ruins through which he loves to wander; nor does the classic scholar derive more inspiration from the pages of Virgil,[16] than such an antiquary from the glowing, rich, and powerful feudal painting of Froissart.[17] His mind being thus stored with information, accumulated by researches into the antiquities of the middle ages, and inspired, as he himself informs us, by the romantic cast of his own habitation, Mr. Walpole resolved to give the public a specimen of the Gothic style adapted to modern literature, as he had already exhibited its application to modern architecture.

As, in his model of a Gothic modern mansion, our author had studiously endeavoured to fit to the purposes of modern convenience, or luxury, the rich, varied, and complicated tracery and carving of the ancient cathedral, so, in the Castle of Otranto, it was his object to unite the marvellous turn of incident, and imposing tone of chivalry, exhibited in the ancient romance, with that accurate exhibition of human character, and contrast of feelings and passions, which is, or ought to be, delineated in the modern novel. But Mr. Walpole, being uncertain of the reception which a work upon so new a plan might experience from the world, and not caring, perhaps, to encounter the ridicule which would have attended its failure, the Castle of Otranto was ushered in to the world as a translation from the Italian. It does not seem that the authenticity of the narrative was suspected. Mr. Gray writes to Mr. Walpole, on 30th December, 1764:[18] 'I have received "The Castle of Otranto," and return you my thanks for it. It engages our attention here (i.e. at Cambridge), makes some of us cry a little; and all, in general, afraid to go to bed o'nights. We take it for a translation; and should believe it to be a true story, if it were not for St. Nicholas.' The friends of the author were probably soon permitted to peep beneath the veil he had thought proper to assume; and, in the second edition, it was altogether withdrawn by a preface, in which the tendency and nature of the work are shortly commented upon and explained. From the following passage, translated from a letter by the author to Madame Deffand,[19] it would seem that he repented of having laid aside his incognito; and, sensitive to criticism, like most dilletante authors, was rather more hurt by the raillery of those who liked not his tale of chivalry, than gratified by the applause of his admirers. 'So they have translated my Castle of Otranto, probably in ridicule of the author. So be it; – however, I beg you will let their raillery pass in silence. Let the critics have their own way; they give me no uneasiness. I have not written the book for the present age, which will endure nothing but *cold common sense*. I confess to you, my dear friend, (and you will think me madder than ever), that this is the only one of my works with which I am myself pleased; I have given reins to my imagination till I became on fire with the visions and feelings which it excited. I have composed it in defiance of rules, of critics, and of philosophers; and it seems to me just so much the better for that very reason. I am even persuaded, that some time hereafter, when taste shall resume the place which philosophy now occupies, my poor Castle will find admirers: we have actually a few among us already, for I am just publishing the third edition. I do not say this in order to mendicate your approbation.[20] I told you from the beginning you would not like the book, – your visions are all in a different style. I am not sorry that the translator has given the second preface; the first, however, accords best with the style of the fiction. I wished it to be believed ancient, and almost every body was imposed upon.' If the public applause, however, was sufficiently qualified by the voice of censure to alarm the feelings of the author, the continued demand for various editions of The Castle of Otranto showed how high the work really stood in popular estimation, and probably eventually reconciled Mr. Walpole to the taste of his own age. This Romance has been justly considered not only as the original and model of a peculiar species of composition, but as one of the standard works of our lighter literature. A few remarks both on the book itself, and on the class to which it belongs, have been judged an apposite introduction to an edition of the Castle of Otranto, which the publishers have endeavoured to execute in a style of elegance corresponding to the estimation in which they hold the work, and the genius of the author.

It is doing injustice to Mr. Walpole's memory to allege, that all which he aimed at in the Castle of Otranto was 'the art of exciting surprise and horror';[21] or, in other words, the appeal to that secret and reserved feeling of love for the marvellous and supernatural, which occupies a hidden corner in almost every one's bosom. Were this all which he had attempted, the means by which he sought to attain his purpose might, with justice, be termed both clumsy and puerile. But Mr. Walpole's purpose was both more difficult of attainment, and more important when attained. It was his object to draw such a picture of domestic life and manners, during the feudal times, as might actually have existed, and to paint it checkered and agitated by the action of supernatural machinery, such as the superstition of the period received as matter of devout credulity. The natural parts of the narrative are so contrived, that they associate themselves with the marvellous occurrences; and, by the force of that association, render those *speciosa miracula*[22] striking and impressive, though our cooler reason admits their impossibility. Indeed to produce, in a well-cultivated mind, any portion of that surprise and fear which is founded on supernatural events, the frame and tenor of the whole story must be adjusted in perfect harmony with this main-spring of the interest. He, who, in early youth, has happened to pass a solitary night in one of the few ancient mansions which the fashion of more modern times has left undespoiled of their original furniture,[23] has probably experienced, that the gigantic and preposterous figures dimly visible in the defaced tapestry, the remote clang of the distant doors which divide him from living society, the deep darkness which involves the high and fretted roof of the apartment, the dimly-seen pictures of ancient knights, renowned for their valour, and perhaps for their crimes, the varied and indistinct sounds which disturb the silent desolation of a half-deserted mansion; and, to crown all, the feeling that carries us back to ages of feudal power and papal superstition, join together to excite a corresponding sensation of supernatural awe, if not of terror. It is in such situations, when superstition becomes contagious, that we listen with respect, and even with dread, to the legends which are our sport in the garish light of sun-shine, and amid the dissipating sights and sounds of every-day life. Now, it seems to have been Walpole's object to attain, by the minute accuracy of a fable, sketched with singular attention to the costume of the period in which the scene was laid, that same association which might prepare his reader's mind for the reception of prodigies congenial to the creed and feelings of the actors. His feudal tyrant, his distressed damsel, his resigned, yet dignified, churchman, – the Castle itself, with its feudal arrangements of dungeons, trap-doors, oratories, and galleries, the incidents of the trial, the chivalrous procession, and the combat; – in short, the scene, the performers, and action, so far as it is natural, form the accompaniments of his spectres and his miracles, and have the same effect on the mind of the reader that the appearance and drapery of such a chamber as we have described may produce upon that of a temporary inmate. This was a task which required no little learning, no ordinary degree of fancy, no common portion of genius, to execute. The association of which we have spoken is of a nature peculiarly delicate, and subject to be broken and disarranged. It is, for instance, almost impossible to build such a modern Gothic structure as shall impress us with the feelings we have endeavoured to describe. It may be grand, or it may be gloomy; it may excite magnificent or melancholy ideas; but it must fail in bringing forth the sensation of supernatural awe, connected with halls that have echoed to the sounds of remote generations, and have been pressed by the footsteps of those who have long since passed away. Yet Horace Walpole has attained in composition, what, as an architect, he must have felt beyond the power of his art. The remote and superstitious period in which his scene is laid, the art with which he has furnished forth its Gothic decorations, the sustained, and, in general, dignified tone of feudal manners, prepare us gradually for the favourable reception of prodigies, which, though they could not really have happened at any period, were consistent with the belief of all mankind at that time in which the action is placed. It was, therefore, the author's object, not merely to excite surprise and terror, by the introduction of supernatural agency, but to wind up the feelings of his reader till they became for a moment identified with those of a ruder age, which

Held each strange tale devoutly true.[24]

The difficulty of attaining this nice accuracy of delineation may be best estimated by comparing The Castle of Otranto with the less successful efforts of later writers; where, amid all their attempts to assume the tone of antique chivalry, something occurs in every chapter so decidedly incongruous, as at once reminds us of an ill-sustained masquerade, in which ghosts, knights-errant, magicians, and damsels gent, are all equipped in hired dresses from the same warehouse in Tavistock-street.

There is a remarkable particular in which Mr. Walpole's steps have been departed from by the most distinguished of his followers.

Romantic narrative is of two kinds, – that which, being in itself possible, may be matter of belief at any period; and that which, though held impossible by more enlightened ages, was yet consonant with the faith of earlier times. The subject of the Castle of Otranto is of the latter class. Mrs. Radcliffe, a name not to be mentioned without the high respect due to genius, has endeavoured to effect a compromise between those different styles of narrative, by referring her prodigies to an explanation, founded on natural causes,[25] in the latter chapters of her romances. To this improvement upon the Gothic romance there are so many objections, that we own ourselves inclined to prefer, as more simple and impressive, the narrative of Walpole, which details supernatural incidents as they would have been readily believed and received in the eleventh or twelfth century. In the first place, the reader feels indignant at discovering that he has been cheated into sympathy with terrors which are finally explained as having proceeded from some very simple cause; and the interest of a second reading is entirely destroyed by his having been admitted behind the scenes at the conclusion of the first. Secondly, the precaution of relieving our spirits from the influence of supposed supernatural terror, seems as unnecessary in a work of professed fiction, as that of the prudent Bottom, who proposed that the human face of the representative of his lion should appear from under his masque,[26] and acquaint the audience plainly that he was a man as other men, and nothing more than Snug the joiner.[27] Lastly, these substitutes for supernatural agency are frequently to the full as improbable as the machinery which they are introduced to explain away and to supplant. The reader, who is required to admit the belief of supernatural interference, understands precisely what is demanded of him; and, if he be a gentle reader, throws his mind into the attitude best adapted to humour the deceit which is presented for his entertainment, and grants, for the time of perusal, the premises on which the fable depends.[28] But if the author voluntarily binds himself to account for all the wondrous occurrences which he introduces, we are entitled to exact the explanation shall be natural, easy, ingenious, and complete. Every reader of such works must remember instances in which the explanation of mysterious circumstances in the narrative has proved equally, nay, even more incredible, than if they had been accounted for by the agency of supernatural beings. For the most incredulous must allow, that the interference of such agency is more possible than that an effect resembling it should be produced by an inadequate cause. But it is unnecessary to enlarge further on a part of the subject, which we have only mentioned to exculpate our author from the charge of using machinery more clumsy than his tale from its nature required. The bold assertion of the actual existence of phantoms and apparitions seems to us to harmonise much more naturally with the manners of feudal times, and to produce a more powerful effect upon the reader's mind, than any attempt to reconcile the superstitious credulity of feudal ages with the philosophic scepticism of our own, by referring those prodigies to the operation of fulminating powder, combined mirrors, magic lanthorns, trap-doors, squeaking trumpets, and such like apparitions of German phantasmagoria.

It cannot, however, be denied, that the character of the supernatural machinery in the Castle of Otranto is liable to objections. Its action and interference is rather too frequent, and presses too hard and constantly upon the same feelings in the reader's mind, to the hazard of diminishing the elasticity of the spring upon which it should operate. The fund of fearful sympathy which can be afforded by a modern reader to a tale of wonder, is much diminished by the present habits of life and mode of education. Our ancestors could wonder and thrill through all the mazes of an interminable metrical romance of fairy land, and of enchantment, the work perhaps of some

Prevailing poet, whose undoubting mind
Believed the magic wonders which he sung.[29]

But our habits and feelings and belief are different, and a transient, though vivid, impression is all that can be excited by a tale of wonder even in the most fanciful mind of the present day. By the too frequent recurrence of his prodigies, Mr. Walpole ran, perhaps, the greatest risk of awakening *la raison froide*, that cold common sense, which he justly deemed the greatest enemy of the effect which he hoped to produce. It may be added also, that the supernatural occurrences of the Castle of Otranto are brought forward into too strong day-light, and marked by an over degree of distinctness and accuracy of outline. A mysterious obscurity seems congenial at least, if not essential, to our ideas of disembodied spirits, and the gigantic limbs of the ghost of Alphonso, as described by the terrified domestics, are somewhat too distinct and corporeal to produce the feelings which their appearance is intended to excite. This fault, however, if it be one, is more than compensated by the high merit of many of the marvellous incidents in the romance. The descent of the picture of Manfred's ancestor, although it borders on extravagance, is finely introduced, and interrupts an interesting dialogue with striking effect. We have heard it observed, that the animated figure should rather have been a statue than a picture. We greatly doubt the justice of the criticism. The advantage of the colouring induces us decidedly to prefer Mr. Walpole's fiction to the proposed substitute. There are few who have not felt, at some period of their childhood, a sort of terror from the manner in which the eye of an ancient portrait appears to fix that of the spectator from every point of view. It is, perhaps, hypercritical to remark, (what, however, Walpole of all authors might have been expected to attend to), that the time assigned to the action, being about the eleventh century, is rather too early for the introduction of a full-length portait. The apparition of the skeleton hermit to the prince of Vicenza was long accounted a master-piece of the horrible; but of late the valley of Jehosophat[30] could hardly supply the dry bones necessary for the exhibition of similar spectres, so that injudicious and repeated imitation has, in some degree, injured the effect of its original model. What is most striking in the Castle of Otranto, is the manner in which the various prodigious appearances, bearing each upon the other, and all upon the accomplishment of the ancient prophecy, denouncing the ruin of the house of Manfred, gradually prepare us for the grand catastrophe. The moon-light vision of Alphonso dilated to immense magnitude, the astonished group of spectators in the front, and the shattered ruins of the castle in the back-ground, is briefly and sublimely described. We know no passage of similar merit, unless it be the apparition of Fadzean in an ancient Scottish poem.[31]

That part of the romance which depends upon human feelings and agency, is conducted with the dramatic talent which afterwards was so conspicuous in the Mysterious Mother. The persons are indeed rather generic than individual, but this was in a degree necessary to the plan, calculated rather to exhibit a general view of society and manners during the time which the author's imagination loved to contemplate, than the more minute shades and discriminating points of particular characters. But the actors in the romance are strikingly drawn, with bold outlines becoming the age and nature of the story. Feudal tyranny was, perhaps, never better exemplified, than in the character of Manfred. He has the courage, the art, the duplicity, the ambition of a barbarous chieftain of the dark ages, yet with touches of remorse and natural feeling, which preserve some sympathy for him when his pride is quelled, and his race extinguished. The pious monk, and the patient Hippolita, are well contrasted with this selfish and tyrannical prince. Theodore is the juvenile hero of a romantic tale, and Matilda has more interesting sweetness than usually belongs to its heroine. As the character of Isabella is studiously kept down, in order to relieve that of the daughter of Manfred, few readers are pleased with the concluding insinuation, that she became at length the bride of Theodore. This is in some degree a departure from the rules of chivalry; and, however natural an occurrence in common life, rather injures the magic illusions of romance. In other respects, making allowance for the extraordinary incidents of a dark and tempestuous age, the story, so far as within the course of natural events, is happily detailed, its progress is uniform, its events interesting and well combined, and the conclusion grand, tragical, and affecting.

The style of the Castle of Otranto is pure and correct English of the earlier and more classical standard. Mr. Walpole rejected, upon taste and principle, those heavy though powerful auxiliaries which Dr Johnson imported from the Latin language, and which have since proved to many a luckless weight, who has essayed to use them, as unmanageable as the gauntlets of Eryx,

————————————— et pondus et ipsa
Huc illuc vinclorum immensa volumina versat.[32]

Neither does the purity of Mr. Walpole's language, and the simplicity of his narrative, admit that luxuriant, florid, and high-varnished landscape painting with which Mrs Radcliffe often adorned, and not unfrequently incumbered, her kindred romances. Description, for its own sake, is scarcely once attempted in the Castle of Otranto; and if authors would consider how very much this restriction tends to realise narrative, they might be tempted to abridge at least the showy and wordy exuberance of a style fitter for poetry than prose. It is for the dialogue that Walpole reserves his strength; and it is remarkable how, while conducting his moral agents with all the art of a modern dramatist, he adheres to the sustained tone of chivalry, which marks the period of the action. This is not attained by patching his narrative or dialogue with glossarial terms, or antique phraseology, but by taking care to exclude all that can awaken modern associations. In the one case, his romance would have resembled a modern dress, preposterously decorated with antique ornaments; in its present shape, he has retained the form of the ancient armour, but not its rust and cobwebs. In illustration of what is above stated, we refer the reader to the first interview of Manfred with the prince of Vicenza, where the manners and language of chivalry are finely painted, as well as the perturbation of conscious guilt confusing itself in attempted exculpation, even before a mute accuser. The characters of the inferior domestics have been considered as not bearing a proportion sufficiently dignified to the rest of the story. But this is a point on which the author has pleaded his own cause fully in the original prefaces.

We have only to add, in conclusion to these desultory remarks, that if Horace Walpole, who led the way in this new species of literary composition, has been surpassed by some of his followers in diffuse brilliancy of description, and perhaps in the art of detaining the mind of the reader in a state of feverish and anxious suspence, through a protracted and complicated narrative, more will yet remain with him than the single merit of originality and invention. The applause due to chastity and precision of style, to a happy combination of supernatural agency with human interest, to a tone of feudal manners and language, sustained by characters strongly drawn and well discriminated, and to unity of action producing scenes alternately of interest and of grandeur; – the applause, in fine, which cannot be denied to him who can excite the passions of fear and pity, must be awarded to the author of the Castle of Otranto.

13. John Dunlop, *The History of Fiction . . . from the Earliest Greek Romances to the Novels of the Present Age*, 3 vols. (London: Longman, Hurst, Rees, Orme & Brown, 1814), Vol. 3, pp. 380–82. Extract.

It is perhaps singular, that emotions so powerful [as fear and superstition] should not have been excited by fiction at an earlier period; for this species of composition cannot be traced higher than the Castle of Otranto, by Horace Walpole . . .

The work is declared by Mr Walpole to be an attempt to blend the ancient romance and modern novel; but, if by the ancient romance be meant the tales of chivalry, the extravagance of the Castle of Otranto has no resemblance to their machinery. What analogy have skulls or skeletons – sliding pannels – damp vaults – trap-doors – and dismal apartments, to the tented fields of chivalry and its airy enchantments?

It has been much doubted, whether the Castle of Otranto was seriously or comically intended; if seriously, it is a most feeble attempt to excite awe or terror; an immense helmet is a wretched instrument for inspiring supernatural dread, and the machinery is so violent that it destroys the effect it was intended to raise.[1] A sword which requires a hundred men to lift it – blood dropping from the nose of a statue – the hero imprisoned in a helmet, resemble not a first and serious attempt at a new species of composition, but look as if devised in ridicule of preceding extravagance, as Don Quixote[2] was written to expose the romances of chivalry, by an aggravated representation of their absurdities.

14. Anser Pen-dragon, ed. [Samuel William Henry Ireland],
   Scribbleomania; or, The Printer's Devil's Polichronicon.
   A Sublime Poem (London: Sherwood, Neely & Jones, 1815),
   pp. 136–8. Extract.

Romancers stand forth: – novel scribes straight arise,
Whose furor consists in retailing *huge lies.*
In mazes monastic of *Strawberry Hill,*
Sir Horace first issu'd the marvellous pill;
His brain teeming hot with the chivalrous rant, O!
Engender'd the *Giant,* and *Castle Otranto:*[1]
A stupid, incongruous, blundering tale,
The *rank* of whose writer[2] alone caus'd its sale;
Since, had Leadenhall's *Lane* seen the work, I'll be bound,
To possess it he would not have proffer'd five pound.[3]

15. William Hazlitt, *Lectures on the Comic Writers* (1819),
   The Complete Works of William Hazlitt, ed. P. P. Howe
(London and Toronto: J. M. Dent, 1930–33), Vol. 6, p. 127. Extract.

The Castle of Otranto (which is supposed to have led the way to this style of writing [that is, the novels of Ann Radcliffe and Matthew Lewis]) is, to my notion, dry, meagre, and without effect. It is done upon false principles of taste. The great hand and arm, which are thrust into the court-yard, and remain there all day long, are the pasteboard machinery of a pantomime; they shock the senses, and have no purchase upon the imagination. They are a matter-of-fact impossibility; a fixture, and no longer a phantom. *Quod sic mihi ostendis, incredulus odi.*[1] By realising the chimeras of ignorance and fear, begot upon shadows and dim likenesses, we take away the very grounds of credulity and superstition; and, as in other cases, by facing out the imposture, betray the secret of the contempt and laughter of the spectators.

16. Lord Byron, Preface to *Marino Faliero: Doge of Venice*
(London: John Murray, 1821), pp. ix–xxi. Extract.

It is the fashion to underrate Horace Walpole, first, because he was a nobleman, and secondly, because he was a gentleman; but to say nothing of the composition of his incomparable letters, and of the *Castle of Otranto*, he is the 'Ultimus Romanorum,'[1] the author of the *Myterious Mother*, a tragedy of the highest order, and not a puling love-play. He is the father of the first romance, and of the last tragedy in our language, and surely worthy of a higher place than any living writer, be he who he may.

17. Thomas Babington Macaulay, Review of *Letters of Horace Walpole, Earl of Orford, to Sir Horace Mann, Edinburgh Review* 58
(October 1833), pp. 227–58. Extract.

The faults of Horace Walpole's head and heart are indeed sufficiently glaring. His writings, it is true, rank as high among the delicacies of intellectual epicures as the Strasburgh pies among the dishes described in the *Almanack des Gourmands*. But, as the *pâté-de-foie-gras* owes its excellences to the diseases of the wretched animal which furnishes it, and would be good for nothing if it were not made of livers preternaturally swollen, so none but an unhealthy and disorganized mind could have produced such literary luxuries as the works of Walpole.

He was, unless we have formed a very erroneous judgment of his character, the most eccentric, the most artificial, the most fastidious, the most capricious, of men. His mind was a bundle of inconsistent whims and affectations. His features were covered by mask within mask. When the outer disguise of obvious affectation was removed, you were still as far as ever from seeing the real man. He played innumerable parts, and over-acted them all. When he talked misanthropy, he out-Timoned Timon.[1] When he talked philanthropy, he left

Howard at an immeasurable distance. He scoffed at Courts, and kept a chronicle of their most trifling scandal, – at Society, and was blown about by its slightest veerings of opinion, – at Literary fame, and left fair copies of his private letters, with copious notes, to be published after his decease, – at Rank, and never for a moment forgot he was an Honourable, – at the practice of Entail,[2] and tasked the ingenuity of conveyancers to tie up his villa in the strictest settlement.

The conformation of his mind was such, that whatever was little, seemed to him great, and whatever was great, seemed to him little. In every thing in which he busied himself, – in the fine arts, in literature, in public affairs, – he was drawn by some strange attraction from the great to the little, and from the useful to the odd. Serious business was a trifle to him, and trifles were his serious business. To chat with blue-stockings, – to write little copies of complimentary verses on little occasions, – to super-intend a private press, – to preserve from natural decay the perishable topics of Ranelagh and White's, to record divorces and bets, Miss Chudleigh's[3] absurdities, and George Selwyn's[4] good sayings, – to decorate a grotesque house with pie-crust battlements, – to procure rare engravings and antique chimney-boards, – to match odd gauntlets, – to lay out a maze of walks within five acres of ground, – these were the grave employments of his long life. From these he turned to politics as an amusement. After the labours of the print-shop and the auction-room, he unbent his mind in the House of Commons. And, having indulged in the recreation of making laws and voting millions, he returned to more important pursuits, – to researches after Queen Mary's comb, Wolsey's red hat, the pipe which King William struck into the flank of Sorrel.

The politics in which he took the keenest interest, were politics scarcely deserving of the name. The growlings of George the Second, – the flirtations of Princess Emily with the Duke of Grafton, – the amours of Prince Frederic and Lady Middlesex, – the squabbles between Gold Stick and the Master of Buckhounds, – the disagreements between the tutors of Prince George, – these matters engaged almost all the attention which Walpole could spare from matters more important still, – from bidding for Zinckes and Petitots, – from cheapening fragments of tapestry, and handles of old lances, – from joining bits of painted glass, and from setting up memorials to departed cats and dogs. While he was fetching and carrying the gossip of Kensington Palace and Carlton House, he fancied that he was engaged in politics, and when he recorded that gossip, he fancied he was writing history.

[Macaulay then describes Walpole's Whig politics as mischievous and superficial, and argues that he was really a worshipper of the aristocracy.]

He had, it is plain, an uneasy consciousness of the frivolity of his favourite pursuits; and this consciousness produced one of the most diverting of his ten thousand affectations. His busy idleness – his indifference to matters which the world generally regards as important – his passion for trifles – he thought fit to dignify with the name of philosophy. He spoke of himself as a man whose equanimity was proof to ambitious hopes and fears, who had learned to rate power, wealth, and fame, at their true value, and whom the conflict of parties, the rise and fall of statesmen, the ebbs and flows of public opinion, moved only to a smile of mingled compassion and disdain. It was owing to the peculiar elevation of his character that he cared about a lath and plaster pinnacle more than about the Middlesex election, and about a miniature of Grammont more than about the American Revolution. Pitt and Murray might talk themselves hoarse about trifles. But questions of government and war were too insignificant to detain a mind which was occupied in recording the scandal of club-rooms and the whispers of the back-stairs, and which was even capable of selecting and disposing chairs of ebony and shields of rhinoceros-skin.

One of his innumerable whims was an extreme dislike to be considered as a man of letters. Not that he was indifferent to literary fame. Far from it. Scarcely any writer has ever troubled himself so much about the appearance which his works were to make before posterity. But he had set his heart on incompatible objects. He wished to be a celebrated author, and yet to be a mere idle-gentleman – one of those epicurean gods of the earth who do nothing at all, and who pass their existence in the contemplation of their own perfections. He did not like to have any thing in common with the wretches who lodged in the little courts behind St. Martin's Church, and stole out on Sundays to dine with their bookseller. He avoided the society of authors. He spoke with lordly contempt of the most distinguished among them. He tried to find out some way of writing books, as M. Jourdain's father sold cloth, without derogating from his character of *Gentilhomme*. [The essay provides examples of these attitudes and criticizes his judgments of contemporary writers before moving on to discuss relations between England and France.]

Walpole had neither hopes nor fears. Though the most Frenchified English writer of the eighteenth century, he troubled himself little about the portents which were daily to be discerned in the French literature of his time. While the most eminent Frenchmen were studying with enthusiastic delight English politics and English philosophy, he was studying as intently the gossip of the old courts of France. The fashions and scandal of Versailles and Marli – fashions and scandal a hundred years old – occupied him infinitely more than a great moral revolution which was taking place in his sight. He took a prodigious interest in every noble sharper, whose vast volume of wig, and infinite length of riband[5] had figured at the dressing or at the tucking up of

Louis XIV, and of every profligate woman of quality who had carried her train of lovers backward and forward from king to parliament, and from parliament to king, during the wars of the *Fronde*. These were the people of whom he treasured up the smallest memorial, of whom he loved to hear the most trifling anecdote, and for whose likenesses he would have given any price. Of the great French writers of his own time, Montesquieu[6] is the only one of whom he speaks with enthusiasm. And even of Montesquieu he speaks with less enthusiasm than of that abject thing, Crebillon the younger,[7] a scribbler as licentious as Louvet,[8] and as dull as Rapin.[9] A man must be strangely constituted who can take interest in pendantic journals of the blockades laid by the Duke of A. to the hearts of the Marquise de B. and the Comtesse de C. This trash Walpole extols in language sufficiently high for the merits of *Don Quixote*. He wished to possess a likeness of Crebillon, and Liotard,[10] the first painter of miniatures when living, was employed to preserve the features of the profligate twaddler. The admirer of the *Sopha*, and the *Lettres Athéniennes*,[11] had little respect to spare for the men who were then at the head of French literature. He kept carefully out of their way. He tried to keep other people from paying them any attention. He could not deny Voltaire[12] and Rousseau[13] were clever men; but he took every opportunity of depreciating them. Of D'Alembert[14] he spoke with contempt, which, when the intellectual powers of the two men are compared, seems exquisitely ridiculous. D'Alembert complained that he was accused of having written Walpole's squib against Rousseau.[15] 'I hope,' says Walpole, 'that nobody will attribute D'Alembert's works to me.' He was in little danger.

It is impossible to deny, however, that Walpole's works have real merit, and merit of a very rare, though not of a very high kind. Sir Joshua Reynolds[16] used to say, that though nobody would for a moment compare Claude[17] to Raphael,[18] there would be another Raphael before there was another Claude. And we own that we expect to see fresh Humes[19] and fresh Burkes[20] before we again fall in with that peculiar combination of moral and intellectual qualities to which the writings of Walpole owe their extraordinary popularity.

It is easy to describe him by negatives. He had not a creative imagination. He had not a pure taste. He was not a great reasoner. There is indeed scarcely any writer in whose works it would be possible to find so many contradictory judgments, so many sentences of extravagant nonsense. Nor was it only in his familiar correspondence that he wrote in his flighty and inconsistent manner; but in long and elaborate books – in books repeatedly transcribed and intended for the public eye. [Provides several examples of contradictions.]

Of such a writer it is scarcely necessary to say, that his works are destitute of every charm which is derived from elevation or from tenderness of sentiment.

When he chose to be humane and magnanimous – for he sometimes, by way of variety, tried this affectation – he overdid his part most ludicrously. None of his many disguises sat so awkwardly upon him. For example, he tells us that he did not choose to be intimate with Mr. Pitt;[21] – and why? Because Mr. Pitt had been among the persecutors of his father; or because, as he repeatedly assures us, Mr. Pitt was a disagreeable man in private life? Not at all; but because Mr. Pitt was too fond of war, and was great with too little reluctance. Strange, that a habitual scoffer like Walpole, should imagine that this could impose on the dullest reader! If Moliére had put such a speech into the mouth of Tartuffe, we should have said that the fiction was unskillful, and that Orgon[22] could not have been such a fool as to be taken in by it. Of the twenty-six years during which Walpole sat in Parliament, thirteen were years of war. Yet he did not, during all those thirteen years, utter a single word, or give a single vote, tending to peace. His most intimate friend – the only friend, indeed, to whom he appears to have been sincerely attached – Conway – was a soldier, was fond of his profession, and was perpetually intreating Mr. Pitt to give him employment. In this, Walpole saw nothing but what was admirable. Conway was a hero for soliciting the command of expeditions, which Mr. Pitt was a monster for sending out.

What then is the charm, the irresistible charm of Walpole's writings? It consists, we think, in the act of amusing without exciting. He never convinces the reason, nor fills the imagination, nor touches the heart; but he keeps the mind of the reader constantly attentive, and constantly entertained. He had a strange ingenuity peculiarly his own, – an ingenuity which appeared in all that he did, – in his building, in his gardening, in his upholstery, in the matter and in the manner of his writings. If we were to adopt the classification – not a very accurate classification – which Akenside has given to the pleasures of the Imagination,[23] we should say, that with the Sublime and the Beautiful Walpole had nothing to do, but that the third province, the Odd, was his peculiar domain. The motto which he prefixed to his *Catalogue of Royal and Noble Authors*, might have been inscribed with perfect propriety over the door of every room in his house, and on the titlepage of every one of his books. 'Dove diavolo, Messer Ludovico, avete pigliate tante coglionere?'[24] In his villa, every compartment is a museum; every piece of furniture is a curiosity; there is something strange in the form of a shovel; there is a long story belonging to the bell-rope. We wander among a profusion of rarities, of trifling intrinsic value, but so quaint in fashion, or connected with such remarkable names and events that they may well detain our attention for a moment. A moment is enough. Some new relic, some new unique, some new carved work, some new enamel, is forthcoming in an instant. One cabinet of trinkets is no sooner closed than another is opened. It is the same with Walpole's writings. It is not in their utility, it is not in their beauty, that their attraction lies. They are to the works of great historians and poets, what Strawberry Hill is to the museum of Sir Hans Sloane,[25] or to the Gallery of Florence. Walpole is constantly showing us things, – not of very great value indeed, – yet things which we are pleased to see, and which we can see nowhere else. They are baubles; but they are made curiosities either by his grotesque workmanship, or by some association belonging to them. His style is one of those peculiar styles by which every body is attracted, and which nobody can safely venture to imitate. He is a mannerist whose manner has become perfectly easy to him. His affectation is so habitual, and so universal, that it can hardly be called affectation. The affectation is the essence of the man. It pervades all his thoughts and all his expressions. If it were taken away, nothing would be left. He coins new words, distorts the senses of old words, and twists sentences into forms which would make grammarians stare. But all this he does, not only with an air of ease, but as if he could not help doing it. His wit was, in its essential properties, of the same kind with that of Cowley[26] and Donne.[27] Like theirs, it consisted in an exquisite perception of points of analogy, and points of contrast too subtile for common observation. Like them, Walpole perpertually startles us by the ease with which he yokes together ideas between which there would seem, at first sight, to be no connexion. But he did not, like them, affect the gravity of a lecture, and draw his illustrations from the laboratory and from the schools. His tone was light and fleering;[28] his topics were the topics of the club and the ballroom. And therefore his strange combinations, and far-fetched allusions, though very closely resembling those which tire us to death in the poems of the time of Charles the First, are read with pleasure constantly new.

No man who has written so much is so seldom tiresome. In his books there are scarcely any of those passages which, in our school days, we used to call *skip*. Yet he often wrote on subjects that are generally considered as dull, – on subjects which men of great talents have in vain endeavoured to render popular. When we compare the *Historic Doubts* about Richard the Third with Whitaker's and Chalmers' books[29] on a far more interesting question, – the character of Mary Queen of Scots; – when we compare the *Anecdotes of Painting* with Nichols's *Anecdotes*,[30] or even with Mr. D'Israeli's *Quarrels of Authors* and *Calamities of Authors*,[31] we at once see Walpole's superiority, not in industry, not in learning, not in accuracy, not in logical power, but in the art of writing what people will like to read. He rejects all but the attractive parts of his subject. He keeps only what is in itself amusing, or what can be made so by the artifice of his diction. The coarser morsels of antiquarian learning he abandons to others; and sets out an entertainment worthy of a Roman epicure, – an entertainment consisting of nothing but delicacies, – the brains of singing birds, the roe of mullets, the sunny halves of peaches. This, we think, is the great merit of his 'Romance.' There is little skill in the delineation of the characters. Manfred is as commonplace a tyrant, Jerome as commonplace a confessor, Theodore as commonplace a young gentleman, Isabella and Matilda as commonplace a pair of young ladies, as are to be found in any of the thousand Italian castles in which condottieri have revelled, or in which imprisoned duchesses have pined. We cannot say that we much admire the big man whose sword is dug up in one quarter of the globe, whose helmet drops from the clouds in another, and who, after clattering and rustling for some days, ends by kicking the house down. But the story, whatever its value may be, never flags for a single moment. There are no digressions, or unseasonable descriptions, or long speeches. Every sentence carries the action forward. The excitement is constantly renewed. Absurd as is the machinery, and insipid as are the human actors, no reader probably ever thought the book dull.

Walpole's *Letters* are generally considered as his best performances, and we think, with reason. His faults are far less offensive to us in his correspondence than in his books. His wild, absurd, and ever-changing opinions about men and things are easily pardoned in familiar letters. His bitter, scoffing, depreciating disposition, does not show itself in so unmitigated a manner as in his *Memoirs*. A writer of letters must be civil and friendly to his correspondent at least, if to no other person.

He loved letter-writing, and had evidently studied it as an art. It was, in truth, the very kind of writing for such a man – for a man very ambitious to rank among wits, yet nervously afraid that, while obtaining the reputation of a wit, he might lose caste as a gentleman. There was nothing vulgar in writing a letter. Not even Ensign Northerton,[32] not even the Captain described in Hamilton's Baron – Walpole, though the author of many quartos, had some feelings in common with those gallant officers – would have denied that a gentleman might sometimes correspond with a friend. Whether Walpole bestowed much labour on the composition of his letters, it is impossible to judge from internal evidence. There are passages which seem perfectly unstudied. But the appearance of ease may be the effect of labour. There are passages which have a very artificial air. But they may have been produced without effort by a mind of which the natural ingenuity had been improved into morbid quickness by constant exercise. We are never sure that we see him as he was. We are never sure that what appears to be nature is not an effect of art. We are never sure that what appears to be art is not merely habit which has become second nature. [Rest of essay discusses Robert Walpole.]

Notes

4. Review of *The Castle of Otranto* (2nd edition),
Monthly Review 32 (May 1765), p. 394.

1. Reviewer's Note: 'From the initials, H. W., in this edition, and the beauty of the impression, there is no room to doubt that it is the production of Strawberry Hill.'
2. *incredulus odi*: Disbelieving revulsion.
3. *cæcum vulgus*: Blind multitude.

6. Voltaire [François-Marie Arouet] to Horace Walpole (15 July 1768);
in *Monthly Mirror* 19 (March 1805).

1. *Voltaire . . . to Horace Walpole (15 July 1768)*: In *Short Notes of the life of Horatio Walpole* (printed in *Correspondence*, Vol. 13, pp. 3–51), Walpole notes: 'June 20, received a letter from Voltaire desiring my *Historic Doubts*. I sent them, and *The Castle of Otranto*, that he might see the preface of which I told him. He did not like it, but returned a very civil answer, defending his opinion. I replied [27 July 1768] with more civility, but dropping the subject, not caring to enter into a controversy; especially on a matter of opinion; on which, whether we were right or wrong, all France would be on his side, and all England on mine' (p. 43).
2. *Locke*: John Locke (1632–1704), English philosopher whose *Essay Concerning Human Understanding* (1689) and *Two Treatises of Government* (1690) laid the foundations for the Enlightenment in Britain and France.
3. *Addison*: Joseph Addison (1672–1719), English essayist, poet, travel-writer and dramatist, best known for his *Remarks on Several Parts of Italy* (1705) and for his involvement with Richard Steele in the periodicals the *Tatler* (1709–11) and the *Spectator* (1711–12). Addison wrote a number of plays in the first decades of the eighteenth century. Of these, his *Cato* (1713) was unquestionably his most successful and influential; his comedy written with Steele, *The Tender Husband* (1705), and his opera *Rosamonde* (1707) also were revived during the eighteenth century with success.
4. *Lopez de Vega*: Lope de Vega (1562–1635), Spanish dramatist and author of approximately 1,800 plays and several hundred shorter pieces. He first established himself as a playwright in Madrid through his 'comedias', the tragicomic social dramas for which he is best known. Cervantes' description of him as 'a prodigy of nature' closely resembles Voltaire's description of Shakespeare in *Letters Concerning the English Nation* (1733).
5. *Caldéron*: Pedro Calderón de la Barca (1600–1681), Spanish dramatist and poet generally regarded as Lope de Vega's successor. His best-known plays are *El médico de*

su honra (*The Surgeon of His Honour*, 1635), *La vida es sueño* (*Life is a Dream*, 1635), *El alcalde de Zalamea* (*The Mayor of Zalamea*, *c.* 1640) and *La Hija del aire* (*The Daughter of the Air*, 1653).

6. *Sophocles*: Sophocles (*c.* 496–406 BC), Greek tragedian and author of 123 dramas, the best known of which is *Œdipus the King*. Only seven of his plays survive in their entirety. His formal artistry and attention to issues of character have made him the most critically acclaimed of the classical Greek dramatists.

7. *mère sotte*: Literally, 'foolish mother'.

8. *Moliere*: Jean-Baptiste de Molière, originally Jean-Baptiste Poquelin (1622–73), French actor and dramatist whose comedies established him as one of the most popular and critically acclaimed French playwrights. His best-known plays are *L'École des femmes* (*The School for Wives*, 1662), *Le Tartuffe* (*The Impostor*, 1664), which was banned until revised as *Le Misanthrope* (1666), and *L'Avare* (*The Miser*, 1668). His theoretical views on comedy appeared in *La Critique de L'École des femmes* (1663).

9. *George Dandin*: Molière's play *George Dandin*, performed in 1668.

10. *Horace . . . Art of Poetry*: Quintus Horatius Flaccus (65–8 BC), Roman lyric poet and satirist. His *Satires* were published in 35 BC, and his *Epodes* and a second book of *Satires* appeared in 30–29 BC. His *Ars Poetica* (written *c.* 19 BC) consists of thirty maxims for young poets, and was generally cited in the eighteenth century as an authority for issues of style and literary purpose.

11. *Boileau . . . Art of Poetry*: Nicolas Boileau-Despréaux (1636–1701), French satirist and leading literary critic of his day. He is best known for his mock-heroic epic *Le Lutrin* (1667) and his *L'Art poétique* (1674), which set out rules for poetic composition in the classical tradition.

12. *Regnard*: Jean-François Regnard (1655–1709), French dramatist and successor to Molière, author of *La Sérénade* (1694), *Le Joueur* (*The Gamester*, 1696) and *Le Légataire universel* (*The Heir*, 1708). His comedies are similar in their raucous nature and depiction of decadent societies to those of Aphra Behn, Congreve and Vanbrugh.

13. *Demosthenes*: Demosthenes (384–322 BC), celebrated Greek orator and champion of democracy who rallied the people of Athens to oppose Philip of Macedon and his son Alexander the Great.

14. *Euripides*: Euripides (484–406 BC), Greek dramatist, usually cited with Aeschylus and Sophocles as the most important of the Athenian tragedians. Of the nineteen plays of his that survive, the best known are *Medea* (431 BC), *Hippolytus* (428 BC), *Electra* (418 BC) and *Iphigenia at Aulis* (406 BC).

15. Translator's Note: 'Voltaire's partiality to England is frequently evidenced in his writings. Voyez la Henriade, Chant. 1.'

16. *The Siege of Calais*: Voltaire refers here to Claudine Alexandrine Guérin de Tencin's historical novel *Le Siége de Calais, nouvelle historique*, 2 vols. (La Haye, 1739). I have not been able to locate the sources for 'Don Japhel of Armenia' and 'Jodolet'.

17. *Almost all Dryden's works are in rhyme*: John Dryden (1631–1700), English critic, dramatist, and poet. Esteemed now for public poems like *Astraea Redux* (1660) and *Annus Mirabilis* (1667) and for verse satires like *MacFleckno* (composed 1678) and *Absolom and Achitophel* (1681), Dryden made much of his reputation in the seventeenth century as a writer of heroic verse tragedies, the most successful of which were *The Indian Queen* (1664), *The Indian Emperour* (1665), and *The Conquest of Granada* (1670).

18. *Cimna, Athalia, Phædra, and Iphigenia*: By 'Cimna', the *Monthly Mirror*'s translator appears to mean Thomas Corneille, *Cinna où la clemence d'Auguste*, published in Paris in 1643. The second, third and fourth plays mentioned are by Racine, and were published in 1691, 1677 and 1675, respectively. In *Short Notes of the life of Horatio Walpole* (*Correspondence*, Vol. 13, pp. 3–51), Walpole notes 'In the summer of 1744 I wrote a parody of a scene in Corneille's *Cinna*; the interlocutors, Mr Pelham, Mr Arundel and Mr Selwyn' (p. 14). The MS is unpublished, and part of the Waldegrave MSS, Vol. 2, pp. 124–34.

19. *Pope*: Alexander Pope (1688–1744), English poet best known for his satirical works *An Essay on Criticism* (1711), *The Rape of the Lock* (1712–14), *The Dunciad* (1728–41) and *An Essay on Man* (1733–4).

20. *Milton*: John Milton (1608–74), after Shakespeare probably the most acclaimed of English writers, best known for his sonnets and his *Paradise Lost* (1667), *Paradise Regained* (1671) and *Samson Agonistes* (1671). He was also a noted historian and political writer during the Puritan Commonwealth, and served as the secretary for foreign languages under Oliver Cromwell's government.

21. *red rose and your white rose*: That is, the houses of Lancaster and of York.

7. Clara Reeve, Preface to *The Old English Baron*, 2nd edition (London, 1778).

1. *2nd edition*: Reeve's novel was originally published without her Preface as *The Champion of Virtue* in 1777.

2. *the ancient Romances, which are only Epics in prose*: Reeve's full treatment of this argument appeared in *The Progress of Romance*, 2 vols. (London: G. G. J. & J. Robinson, 1785), Vol. I, pp. 8–44.

3. *keeping, as in painting*: The maintenance of the proper relation between the representations of nearer and more distant objects in a picture; the maintenance of harmony of composition.

9. Ann Yearsley, 'To the Honourable H[orac]e W[alpol]e,
on Reading *The Castle of Otranto* (December 1784)',
Poems on Several Occasions (London: T. Cadell, 1785).

1. *Manes*: The deified souls of departed ancestors; the spirit of a departed person, considered as an object of homage or reverence, or as demanding to be propitiated by vengeance.

2. *He'd cramp my bones*: See Shakespeare, *The Tempest*, I.ii.325–30.

3. *Morpheus*: Ovid's name for the god of dreams, the son of sleep (often mistaken for the god of sleep).

10. Thomas James Mathias, *The Pursuits of Literature: A Satirical
Poem in Four Dialogues* (London: T. Beckett, 1798).

1. Mathias's Note: 'The late ingenious Earl of Orford, Horace Walpole. The spirit of enquiry, which he introduced was rather frivolous, though pleasing, and his Otranto Ghosts have propagated their species with unequalled fecundity. The spawn is in every novel shop.'

11. Anna Letitia Barbauld, 'Horace Walpole', *The British Novelists*,
ed. A. L. Barbauld, 50 vols. (London: F. C. & J. Rivington et al., 1810).

1. *Mrs. Radcliffe's productions*: Ann Radcliffe (1764–1823), English novelist and the most acclaimed writer of Gothic fiction of her time. Her *Castles of Athlin and Dunbayne* (1789) and *A Sicilian Romance* (1790) appeared anonymously, as did her vastly successful *Romance of the Forest* (1791). The success of this third work convinced her to claim authorship for it in its second edition, as well as allowing her to command large sums for her subsequent works, *The Mysteries of Udolpho* (1794) and *The Italian* (1797). At the turn of the nineteenth century she was without question the most popular and influential novelist in England.

2. *'supped full with horrors'*: The reference is to Shakespeare, *Macbeth*, V.v.13.

3. *His little jeu d'esprit upon Rousseau*: Walpole wrote 'Le Roi de Prusse à Monsieur Rousseau' on 23 December 1765, and the letter circulated in Paris as early as 28 December 1765. Signed in the name of the King of Prussia, it offered Rousseau asylum while at the same time satirizing his fears of persecution. The letter was soon printed in the *St James's Chronicle*, 1–3 April 1766; Rousseau wrote an indignant letter to the editor of that paper in response, which was printed on 8–10 April. Walpole's ruse played a

significant role in the rift between Rousseau and David Hume, about which Hume and Rousseau both published accounts in 1766. Walpole's own account of the affair appears in his *Narrative of what passed relative to the Quarrel of Mr. David Hume and Jean Jacques Rousseau, as far as Mr. Horace Walpole was concerned with it*, written 13 September 1767 and published in Vol. 4 of his *Works of Horatio Walpole, Earl of Orford*.

4. *Count Hamilton*: Anthony Hamilton (*c.* 1646–1720), English courtier and author of *Mémoires du Comte de Grammont*, he also wrote four 'Contes' designed to satirize the stories of the marvellous that were fashionable in the early eighteenth century. In her essay Barbauld most likely refers to Hamilton's 'Le Bélier', which was first published in Paris in 1730 and features a contest between a prince and a giant for the daughter of a druid.

5. *Gesta Romanorum*: Barbauld most likely means *Gesta Romanorum: containing fifty-eight remarkable histories originally (as 'tis said) collected from the Roman Records* (London: G. Conyers, 1722).

6. *Cases of Conscience*: Jeremy Taylor, *Ductor Dubitantium or the Rule of Conscience in all her generall measures; serving as a great instrument for the determination of Cases of Conscience*, 2 vols. (London: R. Royston, 1660).

12. Walter Scott, Introduction to *The Castle of Otranto*
(Edinburgh: James Ballantyne, 1811).

1. *Spenser's fairy web*: That is, *The Faerie Queene* (1590–96), the long allegorical poem by Edmund Spenser (*c.* 1552–99).

2. *Don Belianis*: Scott most likely means the Italian *Libro Primero, del valeroso e inuencible principe don Belianis de Grecia: hijo del Emperador don Belanio de Grecia* (Medina del campo: D. Despinosa, 1564), which was reprinted frequently during the sixteenth century. In eighteenth-century England it survived as a chapbook, *The History of Don Belianis of Greece; containing an account of his many wonderful exploits, and his obtaining the Soldan of Babylon's Daughter in marriage* (London, *c.* 1760).

3. *Mirror of Knighthood*: That is, M[argaret] T[yler], *The Mirrour of Princely Deedes and Knighthood: wherein is shewed the worthinesse of the Knight of the Sunne, and his brother Rosicleer . . . with the strange loue of the beautifull and excellent Princesse Briana . . . Now newly translated out of Spanish into our vulgar English tongue* (London: Thomas East, 1578). The original Spanish title for the book is *Espejo de Principes y Cavalleros*. The earliest copy in the British Library is dated 1583.

4. *Calprenede*: Gaultier de Coste, seigneur de la Calprenéde (*c.* 1610–63), French author of sentimental and historical romances immensely popular in seventeenth-century France, best known for his *Cassandre* (1642–5), *Cléopâtre* (1647–58) and *Faramond* (1661–70).

5. *Scuderi*: Madeleine de Scudéri (1607–1701), French author of historical romances, best known for her *Artamène ou le grand Cyrus* (*Artamenes or the Grand Cyrus*, 1649–53) and *Clélie* (1654–60).

6. *Le Sage*: Alain-René Le Sage (1668–1747), prolific French satirical dramatist and author of *Histoire de Gil Blas de Santillane* (1715–35), one of the earliest realist fictions and influential in making the picaresque novel fashionable in Europe.

7. *Richardson*: Samuel Richardson (1689–1761), English epistolary novelist whose *Pamela* (1740), *Clarissa* (1747–8) and *History of Sir Charles Grandison* (1753–4) are considered foundational realist fictions.

8. *Fielding*: Henry Fielding (1707–54), English dramatist who became a novelist only after the passing of the Licensing Act in 1737, which legislated that all new plays had to be approved and licensed by the Lord Chamberlain before production. His first fiction, *An Apology for the Life of Miss Shamela Andrews* (1741), was a heavily parodic and satirical response to Samuel Richardson's *Pamela*. He is best known for the novels that followed: *Joseph Andrews* (1741), *The Life of Mr Jonathan Wild the Great* (1743), *The History of Tom Jones, a Foundling* (1749) and *Amelia* (1751).

9. *Smollett*: Tobias Smollett (1721–71), English satirical novelist, dramatist, translator of *Gil Blas* (see n. 6 above), and founder of the *Critical Review* in 1756. He is best known for his novels: *Adventures of Roderick Random* (1748), *Adventures of Peregrine Pickle* (1751), *The Adventures of Ferdinand, Count Fathom* (1753) and *The Expedition of Humphrey Clinker* (1771).

10. *'to gaze on Gothic toys through Gothic glass'*: See Appendix, no. 10.

11. *scutcheons*: A shield holding a coat of arms.

12. *lanceolated*: Made to resemble a spear-head in shape.

13. *but pleased his own taste, and realised his own visions*: See Walpole, *A Description of the Villa of Mr. Horace Walpole*: 'But I do not mean to defend by argument a small capricious house. It was built to please my own taste, and in some degree to realize my own visions' (p. iii).

14. Scott's Note: 'It is well known that Mr. Walpole composed his beautiful and lively fable of the Entail upon being asked, whether he did not mean to settle Strawberry-Hill, when he had completed its architecture and ornaments, upon his family?'

15. *Thomas Warton*: Thomas Warton the Younger (1728–90), author of the foundational *The History of English Poetry from the Close of the Eleventh to the Commencement of the Eighteenth Century* (1774–81), generally recognized as the first history of its kind.

16. *Virgil*: Publius Vergilius Maro (70–19 BC), the most acclaimed poet of Rome, best known for his epic, *The Aeneid*, which he began in 30 BC and left unfinished at his death.

17. *Froissart*: Jean Froissart (*c.* 1333–1400/01), European medieval poet and historian. His *Chronicles* provide the best contemporary documentary treatment of chivalry. It was first translated into English by Lord Berners in 1523.

18. *Mr. Gray writes to Mr. Walpole, on 30th December, 1764*: See *Correspondence*, Vol. 14, p. 137.

19. *Madame Deffand*: Marie de Vichy-Cahmrond, Marquise du Deffand (1697–1780), celebrated letter-writer and leading figure in French literary society. Her salon attracted scientists and writers of consequence. Walpole met her in 1765 and visited her several times thereafter. Her 841 letters to Walpole, located mostly in the Bodleian Library, Oxford, are published as Vols. 3–8 of Walpole's *Correspondence*.

20. Scott's Note: 'Madame Deffand had mentioned having read the Castle of Otranto twice over; but she did not add a word of approbation. She blamed the translator for giving the second preface, chiefly because she thought it might commit Walpole with Voltaire.'

21. *'the art of exciting surprise and horror'*: The phrase appears to be a common one in critical writing on Gothic fiction and drama after 1791. See, for example, *Monthly Review* 81 (December 1789), p. 563; *Monthly Review*, 2nd series 8 (1792), pp. 82–7; *Critical Review* 19 (1797), pp. 194–200; *Spirit of the Public Journals. Being an Impartial Selection of the Most Exquisite Essays & Jeux D'Esprits* (London, 1797–1800), Vol. 1, pp. 227–9; *Scots Magazine* 64 (June, 1802), pp. 470–74; and (July 1802), pp. 545–8.

22. *speciosa miracula*: Specious miracles.

23. *He, who ... original furniture*: Volume I, Chapter 10 of Scott's own novel *The Antiquary* (1816) dramatizes precisely this psychological situation.

24. *Held each strange tale devoutly true*: William Collins, 'Ode to Fear' (1747), l. 57.

25. *an explanation, founded on natural causes*: Radcliffe began this practice in her second novel, *A Sicilian Romance* (1790).

26. Scott's Note: 'Honest Bottom's device seems to have been stolen by Mr. John Wiseman, schoolmaster of Linlithgow, who performed a lion in a pageant presented before Charles I., but vindicated his identity in the following verses put into his mouth by Drummond of Hawthornden:

> Thrice royal sir, here do I thee beseech,
> Who art a lion, to hear a lion's speech:
> A miracle! for, since the days of Æsop,
> No lion till those times his voice did raise up
> To such a majesty: Then, King of Men,
> The King of Beasts speaks to thee from his den,
> Who, though he now inclosed be in plaster,
> When he was free, was Lithgow's wise schoolmaster.'

27. *nothing more than Snug the joiner*: See Shakespeare, *A Midsummer Night's Dream*, III.i.27–46 and V.i.219–26.

28. Scott's Note: 'There are instances to the contrary however. For example, that stern votary of severe truth, who cast aside Gulliver's Travels as containing a parcel of improbable fictions.'

29. *Prevailing poet . . . which he sung*: From William Collins, 'Ode on the Popular Superstitions of the Highlands, Considered as the Subject of Poetry' (1749), ll. 198–9.

30. *valley of Jehosophat*: Also 'Jehoshaphat' and 'Josaphat'; Hebrew 'Yehoshaphat' – king (c. 873 – c. 849 BC) of Judah during the reigns in Israel of Ahab, Ahaziah and Jehoram. The 'valley of Jehosophat' is the name given to the valley between Jerusalem and the Mount of Olives, through which the Kidron river flows. See Psalms 83.6–8 and Joel 3.1–9.

31. Scott's Note: 'This spectre, the ghost of a follower whom he had slain upon suspicion of treachery, appeared to no less a person than Wallace, the champion of Scotland, in the ancient castle of Gask-hall. – See Ellis's *Specimens*, vol. 1 [i.e. George Ellis, *Specimens of Early English Metrical Romances*, 3 vols. (London: Longman, Hurst, Rees, and Orme, 1805)].'

32. *et pondus . . . immensa volumina versat*: 'Turns this way and that/The crowds' immense and voluminous folds', Virgil, *The Aeneid*, V.407–8.

13. John Dunlop, *The History of Fiction . . . from the Earliest
Greek Romances to the Novels of the Present Age*, 3 vols.
(London: Longman, Hurst, Rees, Orme & Browne, 1814).

1. *the machinery . . . intended to raise*: Here Dunlop echoes Reeve's Preface to *The Old English Baron*; see Appendix, no. 7.

2. *Don Quixote*: The novel by the Spanish novelist Miguel de Cervantes Saavedra (1547– 1616), the full title of which is *El ingenioso hidalgo Don Quixote de la Mancha* (1605, 1615).

14. Anser Pen-dragon, ed. [Samuel William Henry Ireland],
*Scribbleomania; or, The Printer's Devil's Polichronicon.
A Sublime Poem* (London: Sherwood, Neely & Jones, 1815).

1. Ireland's Note: 'The style of this would-be flight of fancy, like the dull monotonous language of the *Mysterious Mother* before mentioned, is a further convincing proof of its writer's total incapacity to produce any composition bearing the stamp of originality and genius. As a compiler of the Anecdotes of Painting and Engraving, *Lord Orford* appears in a respectable light; but for the accomplishment of any literary attempt beyond the mere drudgery of research he never was intended by nature; and, consequently, the world would have lost nothing had his romance and his drama *existed* only in the mazes of his lordship's pericranium.'

2. *the rank of whose writer*: See Byron's defence of Walpole in his Preface to *Marino Faliero*; see Appendix, no. 16.

3. *Leadenhall's Lane ... proffer'd five pound*: Owner of the notorious circulating library and publishing house the Minerva Press, William Lane (*c.* 1745–1814) had great success in publishing his own line of sentimental and Gothic romances, which were constantly attacked by critics as being of the lowest literary value. Ireland's satire comes from the rumour that in the 1790s Lane would pay £5 for any Gothic manuscript, sight unseen.

15. William Hazlitt, *Lectures on the Comic Writers* (1819),
The Complete Works of William Hazlitt, ed. P. P. Howe
(London and Toronto: J. M. Dent, 1930–33).

1. *Quod sic mihi ostendis, incredulus odi*: Horace, *Ars Poetica*, l. 188: 'That which you show to me openly leaves me incredulous and repulsed.'

16. Lord Byron, Preface to *Marino Faliero: Doge of Venice*
(London: John Murray, 1821).

1. *'Ultimus Romanorum'*: Last Roman, or last of the Romans.

17. Thomas Babington Macaulay, Review of *Letters of Horace Walpole, Earl
of Orford, to Sir Horace Mann*, *Edinburgh Review* 58 (October 1833).

1. *out-Timoned Timon*: Macaulay here refers to Shakespeare's *Timon of Athens*.
2. *Entail*: The settlement of the succession of a landed estate, so that it cannot be bequeathed at pleasure by any one possessor.
3. *Miss Chudleigh*: Elizabeth Chudleigh (1720–88), Countess of Bristol, remarkable for the freedom of her conduct in élite society.
4. *George Selwyn's*: George Selwyn (1719–91), English wit and politician, Member of Parliament for Ludgershall and later for Gloucester, he was a close friend and correspondent of Walpole's.
5. *riband*: Ribbon; a narrow strip of something.
6. *Montesquieu*: Charles-Louis de Secondat, baron de La Brède et de Montesquieu (1689–1755), French political philosopher most famous for his *L'Esprit des lois* (*The Spirit of Laws*, 1750), a foundational political work of the French Enlightenment.
7. *Crebillon the younger*: Claude-Prosper Jolyot, sieur de Crébillon (1707–77), French novelist known for licentious and satirical works like *Les Egarements du coeur et de l'esprit* (*The Wayward Heart and Head*, 1736) and *Le Sopha, conte moral* (*The Sofa: A Moral*

Tale, 1742) and *Les Lettres Athénienne* (*The Athenian Letters*, 1771). He was the son of the acclaimed poet and dramatist Prosper Jolyot Crébillon (1674–1762).

8. *Louvet*: Jean-Baptiste Louvet de Couvray (1760–97), French literary figure prominent as a Girondin during the French Revolution, and the author of the licentious *Les Amours du chevalier de Faublas* (*The Loves of the Chevalier de Faublas*, 1786).

9. *Rapin*: Likely Paul de Rapin (1661–1725), French historian and author of *L'Histoire d'Angleterre* (*History of England*, 1724).

10. *Liotard*: Jean-Étienne Liotard (1702–89), Swiss painter noted for his pastel portraits.

11. *the Sopha, and the Lettres Athéniennes*: See n. 7 above.

12. *Voltaire*: See Preface to the Second Edition, n. 7.

13. *Rousseau*: Jean-Jacques Rousseau (1712–78), French philosopher, novelist and political theorist whose writings are often invoked as foundational texts of the French Revolution. He was the author of *Discours sur l'origine de l'inegalité* (*Discourse on the Origin of Inequality*, 1755), *Julie: ou, la nouvelle Héloïse* (*Julie: or, The New Eloise*, 1761), *Emile: ou, de l'education* (*Emile: or, On Education*, 1762), *Du Contrat social* (*The Social Contract*, 1762) and *Confessions* (1782).

14. *D'Alembert*: Jean le Rond d'Alembert (1717–83), French mathematician, philosopher and writer, known for deriving an alternative form of Newton's second principle of motion, and famous later as one of the editors of the *Encyclopédie*.

15. *Walpole's squib against Rousseau*: See Appendix, no. 11, n. 3.

16. *Sir Joshua Reynolds*: Sir Joshua Reynolds (1723–92), English painter, art theorist and founding president of the Royal Academy, who dominated artistic life in the middle and late eighteenth century. His *Discourses Delivered at the Royal Academy* (1769–91) was among the most influential works of art criticism of the time.

17. *Claude*: Claude Lorrain (1600–82), French master of ideal-landscape painting, an art-form that seeks to present a view of nature more beautiful and harmonious than nature itself. Claude was particularly influential in England after his death, from the mid-eighteenth to the mid-nineteenth century.

18. *Raphael*: Raffaello Sanzio (1483–1520), Italian painter best known for his Madonnas and for his large figure compositions in the Vatican.

19. *Hume*: David Hume (1711–76), Scottish philosopher, historian, economist and essayist, known especially for his philosophical empiricism and scepticism.

20. *Burkes*: Edmund Burke (1729–97), British statesman, best known for his support of the American colonies in the 1770s and his opposition to the French Revolution in the 1790s. His *Philosophical Enquiry into the Origin of Our Ideas of the Sublime and the Beautiful* (1757) and *Reflections on the Revolution in France* (1790) are his best-known works.

21. *Mr. Pitt*: William Pitt the Elder (1708–66), twice virtual prime minister (1756–61, 1766–8), best known for making Great Britain an imperial power.

22. *Orgon*: The character fooled in Molière's *Tartuffe*.

23. *Akenside has given . . . the Imagination*: Mark Akenside (1721–70) published *The Pleasures of the Imagination* in 1744.

24. *'Dove diavolo, Messer Ludovico, avete pigliate tante coglionere?'*: 'Where the devil, Sir Ludovico, did you collect so many imbecilities?'

25. *Sir Hans Sloane*: (1660–1753), British physician and naturalist whose collection of books, manuscripts and curiosities formed the basis for the British Museum, London.

26. *Cowley*: Abraham Cowley (1618–67), English poet and dramatist best known for adapting the Pindaric ode to English verse.

27. *Donne*: John Donne (1572–1631), English Metaphysical poet and dean of St Paul's Cathedral in London from 1621 to 1631, known both for his secular poetry and for his religious verses and sermons.

28. *fleering*: Making a wry face, grimace.

29. *Whitaker's and Chalmers' books*: John Whitaker wrote *Mary Queen of Scots Vindicated* (London: John Murray, 1787); George Chalmers wrote *The Life of Mary, Queen of Scots* (London: John Murray, 1818).

30. *Nichols's Anecdotes*: Likely John Nichols, *Biographical and Literary Anecdotes of W. Bowyer, and Many of His Learned Friends* (London: William Bowyer, 1782). Nichols also published at this time *Biographical Anecdotes of William Hogarth* (London: J. Nichols, 1781).

31. *Mr. D'Israeli's Quarrels of Authors and Calamities of Authors*: Isaac D'Israeli, *Quarrels of Authors, or Some Memoirs of Our Literary History* (London: John Murray, 1814); and *Calamities of Authors* (London: John Murray, 1812).

32. *Ensign Northerton*: A character in Henry Fielding's *Tom Jones*.

READ MORE IN PENGUIN

In every corner of the world, on every subject under the sun, Penguin represents quality and variety – the very best in publishing today.

For complete information about books available from Penguin – including Puffins, Penguin Classics and Arkana – and how to order them, write to us at the appropriate address below. Please note that for copyright reasons the selection of books varies from country to country.

In the United Kingdom: Please write to *Dept. EP, Penguin Books Ltd, Bath Road, Harmondsworth, West Drayton, Middlesex UB7 0DA*

In the United States: Please write to *Consumer Services, Penguin Putnam Inc., 405 Murray Hill Parkway, East Rutherford, New Jersey 07073-2136.* VISA and MasterCard holders call 1-800-631-8571 to order Penguin titles

In Canada: Please write to *Penguin Books Canada Ltd, 10 Alcorn Avenue, Suite 300, Toronto, Ontario M4V 3B2*

In Australia: Please write to *Penguin Books Australia Ltd, 487 Maroondah Highway, Ringwood, Victoria 3134*

In New Zealand: Please write to *Penguin Books (NZ) Ltd, Private Bag 102902, North Shore Mail Centre, Auckland 10*

In India: Please write to *Penguin Books India Pvt Ltd, 11 Community Centre, Panchsheel Park, New Delhi 110017*

In the Netherlands: Please write to *Penguin Books Netherlands bv, Postbus 3507, NL-1001 AH Amsterdam*

In Germany: Please write to *Penguin Books Deutschland GmbH, Metzlerstrasse 26, 60594 Frankfurt am Main*

In Spain: Please write to *Penguin Books S. A., Bravo Murillo 19, 1°B, 28015 Madrid*

In Italy: Please write to *Penguin Italia s.r.l., Via Vittorio Emanuele 45/a, 20094 Corsico, Milano*

In France: Please write to *Penguin France, 12, Rue Prosper Ferradou, 31700 Blagnac*

In Japan: Please write to *Penguin Books Japan Ltd, Iidabashi KM-Bldg, 2-23-9 Koraku, Bunkyo-Ku, Tokyo 112-0004*

In South Africa: Please write to *Penguin Books South Africa (Pty) Ltd, P.O. Box 751093, Gardenview, 2047 Johannesburg*

READ MORE IN PENGUIN

A CHOICE OF CLASSICS

Oliver Goldsmith	**The Vicar of Wakefield**
Gray/Churchill/Cowper	**Selected Poems**
William Hazlitt	**Selected Writings**
George Herbert	**The Complete English Poems**
Thomas Hobbes	**Leviathan**
Samuel Johnson	**Gabriel's Ladder**
	History of Rasselas, Prince of Abissinia
	Selected Writings
Samuel Johnson/	**A Journey to the Western Islands of**
James Boswell	**Scotland and The Journal of a Tour of**
	the Hebrides
Matthew Lewis	**The Monk**
John Locke	**An Essay Concerning Human**
	Understanding
Andrew Marvell	**Complete Poems**
Thomas Middleton	**Five Plays**
John Milton	**Complete Poems**
	Paradise Lost
Samuel Richardson	**Clarissa**
	Pamela
Earl of Rochester	**Complete Works**
Richard Brinsley	
Sheridan	**The School for Scandal and Other Plays**
Sir Philip Sidney	**Arcadia**
Christopher Smart	**Selected Poems**
Adam Smith	**The Wealth of Nations (Books I–III)**
Tobias Smollett	**Humphrey Clinker**
	Roderick Random
Edmund Spenser	**The Faerie Queene**
Laurence Sterne	**The Life and Opinions of Tristram Shandy**
	A Sentimental Journey Through France
	and Italy
Jonathan Swift	**Complete Poems**
	Gulliver's Travels
Thomas Traherne	**Selected Poems and Prose**
Henry Vaughan	**Complete Poems**